Gioconda

Gioconda

Lucille Turner

GRANTA

Granta Publications, 12 Addison Avenue, London W11 4QR

First published in Great Britain by Granta Books, 2011
This paperback edition published by Granta Books, 2012

A CIP catalogue record for this book
is available from the British Library.

1 3 5 7 9 10 8 6 4 2

ISBN 978 1 84708 359 3

Typeset by M Rules

Printed and bound by CPI Group (UK) Ltd, Croydon, CR0 4YY

For my mother and sister

Obstacles cannot crush me. Every obstacle yields to stern resolve. He who is fixed to a star does not change his mind.

LEONARDO DA VINCI

It is amusing to think that he, Leonardo, has stolen his own painting. As he places it carefully down, he considers the consequences for a moment. There will be discovery, displeasure: talk. But pleasing others was never his way, and he is used to talk. He pulls back the cover and leans the unfinished portrait of Lisa against the wall.

Her eyes, which stare back at him from the panel, register anything but surprise. They appear to understand his half-planned impulse, condone it. He lingers on this thought for a moment, but a memory breaks through: a handful of shells in the folds of a dress, a clutch of laughter. He abandons the theory of complicity. If she could speak she would probably say that this old habit he has of keeping things – shells, butterflies, annotations, and now her – is a path to destruction. Isn't that what he has drawn at her back? Exposure, erosion, attrition? He follows the course of the river until it disappears behind her face. The breaking down of cliff and rock; the wearing down of stones by river and stream. Those mountains at my shoulder, she tells him. They are you. Summits in the sky. Lonely heights.

He moves in closer, lights a lamp, changes the angle of light on her face and thinks about colour. No delivery means no compromise, no complaint, no delay. He is free of time; she is timeless. She will never change; he will grow old. He only has to open the pages of his notes to know how. Pages of annotations to flesh, bone and muscle show the markers of old age: thinning skin, flaking bone, hardening tendons. If he puts his hands to his face, the signs are there already. He picks up a shard of mirror from his workbench, sees the face of a man in the middle of his life. These lines will become crevasses and ridges. The landscape of his face will alter as every landscape does.

He puts wood in the stove, stokes the embers, finds herbs; enough Hypericum to raise the spirits of the dead. He decides on an early departure. Up before the birds, out before the monks. The question of where he will go is an old one that does little to change the set of facts. Out of Florence, certainly. Out of Italy, perhaps. Out of sight? The last is the more appealing.

He pours water in a pan and, in a gesture of habit, stirs it into a vortex with his finger. He drops in the grainy flowers and watches as they gather into the centre of the eddy and submerge. His mind fills with water: lakes, rivers, streams. He is six, nine, twelve, standing at the banks, throwing in sticks, a piece of bark, a leaf boat. What has changed? Nothing. Where is he now? Still waiting. He closes his eyes. The stream leads on, he follows. Through rock, over gravel, into banks of cilantro, grass and mint.

Ahead is a small boy holding a net. A multitude of wings pushes up through the air, sending the boy leaping from one set to another. The net falls. Air becomes water. The vortex slackens. The flowers rise to the surface. Where is he now? Anchiano. The seventh day of the Calends of June 1463. *Papilio Macaone.*

Anchiano

I

A small boy knee deep in meadow flowers of humming violet, blazing white, is lost in a cloud of butterflies. He holds out his net, a sheet of gauze held by wood sap around a frame, and waves it through the air, making eddies and currents but catching only sunlight. He flies this way and that, chasing wings that do not want to be caught, until finally he gives up, sits on a clump of moss and watches the stream instead. The water slows at the pile of stones he has made, becomes a murky pool and trickles out the other side in a thin line of cloudless green. He lies down beside it, opens his mouth and drinks.

Time for another approach, he thinks. *Let the butterfly come to you*. He sits still and waits. Late sunlight sharpens the grass. At length, a small yellow and black butterfly lands near his leg. He moves his hand forward slowly. The butterfly remains motionless, wings folded. With his finger and thumb, he gently grasps the wings and picks the insect up. He holds the butterfly up and observes its shape. He would like to spread the wings out in the palm of his hand but knows from past experience that the insect will struggle and they will break. Moving his forefinger and thumb gently around the middle of its body, he feels the pulsation of life between his fingers. He takes a breath and gives a sudden sharp pinch.

He opens his hand. The butterfly lays motionless but perfectly intact. Two orange spots, with pointed back wings: *Papilio Macaone*, he says, satisfied. Folding the wings together, he wraps the dead butterfly in a piece of gauze, and returns the way he came, along the riverbank until water vanishes into rock, then a short climb in the shadow of the hill. Behind him is Anchiano. His mother's house is ahead of him. He makes his way to a pot boiling over the stove. Holding the butterfly by its wings, he immerses its body in the soup and leaves it there for a while.

'If that's another of your flying creatures I don't want to see it in our supper.'

'Too late,' he mutters. He leaves the stove and the parlour, makes his way round the back of the house and shuts himself in the barn. He takes out a piece of board and a small sharp stick from a makeshift table erected in a corner of what he now refers to privately as his own *bottega*. Spreading the wings of the butterfly carefully so as not to break them, he fixes the wooden pin through the centre of its body onto the wood, in the space he has reserved for it alongside the other specimens. With the chalk in his left hand, he notes the day, then he reads it aloud.

He taught himself to read from a book on natural history that he found in the study of his father, at the big house in Anchiano with the wall of books. He doesn't live there; his father does. So does Albiera, his father's wife. He lives with his mother. And Antonio, her husband. Sometimes he goes to his father's house, but only on feast days and on the days when he sees his tutor, Fra Alessandro, a fat and lazy man, a *grassone*, who makes him sit still until his legs ache, and read passages from the book of Golden Legend over and over. It's not that he dislikes the stories about God. Some of them, particularly Genesis, make him sit up and read faster, until Fra Alessandro tells him to slow down or start again. But what Fra Alessandro hates most is an interruption.

This morning was especially difficult. He wondered whether Fra Alessandro would keep him in all day, copying letters. They had read about the Great Flood. He sat there with questions bursting his head, holding them back as long as he could. When they finally came out, it seemed to perplex and even anger the man, so that his beard twitched and sweat beads accumulated on his brow, in valleys and streams that flowed down either side of his face until water dripped onto the paper in front of them both. What was wrong with his questions? He could not be sure.

'Where did the water go when the flood went away?'

'Not important,' declared his tutor, waving his arm and tapping with his teaching stick. 'It went away. Away.'

He thought of the stream in the valley below that dried up after long hot summers. 'In the ground?' he added, trying to help. His tutor nodded. But then he thought of the volume of water in the stream as compared to the vast flood of the Golden Legend. 'That's a lot of water,' he began, but Fra Alessandro turned the page firmly. He swallowed his next question, so as not to provoke the man, and chose another.

'What was the Ark made of?'

'Wood,' said his tutor. 'All boats are made of wood.'

He thought of all those pairs of animals: cows, horses, wolves, sheep, moving, jostling, eating ... 'All those animals?' he said, staring at the book. 'How big was the Ark?' He read on. 'Three hundred cubits long; fifty cubits wide; thirty cubits high.' He looked at the illustration in the book. 'That's far too small,' he muttered.

At such moments Fra Alessandro would flick the pages of the book further along to some other part, but this did not deter him.

'What about ants and bees?' he asked. 'They never go two by two. Just the other day I saw a whole nest of them, making a line to a trail of sugar.'

'Who, I wonder, put out the sugar?' said Fra Alessandro. It was just before lunch, one of those times when his tutor looked tired. His tutor waved his teaching stick – a length of thin oak wood, which the old man liked to point whenever Leonardo made a mistake.

He stared back at the *grassone* with wide eyes. 'Monna Albiera,' he said, 'just after she gave you the jug of wine and six sweet cakes. It was the sugar left on the plate.'

He hides the butterfly board behind a pile of wood, covered so that Antonio won't find it, leaves his *bottega* and takes a narrow path away from the house. In the distance, he can just make out the flow of the river, where it passes through a belt of trees and emerges the other side in more of a hurry. He tightens his belt, where he keeps his chalk and a piece of wood for drawing, as well as a small leather pouch for collecting new plants he sees.

As he walks, he wonders what his tutor could possibly know about floods and water, since Fra Alessandro always avoids the river when they walk back to his mother's house on the other side of the valley after lessons, because the ground is too muddy. Sometimes, on days when Fra Alessandro has been particularly busy with his teaching stick, he takes his tutor down an unfamiliar route, to see how much mud will gather on his tutor's robe without the old man noticing. Last time, the robe – heavy with mud – began to trail over the ground like a harrow gathering kindling and he had to devise a short cut so the long grass would brush it off.

Water has become a difficult subject, but he can't stop thinking about it. Once he asked Fra Alessandro how much water there was in the Arno River. His tutor sighed and suggested that however much there was would not make a blind bit of difference to Leonardo, who would do better to learn how his father's accounting worked so that he may be, if not a notary, then at least not a pig farmer. Fra Alessandro did not think the Arno was important, and yet the old man must have known that floods were dangerous. Even after one day of rain the stream became wider. When there was heavy rain, Leonardo's mother kept him indoors, and Antonio came in from the fields cursing. Then there was the Ark. If Noah went to all that trouble, surely water levels mattered?

Tired of worrying about what goes on in other people's heads, he squints at the blue line of the river, and adjusts his route. He finds a wild iris, the only flower in a clump of leaves, takes a stick of charcoal from his pouch and draws it on a smooth flat stone he kept from his last journey there. He holds the stone up at eye level, against the backdrop of the flower. Satisfied, he leaves it on the ground beside the plant, as a marker.

As he pockets his charcoal, he considers that for all his sighing and stick pointing, Fra Alessandro made one good point. Rather an accountant than a pig farmer. He remembers the smell of Antonio when he has been out with the pigs. He decides to take Fra Alessandro's advice, and concentrate his mind on what is, in any case, by far his favourite subject: mathematics. Mathematics allows only one answer. If his tutor says no, he will find the solution later. You can't argue with mathematics.

He takes the last slope of the hill at a run. Scattered poppies and violets make a sunset in the grass. The slope drops into the Arno valley beyond a belt of cypress trees, black against the paler green of the hill. Around him pulse the colours of the trees and the grass, the shapes of the hills and the valley, and running through it all, the serpentine blue line of the river. But he knows that what he sees is only part of the picture; the grass and the water are not the colour they are because they are water and grass. He knows this because when grass is in the half shade of afternoon, when the sun has dipped over the hill and the shadows are everywhere, the grass is not green but blue. Then, when the sun is high in the sky, without clouds chasing across it, the grass shines too; the colour moves from green to yellow. In his mind it is a simple step of no great understanding that the grass is the colour it is because of the sun. Green is only one part of the picture of colour, made and remade every day according to season, weather and light. He imagines a conversation with Fra Alessandro, explaining to his tutor that grass is not green, or that water has no colour of its own: it is cobalt in the shallows, blue grey in the depths. It would be like trying to tell Antonio that pigs can fly.

He reaches the river. Water is the best tutor. He watches it move; its power: frothing, churning. It runs over the rocks making eddies that capture stray twigs and leaves and turn them into tiny Arks, where clinging beetles wrestle with Fra Alessandro's stories. Clouds race overhead. The water darkens, brightens, darkens again. He likes to sit on the eastern bank of the river at this particular spot, where the current turns in and the water becomes deep and calm. Sometimes water moves like a snake; wherever the river turns, the water on the outer side stretches, fast and thin, babbling over stone and silt, while on the inside it slackens and slows, barely moving. As it slows it muddies, clouds then clears to become almost a pond, where beetles can be caught and miracles can be observed.

He sees one of these now: a stick-like insect walking on water without sinking. Lying on his stomach at eye level with the surface gives him the answer: water bends. He thinks of the drips of water from leaves after rain, of round droplets of water trembling on spiders' webs. He remembers Fra Alessandro's Golden Legend, and the miracles of Moses, who made the waters part. Perhaps it was the bending water that made the miracle, not the man. He gives the stick-like insects a new name: the Kings of the Flood. He must tell Fra Alessandro that Noah could have saved himself the bother with this pair. He takes off his pouch and decides to catch one to make his point. As though it were just another butterfly, he scoops up the insect. He watches it flounder in the tiny pond of his palm, and just as he wonders how to get it safely back in one piece, the bushes part beside him to reveal a human face.

A small girl fixes him for a moment with curious eyes, as though he is something new, then glances down at his hand, and disappears as fast as she came. He covers the pond in his hand

and darts round the other side of the bush as she runs off. 'Frightened?' he calls after her. Too late. What is she afraid of? He looks down at the fragile insect now marooned on its island of flesh, and shakes his head.

II

He sits on the horse's back. His father has come back early and told Fra Alessandro, 'Enough reading for one day; the boy needs some air.' He has been on a horse before, but always sitting behind his father. His legs dangle down either flank of the animal, and with his calves he can feel the swelling of its breath and the throbbing of its body; it passes through his legs and into his own body. The breath of the horse comes quicker than his own; perhaps because it is stronger than him; or perhaps it is stronger because of the throbbing? He wants the horse to run. Grabbing a clump of the black mane with his hands, he shouts, '*Va, va!*'

The horse twitches its ears curiously. He shifts on its back. 'Why won't she go?' he asks, hurt.

'For the simple reason that you're wriggling around,' replies his father, walking over. 'If only you would sit quietly, the horse would feel that you are safe and he would move.'

Taking this in, he stares ahead, motionless. 'Go,' he whispers. The horse twitches and stamps its foot. Leonardo drops his shoulders in disappointment. As though this were a signal, the horse moves forward at a walk. His father claps and approaches the horse with a rope. Tying the rope around its head, his father makes a bridle and hands him the end of the rope. 'Lay the rope right across the mane like this,' his father says, showing him, 'and you go right. The same the other way.'

'And the same with the shoulders,' Leonardo says, 'like this.' He hunches his shoulders then drops them. The horse shifts on its feet.

'How does that work?' says his father.

'Simple,' he says. 'If my shoulders are down, my body is safe, then the horse knows I'm ready to go.' His father looks surprised.

'Yes, you're right. Well noticed. Go then.'

The wind sweeps his face. It is easy to keep his balance. He feels the body of the horse move beneath his: the horse stretches out. He waits for the next upward movement.

'Are you enjoying it?' calls his father.

The rope holds the horse's head so he lets it out. 'Hold her in,' his father shouts.

He trots the mare back. 'I've had enough now.'

'But we've only just got going. You want to stop already?'

'I want to take her to the stable.'

He leads the mare across the field. His father follows behind. There are two stalls in his father's stable. One is occupied by a goat; the other is empty. He ties the mare at the stall and runs his hand along her flank, feeling the muscles.

His father tosses him a piece of cloth. 'Use this.'

'It's alright, Father, it's better with my hands.'

'For you or the horse?'

He starts at the top of the withers and lets his hand run downwards. Then he starts on the other side. After a while, he doesn't know how long, he has covered the whole body, where it curves and knots, bends and flows.

His father, watching him, says, 'Fra Alessandro tells me you're not enjoying mathematics. Is that true?'

'I love mathematics,' he replies with surprise.

His father nods. 'I can see that you love horses too. And butterflies?'

'I like to keep them,' he says. 'I have lots already.'

'Tell me,' says his father, 'why do you like to keep them?'

It seems obvious, but his father is asking. 'To remember what they are,' he says.

'That's enough rubbing down now. Albiera will want you to come inside.' He can hear his father in a corner of his head, but the rest is filled with the body of the horse. For a moment he wonders why they must worry about what Albiera wants. Besides, coming indoors is not important. Other things are, but his father doesn't worry about them. Just the other day his mother had said, 'Ser Piero, the roof has not been repaired and the bad weather is not far away.' His father had nodded, but he could see in his face that his father's mind was filled with other thoughts, just as his is now.

He moves his hand along the shoulder of the horse and down the foreleg, stopping at every joint. He doesn't look up for a long time. When at last he does, he notices that his father has gone, and that the air moves with dust. Floating, dancing specks make the light thicken, and he runs forward to touch it.

From the corner of his sight, he sees the girl from the bushes again. He stops in the middle of a cloud of light and weighs up whether it is worth leaving that and the horse to tell her about the Kings of the Flood. He moves towards her.

The girl – tall for her age but nearly half his – has a habit of retreating. Long grass swallows her up beyond the dust and sunlight, where the yard ends and the orchard begins. He has a glimpse of green fabric mixing with bark and shrugs his shoulders, annoyed by the feeling that she is enjoying this more than he is. He finishes with the horse, takes a piece of wood from his belt, and finds one last scrap of charcoal in his pouch bag. Then he starts to draw.

'What have you got in your belt, Leonardo?'

Fra Alessandro looks at the piece of wood. He watches the old man's face closely. His tutor never seems pleased when he brings him things from his *bottega* or from the river. When he showed him the butterflies, Fra Alessandro's face had twisted into a sort of snarl, as it does when you eat old meat. Fra Alessandro understood the butterflies even less than the mathematics of the Ark.

'What do you want to do with them? Feed them to the kestrels?' the tutor said.

'I'm catching them until I've one of each kind.'

'One of each kind of what?'

'One of each kind of butterfly. There is more than one kind.'

Fra Alessandro had looked perplexed. 'I've only ever seen the white ones.'

'Look, here is a white one.' He pointed to his board. 'That one you see most of. They're always on this flower, see.' He indicated the flower carefully dried and pinned beneath the white butterfly. 'They like to sit on the honeysuckle. And these like the grape vine.'

'The grape vine,' Fra Alessandro echoed.

'Yes, but only these grapes, not the ones Fra Bartolomeo has planted next to his barn.'

'Not those grapes . . .?' For a moment his tutor had looked as though he wanted to know why, so he opened his mouth to continue, but the old man shook his head and threw up his hands, then picked up his teaching stick, the way he always did when he had had enough of Leonardo's ideas and wanted to talk about his own. 'That will do for now.'

The horse seems to have a different effect.

'When did you draw this?'

'This morning.'

'Hmm. Not bad, not bad.' Fra Alessandro keeps on looking at it. He puts out his hand to take it back, but Fra Alessandro brushes it away.

'Can I keep it?'

'If you want to.' It is not that he particularly likes Fra Alessandro. He doesn't like the way his mouth turns down at the corners. The only thing he likes about Fra Alessandro is his skin. His face is like a piece of bark or cork: cut up by waves of lines that run across his forehead and dotted with small holes like a rotten turnip. Still, all things considered, Fra Alessandro can have the picture. He has drawn the horse, and it is over. Keeping the picture doesn't matter. What interests him is the horse, not the drawing of it. He only drew it to understand it. Now it's done. It's not like the butterflies, which he keeps because there are so many kinds.

His tutor puts the piece of poplar wood on which he has sketched the horse down beside their books and slides a page of arithmetic on the table in front of them. He takes his charcoal up in his hand. 'Wrong hand!' says his tutor. 'Right, not left.' He moves the charcoal to the other hand and looks out of the window. The line of cypress trees is black; olive groves spread out grey to the right, and from the other side of the trees flashes of purple grape peep from rows of vines. He knows that Fra Alessandro will not let him get back to his butterflies unless he presents him with this page of added numbers. The sooner he gets it out of the way, the better. At least there may be some extra time after for something interesting. He wonders whether to bring out from his purse the page of calculations he has elaborated since their last conversation about the Ark. He has it all worked out: the number of animals, the size the boat would have to be to accommodate them, the food and water Noah would need for his siege. He sighs and takes up his chalk. Fra Alessandro paces the study, tapping the stick on his hand and pointing with the other end of his baton to the long list of numerals. Leonardo speeds up. To make it more fun, he imagines that the numbers are lines of elephants, or groups of growling polecats. By the time Fra Alessandro has done a lap of the study, he has finished.

'Already?' says his tutor with a frown, pulling the page towards him and checking the figures doubtfully. Finally, the old man looks up and says quietly, 'All correct.'

'Can we do something else now?' he cuts in, seeing a chance for something more interesting. 'Numbers can do other jobs,' he offers, eagerly.

'I suppose we could start on geometry,' says his tutor, laying his stick down on the table.

'Pythagoras?' he asks, 'you did say . . .'

'Basic principles first,' replies his tutor, his hand wavering over the stick.

'But I already know basic principles. I know how to measure the inside space of a box. I can draw triangles. I can measure a circle. Apples make a lot of circles. If you cut one up all the way round, you get a circle every time.' Fra Alessandro normally talks in terms of a hundred apples added to a thousand, but one apple on its own is far more interesting than a whole bag of them. 'What about less than one apple?'

Fra Alessandro has picked up the stick again; Leonardo is talking too much. He quietens down and wonders whether he might find better answers outside the study. He thinks of his butterfly board and the spaces left to fill. But an interruption of another kind cuts into his thoughts. It is his father.

'Come, Leonardo,' his father says, 'I have a task for you. I thought it would make a change from butterflies.'

He follows his father into the study. His father points to the sketch of the horse that lies on his desk. 'Fra Alessandro showed me your drawing.'

'Do you like it?' he asks. He is pleased that his father has taken it off Fra Alessandro. His father likes horses; Fra Alessandro doesn't. Horses' backs sink beneath his tutor's weight. When he watches his tutor eat sweet cakes after lunch before the start of lessons, he worries that his horse will not be up to the job.

'Like it? Yes, I like it. I think it's excellent.' His father smiles and points to the shield on his desk. 'Soldiers use this to frighten off their enemies and protect themselves when they go into battle.'

His father picks it up and gives it to him. It is round, made of slats of wood, and covered with hardened leather. The wood is strapped up with sinews at the back. The front is studded with thick metal pins, leaving a large circular space in the centre. He holds it up and looks at it.

'I want you to draw something on the centrepiece,' his father adds, 'like you did on the wood.'

He stares at it.

'I thought you could draw something on it to frighten away our enemies,' continues his father, 'Can you do that?'

'Is it yours?'

'It is mine, although it doesn't get much use now,' his father says, smiling again. Then, more seriously, 'But you never know, I may need it. Enemies are everywhere.'

He sees his father astride a horse, a sword flashing against the sky, the wooden shield strapped to his chest. Sudden fear strikes him. 'How does the shield help?' he asks. He thinks of other places: arms, legs, throat, face.

'They carry it on their armoury, like this.' His father holds the shield up against his chest. 'If an enemy soldier throws a spear, it will hit the shield before it hits the soldier. See?'

'But what about his face?' he asks. The more he thinks about it, the more the shield worries him.

'Most of the time an enemy will aim for the heart, like this.' His father points his finger at the middle of Leonardo's chest.

'Why aim here?'

His father seems confused. 'Because it's the biggest place,' he says. 'Everything that you are, Leonardo, is there. If your heart dies then your soul is lost. That is why shields are important.'

He considers his father's heart. He thinks of it beating in his father's chest. Other animals have hearts too. What happens to them? 'Fra Alessandro told me that a man's soul either goes to heaven or hell, but I think he's wrong. I saw Antonio kill a pig last week in the barn. When he pulled out its heart there was blood coming out of it. If that was the pig's soul then it just dripped onto the straw and then Antonio put the straw on the fire. But then,' he says, talking out loud as he often does, 'perhaps the fire was like hell?'

His father does not answer at once, so he carries on. 'Don't soldiers feel bad taking another man's soul away?'

His father shrugs. 'Sometimes a man has no choice.'

'Does that mean that when I cut my finger, like this—' he holds up his own finger; there is a small gash in it '—I lose some of my soul? What is a soul, anyway? Fra Alessandro says . . .'

'Never mind about all that,' his father interrupts, frowning.

As he leaves his father's study, shield against chest, he thinks about his task. He is pleased that he has been entrusted by his father with saving his life, but on the other hand, he finds it hard to understand the whole idea of fighting. He thought his father worked as a notary in Vinci, but clearly even the job of notary is dangerous commerce. He stops in his tracks. *Men need saving from each other.* He will draw a picture on the shield so unlike anything they have seen before, so terrifying, that the soldiers who look at it will see themselves in the full throes of battle *as they are*: hideous monsters, takers of the souls of men, destroyers of their own.

This brings with it another idea: *Men need saving from themselves.* Not yet sure which thought is the most accurate, a third, more powerful one hits him. He holds his breath, his mind bursting. He will make a solemn vow – to do everything he can to remedy this dread. First there is the shield, but there are others things he can do too. He thinks of his tutor and the horse. He can hide the sweet cake jar, so that Fra Alessandro will no longer eat them and the horse will be saved. He grips the shield in delight; he has the feeling that he has come across something wonderful quite by accident, like when you find a perfect flower at the right moment, when it has just opened, or when a new kind of butterfly flies past and settles at your feet.

If people knew things as they really were – if they knew about hearts, if they understood about souls, if they knew that the butterfly's wing will break and the horse's back will bend – then other things might change too. His father could put away his sword; Fra Alessandro would smile more often and they could become friends. His father could stop frowning. He wouldn't have to listen to his mother crying at night when he is in bed, after Antonio has drunk the rest of the flask and fallen asleep.

Without waiting for Fra Alessandro to escort him, he puts on his cap, picks up the shield and leaves for his *bottega* and his mother's house. He tries to run but the shield is heavy; he has to stop twice to catch his breath. He spends the rest of the afternoon wondering what frightens people most. The girl in the bushes was frightened by the idea of the insect, not by the insect she couldn't see. The idea of the thing, rather than the thing itself, he concludes, is the more frightening. Fear is in the head. He imagines fabulous monsters, creatures with two heads, the faces of wolves and the bodies of goats. But not one truly terrifies him. He casts around for some other source of inspiration, and picks up his butterfly board. *Nothing terrifying about you*, he whispers, stroking the wings of *Papilio Macaone*. He stares at the butterfly's body. Its legs are spread out either side of its wings; its eyes stare back at his – wide, black pupils. He puts down the board and smiles. If you want to understand the meaning of terror, you have to draw it as you see it. From body, to head, to hand.

Dawn next day. The sun is not up and the ground smells of last month's rain. An earthworm squirms beside his feet. He nudges it away from his foot, his eyes scanning the ground for any other signs of movement. By the time the sun has risen, he finds what he's looking for. The rapid movement of a lizard catches his attention. Lowering his flask to ground level, he places it in the path of the creature and ushers it inside with his free hand. He runs back to the *bottega*. Unsure about the most painless way to kill it, he decides in the end on the quickest method. Taking a knife he finds in the barn next to his *bottega*, he cuts the lizard's head off in one stroke. The tail continues to jerk for a few moments. He sits and observes this for a while, nearly forgetting about the head, then places both parts back in safe storage. Now for the rest. He wipes his hand on the side of his tunic, leaving blood smears on the brown wool. He runs to wash them off in the trough at the back of the barn.

He feels bad about killing the lizard, but it was necessary: he is saving his father's life, and his father is more important than a lizard. Then, just above the stream where he first saw the Kings of the Flood, he sees a mass of flies on the ground. He waves them away and finds a dead dog. One black eye stares up at him. The dog's jaw is open in a fixed snarl. The flies come back. He backs away feeling slightly sick, the lizard bumping around in his pouch. Terror he can deal with. Decay needs a stronger stomach.

He watches his mother filling dishes at the fire in the corner. The tin catches the lick of the flames and she burns her hand. Antonio sits at the head of the table. The pig farmer picks up bread with his fingers, his nails short and filthy.

Leonardo looks down at his plate.

'Why won't you eat it? It is meat,' his mother says. 'Think yourself lucky that you have meat.'

'The boy should be more grateful,' says Antonio, pushing his plate along the table towards Caterina, who refills it without looking and pushes it back to him.

Leonardo shakes his head silently at his mother and glances at Antonio. She takes his plate, says nothing and goes into the kitchen.

'I have decided not to eat meat,' he says. He has been thinking about it for a while, but now that he's seen the dead dog, there's no going back. He will leave meat to the flies.

'If you're not going to eat meat, what are you going to eat?' His mother comes back and sits down, with that worried look she has whenever he comes back from his father's house over the hill and whenever he leaves.

'Berries,' he says, vaguely. He can't remember when he last ate a berry, but is sure they taste better than meat.

'Berries,' snorts Antonio. 'Now the boy has become a bird! Still, perhaps it's a good thing; at least you'll have no trouble feeding yourself once you're older.'

'When Leonardo is older he will go and work with his father,'

Caterina says. He thinks fast. If he doesn't change the subject soon there will be trouble.

'I don't want to be a notary,' he says.

'Just as well,' Antonio says, 'because a bastard notary is no good to anyone. If you can't be legitimate in person, then what hope is there for any other business?'

It is time to leave. He gets up. His mother grabs his arm and points to his tunic.

'What is that?'

'Blood.'

'Blood of what?' She casts her eyes over his arms and legs.

'Don't worry, not mine,' he replies. Antonio snorts again. Before anyone can think of anything else to say, he slips out of the door.

III

His *bottega* now resembles a butcher's shop. The blood of course belongs to other creatures than him. He has not yet decided which part of the dog to salvage. The head is intact, although the expression is a sorry one. This is not good, and he spends time trying to prise the jaw of the dog open further, with little success. It had been limp at first, but now it has stiffened like wood. He decides the dog must have died shortly before he came across it, and notes this down on his piece of paper, along with a quick drawing.

He notices too, now that he has brought the dog indoors, that the decay has speeded up. The tiny movements of maggots give the creature ghostly life. Then there is the smell. The longer he keeps the dog, the worse it reeks. The next day he is driven outside, as much to avoid the stench as anything. In any case, a dog and half a lizard is not enough.

He wanders off into the hills, in search of the unexpected. He looks out for kestrels, waits for them to swoop, then rushes to the spot. But by the time he scrambles over rock and shrub, the bird has beaten him to it and the meal is over. Then he finds a dead squirrel curled over the branch of a tree, not yet prey to anything. Pleased, he gathers it up, only to find that the whole thing falls apart in his hands. In the end, he keeps the feet, grateful that at least he has been spared the task of cutting them off, and surprised at how much harder things are when you want to do them perfectly.

He makes for the river, partly to wash his hands, which smell so bad that he fastens them behind his back as he walks, and partly because he has the vague hope of finding something else, although if you asked him what, he would not be able to say.

A face appears through the foliage and a body follows. He looks up from the water.

'Why are your hands all bloody?' The girl watches him from along the bank, unwilling to move closer. 'Well, aren't you going to tell me?'

'I'm not sure I need to,' he says. 'You've been watching me for long enough.'

'I watched you ride the horse. That was the only interesting bit.' She moves closer. 'But I don't think you're very good at it.'

He stands up and wipes his hands behind his back. 'I don't see why not.'

'You weren't enjoying it. People don't enjoy things when they can't do them, or when they are afraid of doing them. You were afraid.'

He looks her straight in the eye; she looks back without flinching. He thinks of the King of the Flood in his hand and her flight. 'I'm not the one who's afraid,' he says.

'Prove it,' she demands.

'I don't need to prove it,' he says, irritated. 'I know, and that's enough.'

The girl picks a long stalk from the bank and dips it in the water. 'Then I know for sure that you definitely are afraid,' she says. 'If you weren't, then you would jump into the river.'

Blood rises to his face. 'That wouldn't make me brave; it would make me stupid.' His back supported by the thin trunk of a poplar, he brings his hands in front of him and folds them. 'Only a fool does things for no reason.' At his feet a beetle stirs; he watches it furrow a path towards the mush of the bank. 'I can think of something much more interesting than throwing myself in the water and getting wet for nothing except a stupid idea,' he finishes.

For a moment the girl looks about ready to leave, but it is as he suspects: curiosity holds her back. 'What, then?'

He bends down and picks up the beetle. He spreads out his hand. 'See this beetle? I can make it travel to the other bank without it getting wet.'

'I don't believe you,' she says. He casts his eye along the course of the river. The water flows fairly steadily where they are stood, before speeding up again as it reaches the bend ahead. There's a natural dam on the other side, of leaves and twigs beneath the large birch just where the water slackens at the turn. He looks round and finds what he needs: dock. He pulls off a large leaf and bends it by twisting the ends and fixing them with twigs, so the leaf forms a boat. He places the beetle carefully on the boat and steps down the bank. The girl follows, the hem of her dress gathering a good deal more mud than Fra Alessandro's trailing gown.

He places the boat in the water and they watch as the beetle, squatting in the hollow of the dock, begins its journey downstream. The boat reacts to the flow of the river exactly as he anticipated it would; once it reaches the dam, it swings in as the current slows and drifts onto the pile of leafy twigs on the opposite bank. They hurry to draw level with it. Sensing the solid bark beside it, the beetle moves forward, edging its way off the boat and onto one of the twigs. It scurries along the twig until it finds another, its senses taking it away from the water and towards the smell of dry ground. The girl watches intently. He turns away and smiles. 'Wasn't that more interesting?'

'Perhaps,' she says airily, as though she's not interested. Then she notices the tail sticking out of his pouch on the ground where he left it to collect the beetle. 'What's that?'

'Nothing – just a thing I found.' He doesn't want to tell her about his monster, or about the dead animal in his pouch, sensing that it will not produce the same effect as the beetle. His evasive reply makes her keener to know.

'Show me,' she demands.

He thinks fast. 'If I did, you'd be afraid.'

'I'm not afraid of anything.'

'Aren't you afraid of monsters?' he says.

She throws him a look of scorn. 'There are monsters with snakes for hair and others with only one eye. Don't you read Greek?' Now it's his turn to feel stupid. 'Anyway,' she continues, 'whatever it is, it doesn't look like a monster.'

'It will. Come with me.'

They follow the course of the river. It widens, forming into a lake. On the far shore rock has burst from the muddy riverbank. It rises vertically into sharp fingers pointing skyward. With every step they take he's conscious of movement: creatures stirring in the undergrowth, fish gliding, hidden beneath the water line; while around them the air swims with unheard vibrations. The wings of birds and butterflies, the sudden flight of dragonflies and the steady hum of bees.

They walk in silence, her dress catching the grass here and there. Leonardo comes to a halt. The girl stops close behind him.

'So what about this monster?' she says. 'Where is it?'

'My father's house is beyond that hill,' he replies, 'but my mother lives there.' He points to the house on the hill with its out buildings crumbling around it like the body parts of a broken animal. 'My *bottega* is there too: at the back of our barn. If you come there in two days' time, I'll show you one.'

He can't begin to understand why he invited the girl to his *bottega*. He returns at a run, banging the barn door behind him, running round the back, where his chalks and sketches lie in rows on the table, the shield waiting in the middle. He places what remains of the squirrel on top of a wooden plinth and closes his eyes, astonished at his own impulses. Removing her face from his mind, he keeps his eyes closed and thinks of other things: the shield on the table, the head of the lizard. He catches his breath then wishes he hadn't.

He dashes out of the barn and gulps fresh air. Returning inside, he sets to work, arranging the animal parts this way and that in the hope that the fear in his head will take form. But the only thing that comes to him is the stench. He goes to the far end of the barn and vomits. Then he dips his face into the trough and returns to the plinth to take in a deep breath of the sickening air. After a few more breaths he finds that he can't smell a thing. It must be the same for Fra Alessandro, who can drink several glasses of wine after sweet cakes without feeling sick. He decides to try several glasses of wine himself at some point in the near future. Perhaps it's just a matter of repetition.

He swaps body parts, a tail here, a head there, but in the end it comes down to expression. The dog incites pity more than fear, although the teeth are quite good, if he could just get them out. The lizard's head is perfect, but the squirrel's feet are not as effective as the cockerel's. Sizes are irrelevant, he thinks. He can change those himself. Within a few hours, his creation is complete. It squats on one of the plinths in the middle of the *bottega*, staring back at him with dead eyes. Now all he has to do is draw it.

He takes the shield and begins to trace the outline. Something is not right. He moves this way and that, changes position and angle, to no avail. He looks around the inner room that the *bottega* occupies at the end of the barn. Then he understands. On one side of the barn, at the back, logs are piled up against the only source of direct sunlight. He shifts the wood, piece by piece. It takes a long time. He forgets to be hungry or thirsty because he's thinking of the shield and the wood and the creature on the plinth. Suddenly he looks up and it's dark already. He washes his hands in the trough and closes the barn door. He crosses the turf of the field at a run, slipping on a patch of something in the dark. When he pushes open the door, his mother is angry.

'Where have you been? I sent Antonio to look for you. If he finds you he'll take a strap to you. Now go to bed.' As he drifts off to sleep, he hears Antonio slam the door. His mother is weeping. He thinks of the monster in the barn. Then he thinks of Antonio. Then he turns over, closes his eyes and thinks of nothing.

Before dawn he is up and back in his *bottega*. He has moved all the wood blocking the side of the barn, and now the light streams in through the side opening. He wipes his hands on his tunic and goes outside, to check the path of the sun. Halfway through the morning it will rise over the top of the line of cypress trees that runs along the side of the field. If he waits till then, he will have plenty of light.

He moves the plinth round to get the best angle, opposite the gap in the wall that the wood had been blocking. Early sunshine streams in through the gap and hits the floor, softened by wood chips from Antonio's axe. He waits patiently until the monster is fully illuminated then begins to draw, his attention focused utterly on a subject that now seems more real dead than it did alive, with a hideous beauty that rises out of the wood-soaked light and begins to take its place upon his father's shield.

The prickly sensation at his back nags him for some time before he bothers to turn around. In the end he does. The girl is planted there, at the entrance to the *bottega*. She is examining his drawing with quiet curiosity, beyond the rays of light that illuminate both him and his creature.

He wants to say, 'Well, are you afraid?' but doesn't. It is not that he doesn't want to know – in fact he does – it is just that he has no time to say so, because from the back of the *bottega*, a lung-breaking scream rips the air.

His mother is standing at the door. Alongside her stands his father.

'Santa Madonna!' His father crosses himself. Caterina swoons.

'The stench, the stench!' his father cries wildly, his eyes fixed on the body parts decomposing on the wooden plinth.

'It's all right,' he says, 'I finished the first sketch before they started shrinking.' He holds up the shield, pleased to note that the creature, a terrifying combination of dog, lizard and cockerel, appears as alive on the shield as it does dead on the plinth: the proportions are perfect.

'*Santa Madonna!*' his father repeats, lost for words. He observes with satisfaction the puckered expression on his father's face, as this can only signify, in every sense, a total success: his father is terrified.

The smell of the monster elicits an instant response. His father apparently does not have the same ability as Fra Alessandro to become indifferent to sensations, and calls for Antonio. He watches in dismay as Antonio arrives in his *bottega* looking grimly pleased, picks up and removes the monster, stokes up a fire at the bottom of the field and brushes the monster onto it with one sweep of the plinth. His father holds the shield and looks at it for just a moment, then, without another word, places it under his arm and walks back up the field to the house, Antonio following behind.

He runs to catch them up. 'Aren't you going to use it?' he asks his father, staring into the grey eye of his monster locked beneath the strong arm. His father stops striding and looks at him, his face sad. 'What am I to do with you, Leonardo?' his father says, and turns into the wind, his hand tight on the shield. 'No more questions. Go to your bedchamber and wait there.'

He follows, dejected, his mind numb. From the corner of his eye he sees a figure lingering at the edge of the field. It's the girl, gone unnoticed in the commotion. She gives a brief wave. Her face is worried. He tries to make light of it, even smile, but all he can manage is a grimace. Heavy splashes of rain spill from the clouds above. The girl disappears. Antonio is hurrying his mother to the shelter of the house. Leonardo hangs back. The rain falls faster. He looks up, eyes wide open, and imagines it all differently. The drops aren't falling, he is. He spreads his arms, closes his eyes, falls into cloud, water and mist. When he looks again, he's alone. Everyone has gone indoors. From the middle of the field the fire billows bitter smoke, which hovers beside him in phantom drifts of brown and grey, and drives him back to the house.

Later that day, he puts his ear to a crack in the wall of the main room and listens to his father's voice. 'This impious, out-of-the-normal way of raising a child will have to stop,' his father says. From now on, Leonardo will live with him at Anchiano. He moves back from the wall, wondering what impious is.

He is sitting in his new bedchamber at Anchiano. Fra Alessandro came to fetch him and they walked the path away from his mother's house in silence. His mother didn't come out. As they rounded the corner, he looked up and saw her face half-hidden behind the window. The face watched him for a moment and then it was gone. As he walked away he regretted the monster. He felt sick and his eyes were hot and stinging.

He wishes himself back, for just a moment, to find the face at the window and ask it whether he will be back for supper the next day, or the one after that. But the finality of his packed trunk answers the question for him. The painting of the shield has exacted a heavy price. Fear has turned sour. He thinks over his father's reaction till his head hurts. It is more than unfair. In place of praise and thanks, he receives nothing but punishment and anger; after saving his father's life he is removed from his *bottega*. What should he have drawn?

Life takes on a new pattern. His lessons with Fra Alessandro grow longer: afternoons become days, broken only by riding lessons when his father is home. Summer evenings are long, spent thinking of the *bottega* at the back of the barn and the evenings when Antonio and his mother will sit down without him. Now he sits down with Albiera. Sometimes his father is there, sometimes not. Mealtimes are quieter. He doesn't have to look at Antonio's filthy hands, or weigh up the likelihood of a strapping. But this new silence is somehow worse. Albiera shows him how to eat with a knife and fork, how to drink, how to sit. He listens politely and does as she says. Sometimes he examines her face when she isn't looking and tries to understand why his father likes it more than his mother's. It is a sad face. He measures, in his mind, the distance between the top of Albiera's forehead and her nose, then that between her nose and her chin, and decides that her forehead is too broad, her chin too short.

One evening, he sees something that makes him change his mind about Albiera's face. They have eaten; it is late. He passes her chamber and stops at the partly open door. There she is, forehead on hands, praying. He sees something else too: a cradle for a baby. Since there is no baby, the cradle is a riddle – but an easy one to solve. It's sad to want something you can't have. He thinks of the face at the window and the memory of the hole in his stomach as he walked away from it. He looks at Albiera the next day with new eyes. You have to understand a face to like it.

Perhaps his father guesses the importance of his room at the back of the barn, because an alternative is provided, a space in a corner of his father's study, with a small desk, a chair and access to the library. But on other matters his father remains silent. Sometimes, Leonardo asks Fra Alessandro to let him go back, since he has left some of his things – the butterfly board and his drawings – and anyway, he wants to go back. His tutor understands that there is more to the trip than butterflies and drawings, and tells him that his mother is working all day in the fields and has no time to see him and that was why he had to move away. But he knows it isn't true. His move is punishment for the monster.

In the end Fra Alessandro promises to collect the board himself, next time he passes by Caterina's house. And to his credit, the old man keeps his word. It is perhaps the only time that his tutor has shown any interest in the board. Fra Alessandro lets him explain each butterfly, its habitat and markings when he is reunited with it. The old man is not as bad as he used to think. He almost asks Albiera to make sweet cakes for him, but then he remembers the vow. No sweet cakes for Fra Alessandro. If the monster has taught him anything, it is that saving people's lives is never going to be easy. He thinks of his father taking back the shield and hiding it, his mother at the window, the long walk down the path from the house. He has paid the price of the vow, so has to keep it. To compensate for the sweet cakes, the next time Fra Alessandro comes with him for a walk he will avoid the mud and take the dry, open ground to the pasture where he found the *Papilio Macaone*. But the walks stop. Every day is spent indoors, away from the sights and sounds of the countryside.

Reward for saving his father's life comes from elsewhere. His tutor opens books from his father's library. He has always marvelled at the rows of books neatly arranged with titles written in languages he can't understand. The unfamiliar words that cover the pages mean that he can only look at the pictures, most of which show scenes of men and mountains, oceans rising and parting, boats and animals he has never seen.

'It's Greek,' Fra Alessandro tells him. 'If you're good, I shall teach you one day.' His tutor turns the thick leather binding of the book to a page where Greek writing stands out in black alongside a small, finely drawn picture painted in colours bluer than a cobalt stream and brighter than a sunrise. 'The first book of Moses. The Ten Commandments. First you finish Latin, then I will teach you Greek. But for now, you must learn the word of God.'

Leonardo's father appears at the door, puts his hands on his shoulders. 'I'm going away for a while now, and will leave Fra Alessandro in charge, with Albiera of course.' His father turns to Fra Alessandro. 'I will rely on you.' His father takes up his cloak and leaves. For the first time in Leonardo's life, it is hard to watch him go.

He imagines his father's shield stashed in safety beneath the cloak, ready to be drawn in battle in the face of fearful enemies on blazing mountaintops. He knows the story of Moses and the Ten Commandments because Fra Alessandro has mentioned it once before. He runs his fingers over the Moses painted on the paper. The bearded figure is holding a stone tablet like a shield. Clearly Moses' shield is better than his. He concludes bitterly that his shield is not under his father's cloak. Perhaps his father has destroyed it, burnt it along with the animals on Antonio's fire without him seeing? Dangerous things are burnt. Once, a child from Vinci died because he was ill. They took everything out of the child's home and burnt it on a big fire; even the child's clothes were burnt. Did his father burn the picture on the shield because it was dangerous? What is his father afraid of?

His mind goes back over the scene in the *bottega*. His father striding down the field with the shield locked under his arm, wondering what to do with it. He remembers the girl: she had understood. Is she the only one who understood the message of the monster? It was no more than a thing he had seen in the hearts of men – even in the heart of his father – but it was enough to banish him from his mother's house.

Once outside, he takes deep breaths of air. It is late afternoon. The sun is dropping over the distant hill of San Pantaleo. His mother and Antonio will be back from working in the fields. His mother will be standing over a pot by the stove. He wonders what they will be eating. He turns away and walks round the back of the house to the stable. The black mare stamps her foot. She's only a foal and not yet used to the bites of flies. She needs brushing. He takes a handful of straw and begins to rub. Beneath his hand, her back softens. Horses make more sense than people. From now on, whenever he draws or writes anything, he will keep it secret. He sits in a corner of the barn, takes out a scrap of paper and holds the piece of charcoal in his left hand, where it's more comfortable. Fra Alessandro is not here now. He writes his name. Then he writes it backwards: right to left. It's easier than he expected. He writes a whole line of words the same way and signs his name at the end. He folds the scrap of paper up and puts it in his belt pouch.

He stands at the stable door and gazes out across the valley and the hill of Mount Albano. The evening light settles on the tree canopy, brightening the uppermost branches and darkening the layer beneath, leaving bark and brushwood in shadow. Then, higher up the mountain just above the tree line, the outline of holes in the hillside: recesses in rock – caves. He remembers the Bible illustration. Moses stood with his stone tablet at the mouth of one of these. But these mountains have more to tell than any number of stone tablets; the animals that inhabit them are part of another story and the world is more than a book. Valley, mountain, river and forest, beast and bird: he must look to them for answers. He unties the mare and leads her into the field. He slips the rope from her head and watches her run until she reaches the olive grove and can go no further. He shades his eyes with his hand against the angle of sunlight. There is the hill of his father's house, there is the next hill, and there is the mountain. He follows the line of the slope to the peak. How far do you have to climb to see everything? Tomorrow he will find out.

He's halfway up Mount Albano when he realises he has company: a kestrel and its mate riding the currents of the warm wind, searching the ground for prey. He shades his eyes and watches them. A little way off, poised on a patch of grass beside a rocky ledge, a young hare is unsure which way to run. He holds his breath. Something brushes his shoulder. He turns and the hare scatters. Perched on the rocks beside him is the girl from the river.

'I'm glad they didn't get it,' she says, looking up at the kestrels.

'They aren't so glad.'

'No,' she replies, staring at him, 'but if I were you, I'd have had enough of dead animals.'

He shrugs his shoulders. 'I know your name by the way. I know where you live too.' He takes a stick and points to a pale speck of stone in the valley below, the other side of the river. He went as far as the perimeter of her gardens, but stopped at the wall. 'I happened to be passing,' he adds. 'I go there for herbs.' Albiera sent him out for mint and cilantro. The other side of the river, of course. He turned his back on San Pantaleo and his mother's house, and went without argument.

'So you live there now?' Lisa asks him, looking over at Anchiano. 'I saw you leave,' she adds. 'The next day.'

His face heats up in the sun. He busies himself with a small sketch of a clump of violets, thinking how almost every conversation can become difficult once it gets started. Looking over his shoulder, she watches him sketch. 'What are you doing that for?' she asks.

'To remember it.' He looks up. 'I can measure the height of the sun. Shall I show you?'

She nods. They walk on together. He talks fast.

'First, we must find two mountains as far apart as possible and of the same height. Then we must position ourselves on the summit, one of us on each.'

Lisa stops walking. 'How are we going to do that?'

'Never mind. So, as I was saying, we then must build wooden shelters and make a small hole through which the sun can shine.'

'And then what?'

'And then, when the sun makes a perpendicular angle in the

first shelter – mine, say – I signal to you, like this, see.' He stops
and waves his arms vigorously.

'And if I don't see you?'

He thinks quickly. 'In case you don't see me, I have a fire ready
and I light the fire and send up smoke to warn you.'

She seems satisfied, so he continues. 'When you see the signal,
you mark the spot where the sun shines into your shelter.' He
turns to her triumphantly and smiles.

'And then what?' she says.

Patience is necessary. He looks round for a stick and finds one:
a thin twig – oak. He kneels on the ground and begins to draw
methodically.

Lisa stares at the shape and laughs.

'What is it; what's funny?' He throws the stick aside and stands
up.

She stops laughing.

'It's a triangle. I can measure with it. Look.' He draws more
lines with his finger, and at the top of the triangle he traces the
circle of the sun. He points to the two angles at the bottom.
'There you are and there am I.' He runs the stick along the sides
of the triangle. 'The height of the sun is the same as this. Shall I
show you how it works?'

She loses interest in his drawing. 'Tomorrow,' she says. 'If I stay
out too long, I'll get in trouble.' Then, 'In any case, I don't know
why you want to know about the height of the sun. It's too hot
already. Can't you think of a better idea?'

He looks across at the opposite hillside, thinking how hard she
is to please. 'All right.' He looks at the sky. 'I know a place where
there's no light at all.'

'What sort of place is that?'

He stands up and throws the stick into the bushes. The kestrels are back, circling a stretch of jagged rock high above the tree line. 'It's a shelter. A sanctuary. Come back tomorrow, and I'll show you.'

IV

The cave, cut into Mount Albano far above the level of the Arno River, smells of musk and moss. It leaches darkness. He hesitates. Behind him, Lisa stands waiting. He can hear her hesitant breathing at his back. There has to be a better way.

He steps back. 'Wait,' he says, 'I know.' Blinking in the sunshine, he searches the ground for brushwood.

'What are you going to do?' she asks.

'You'll see.' He reaches into his purse and pulls out a piece of glass. Scooping together a small pile of leaves and brushwood, he looks up at the sun. He turns the piece of smooth glass, the remnant of a window pane he keeps in his pouch, this way and that until the angle is right. Soon a thin white trail of smoke rises from the pile of leaves.

'Get me a branch – no, a dead one from the ground.'

He rips off a corner of his tunic discreetly while she is searching, wondering all the while how he is going to explain it to Albiera, and wraps it around the branch she brings him.

'Perfect!' The flame devours the wood. Satisfied, he leads the way back into the cave with Lisa following.

He shines the torch into the darkness. Ahead, shadows flicker and recede, to reveal a deep hole. He advances until the light settles on plain earth. He feels Lisa's hand on his arm.

'Where does it end?'

'Why,' he says, 'Scared?'

'No.'

He turns to examine the rest of the cave. In front of the opening, a bird of some kind flits by – the dry and rhythmical sound of flight. Distracted, he looks out.

'See this.' Lisa takes the torch and shines it on the walls. He runs his hand over their surface. A piece falls away and he seizes it. The earth crumbles between his fingers and he is left with a stone: a strange stone that swirls into a round pattern of lines. He takes up a piece of rock and begins to chip away at the wall until similar stone shapes fall away.

'What are you doing?'

'Pick them up,' he says, 'I need them.'

It is full summer. Outside the cave, sunlight explodes. But caves that are deep keep the warmth out even if they are dry. This one is damp.

'I don't see why you need them.' She holds one up to the torch and evidently, as girls do, decides that the stone is pretty and worth keeping, so begins to gather them in the lap of her dress. Still she sighs. 'Why must you collect things you find? It will only get you into trouble. Those dead animals . . .'

'Shh . . .' he says, irritated. He holds up his hand. Is that a bat? He strains his eyes in the dark but can make out nothing, other than a chunk of rock like the shoulder of a huge animal lying above them. 'One day it won't,' he says.

'I don't see how you can be so sure,' Lisa continues. She strokes the rock and clusters of fragments fall at her feet.

He listens harder. He wonders about bats. He makes a note

in his mind to find out how they see in the dark. Then he wonders how to find out. He turns to Lisa; she is waiting for a reaction. Distracted, he says, 'Sometimes people can't see things because they are blind. Not blind in their eyes but blind in their heads.'

Lisa bends down to pick up pieces of stone. 'People can't be blind in their heads,' she says, scornfully. Then, doubtfully, 'Can they?'

He picks up one of the stones and stares at it. 'Sometimes. But only when they're scared.'

'Like with the monster?'

'Yes,' he says, considering. 'Like with the monster.' He remembers the look of fear on his father's face. A thought takes hold of him, nags at his mind and settles there. He looks deep into the cave and fancies he can hear the sound of squeaking, high and thin like the creak of a branch on a windy day. The flaming torch he has left propped up against a rock on the ground begins to die. 'When the light goes out, you want to leave because you can't see,' he says. 'But the cave is just the same as before. It's only the dark, that's all.' For an instant he sees himself going up to her and taking her hand in the dark. Another bat jolts him out of it.

'So one day they won't be?'

'Won't be what?' Blind? he wonders. Scared?

He looks down at the stones she has gathered. She's pulled up her dress to make a nest for them. But they're not stones – they're something else: something more beautiful, something with a purpose. He picks one up and examines it closer. Something about it bothers him. It feels like a stone, but doesn't look like one.

Pebbles come from stones; stones come from rocks; rocks come from crags. You only have to look at a crag to see that. But this stone is different. Not part of something bigger. Complete. He turns it over in his hand. It's pitted with holes and wrinkled like the skin of an old man's face.

She takes it from his hand. Her fingers brush against his. 'That's a pretty one. Will you make me a keepsake?'

He looks at her in confusion. 'A keepsake? What for?' The thought enters his mind and hits a wall. He looks at the stone. 'I'm going to break it open to see what it's made of.' The moment the words come out he knows they were the wrong ones. Lucky that he has kept some of their harvest of stones back, because, on hearing him, she runs off with the rest – as if it's another game he's misunderstood. The light snuffs out and he's left in darkness.

Better off without her, he trudges back down the mountain-side, speeding up at the easy parts and all the while looking ahead. The kestrels are back, soaring overhead on currents he cannot see. He stops in his tracks. Clouds cross the sky, casting their shadows over the plains below and changing the hue of the countryside they cover. The fields move with colour. Gold floods green. Alders quiver with wind-blown shadow. A group of pines shoots into bold relief, fading as the cloud moves on. More light, more colour. He closes his eyes, stamps it on his mind and tightens his hand over the stones. He races down the hill.

He spends the rest of the day considering the stones and finds his answer. They are not stones but shells: seashells. Albiera tells him.

He has only seen pictures of the ocean in books; she has been to the coast.

'What is their purpose?' he asks.

'Some people use them for decoration,' Albiera says. He nods. Albiera doesn't know. He hurries away to scour every book he can find in the library about the sea. Fra Alessandro catches him wading through the shelves and seems pleased. 'I can see that you're taking your work seriously,' his tutor says, nodding with pleasure, 'although I don't see what such volumes have to do with your Bible studies.'

'The Great Flood,' he says, without thinking.

Alessandro looks over his shoulder and sees pictures of water. 'Ah, yes. But if it's a drawing you're thinking of doing, you'd do better to copy something from God's Book than this.' They both look at the book; Poseidon stares back, his mane a shock of illuminated gold. The old man turns the page.

'Venus,' he points, 'goddess of great beauty.' Fra Alessandro closes the book firmly. 'Geometry,' his tutor says and yawns. 'But first a nap.'

By the following day he has discovered the purpose of shells. He runs back to Albiera and – since she doesn't know – tells her. 'See,' he says, showing her the picture of a shell alongside a drawing of Poseidon. The body of a crab is poking out of it. 'They're houses.' Albiera holds one in her palm and looks at it with interest. He looks up at her face and thinks about the empty cradle. 'You can keep it, if you like it.' He looks at the shell as she closes her fingers over it. His shell houses are not like those in the picture. This one is hard and wrinkled. He thinks of the dog that died and went stiff. His shells, which once contained living creatures, have also been transformed. He imagines the dog after one week, then a year, then even longer. He turns away and smiles with new understanding. Not death. Time.

Days lengthen, midsummer passes. Albiera says she will take him to the city of Vinci. He wonders: will he see his mother? So he says no, he doesn't want to go. He has decided not to think about the face at the window, and doesn't want to have to. Albiera looks at him closely. She says, 'All right then. I'll give you bread and cheese and you can play in the field.' He nods, thinking how small the field is and wondering whether Albiera really thinks he stays in it. He looks outside. Plenty of daylight left yet. He says, 'Fra Alessandro is feeling too hot. Should I take him some wine?' Albiera hands him the terracotta flask with a knowing look. 'If it gets dark and you are not back . . .'

'. . . you will take away the chalk and remove the paper.' He finishes the sentence for her, with his best smile.

With the help of the wine, Fra Alessandro snoozes his way through a month of lessons. This leaves Leonardo free to find more answers to his questions, and more questions to ask. Each question drives him out. He makes his way through woods and groves like a denizen of the forest, stopping to draw not from books, but from nature. He examines soil and cliffs, explores new caves and follows the course of rivers and brooks. He feels the presence of fox and boar, hears the music of water over stone and smells the colour of leaf and bark. The play of the wind on long river grasses, the hollow sound of winged flight – one the response to the other: easy conversations. At nightfall he somehow finds his way back to the house on the hill, guided by the light of the candle in the window, which Albiera leaves out at dusk.

In his prayers before sleep he asks God to bring him another surprise in the morning. Today he brought a miracle.

The sun was warm, the air still and heavy. He was climbing Mount Albano. He broke through the trees and hit the path that winds around the cusp of the hill past a line of pine trees. He stopped to sketch a pine cone. As he made the first trace a drop of rain fell onto his hand. Worried about his paper, he rolled it up and slipped it carefully into his pouch. More drops fell on his arms and his head. He found a broad pine and sheltered underneath it. He looked up.

Around him the sky painted two pictures: one rainy and one sunny. There, where the two pictures met, a third unfolded. Chest thumping with excitement, he pulled out his paper; then looked at his grey chalk in despair. He must cast it aside and observe. The shades of colour curved across the sky in an arch. He followed it through every different kind of green to every different shade of pink and violet. A watery cloud swallowed the colour; then it reappeared again as before, except that the colours had changed. They formed a circle and vanished.

He ran up the path to get a better view, his mind racing. But the sun was in his eyes. He stopped. He took out his chalk and paper, squatted down and began to write. A round drop of rainwater settled on his paper. He brushed it away and noted the place: *Mount Albano, late summer, tenth cave visit. The Sky*. Then he wrote: *The colour is caused by the sun and the rain*. He looked at the sun; it was well past noon. In the east the light was fading. A glassy cloud scudded over the sun, putting it out like a dampened fire. The colour melted away. He pulled out his penknife and deftly sharpened the chalk. *The colour is caused by the sun and the rain.* He creased his brow; the thought took shape: colours change with the light. He thought of grass under the sun; grass under cloud. He wrote: *The colour is in the light. The light goes through the rain. The rain* – he smudged out the words – *The raindrops change the colour.* He thought of the curved glass he used to make the fire at the entrance of the cave. He looked at the stain on the paper; the rain has made a round damp patch. He wrote: *The raindrops are round.* Then he wrote: *So is the colour.*

He folded up the paper and put it in his pouch. When he got back he would add it to the other notes he had kept. He left the mountain earlier than usual, tearing down the slope with a head full of colour. When he opened the door, Fra Alessandro was waiting for him in the study.

'Where have you been all morning?' the old man asked, curiously. 'What have you been doing?'

'Watching things.'

'What things?' Fra Alessandro's expression changed to one of concern; it reminded him of the moments that he sits down to sketch, or has the beginning of a thought. 'So,' the tutor said, 'what have you been watching?'

'The sky.'

'The sky?' Fra Alessandro appeared relieved. 'What did you see in the sky?'

'Colour,' he replied. Wrong answer. More dismay. He sat down at the desk and pushed a page of arithmetic towards his tutor. 'Shall I start on this?'

His tutor cast his eyes over Leonardo, his page of sums, and his hands. 'I suppose you should.'

He looked down. His hands, strong, brown from the sun, were scored with grazes from scraping shells from cave walls, sharpening chalk and collecting samples. He hid them in his lap. Hurt welled up in his head and dropped into his throat. His eyes burned with tears that wouldn't fall. The words burst out and he couldn't stop them. 'I don't care, I don't care.' He jumped from his seat and marched towards the door. 'I don't want to do any more. The sums are too easy.' He glanced back; Fra Alessandro had raised his hands to the sky and then dropped them at his side.

At length Fra Alessandro stops waiting for his return. Lisa too is no longer waiting for him, either by the river or on the mountain. For a moment he wonders whether she too is in trouble at home, but he is sure that whatever it is, it must be his fault — keepsakes he didn't make; something he said or didn't say. Things are easier this way, he tells himself. Who can say whether Lisa would have liked the rainbow, or whether Fra Alessandro would have been able to see it?

It is late at night. People are asleep but the other world — the one in which he lives — is still awake. Night creatures move unseen beyond the walls of the house. Only the flicker of his candle makes shapes and shadows on the walls. On the small table in front of him beside the candle is a picture he has drawn of the river. He drew it one day after a summer squall, when rain had fallen all at once and swollen the river. Albiera told him about times past when the water from the river burst from its banks and washed into houses and barns, drowning animals and spoiling food and crops. It was punishment from God, she said, for those of the city who had not confessed their sins or had sinned too much.

Beside the picture are the notes he made about the rainbow. Then there are others, much more prolific. Many rolls of paper tied together with string. He takes out the small, cracked mirror from his pouch. He has smoothed off the edges so that it's nearly round. He holds up the mirror to the paper and smiles. The words, written from right to left with the help of the mirror, now become legible. Only those who truly want to understand will be able to read them. His message is safe.

He returns to bed, blows out the candle and closes his eyes. He sees wolves roaming the woods and voles curled up in holes beneath the warm earth, in the cavities of stone walls and in the river banks. They are plucked from their sleep by torrents of raging water and mud where horses flounder, their heads straining above the water line. Then suddenly, from the sky above, lightning strikes: a bright shafting fork. The flood becomes fire; the people scream and cry out, their arms skyward. And there, high up and far, far above it all, curves the gentle arc of a brilliant rainbow, glinting in the sun.

He wakes with a head full of water, his mind surging with Albiera's flood and God's punishment. He creeps into the kitchen and steals a piece of bread from the shelf. By dawn his legs are halfway up Mount Albano. By noon his head is in the clouds. By dusk he is still out there. Albiera has sent the stable hand to find him. He can see the light of an oil lamp from where he is sitting on the ridge of the hill. The lamp travels along the ridge towards him, in the growing dark. It's getting cold, but he's in no mind to go in. From the trees above him the soft, warm call of a barn owl fills the frozen air.

'Messer Leonardo!'

He sits quietly still. The voice, a hollow echo, moves over the ridge towards him. Another joins it: Albiera's. One light becomes two. For the first time in months he has a memory of his mother waiting at the table for him to open the door. Somewhere in the undergrowth the owl has taken a mouse or a shrew. There's a flurry of movement, squeaking. In a surge of feathers and weight the bird flies off. He shivers and stands up. He picks up his pouch, heavy with shells and stones, cuttings and notes, and walks back along the ridge in the colourless moonlight.

The next day his tutor sits him down before the First Book of Moses.

'I've read it,' he announces.

'All of it?'

'Enough.'

'Really?' Fra Alessandro replies, his hand twitching the teaching stick. 'You are familiar with the teachings of God to Moses on the mountain?' The tutor looks doubtful, but pleased too. Leonardo feels a rush of enthusiasm.

'Good.' Fra Alessandro sits down. 'In that case you can recite the Ten Commandments to me.'

He takes a breath. 'You shall have no other Gods but me,' he begins. 'You must not steal or kill' – he remembers the lizard – 'unless it is really necessary.'

Fra Alessandro holds up his hand, frowning. 'Stop right there,' the old man says. 'I don't think that is quite what was written.'

The eyes of his tutor flicker over his bulging pouch. 'Let me see your work.'

He hesitates. What use is knowledge if you have no one to share it with? How is Fra Alessandro ever to see that the world is more than a book if he, Leonardo, does not explain? Isn't the truth important? It must be; if it weren't, surely Fra Alessandro wouldn't be there? A sense of urgency grips him. He pulls the wad of paper from his pouch and hands it to his tutor.

Fra Alessandro becomes quiet. He stares at the first page of the notebook without turning it over. The rivulets and streams of his face have dried up, but new lines have formed; his brow furrows like a ploughed field. Eyes squinting, the tutor stammers, 'But, what is this?'

'Writing,' he replies. Thinking that perhaps he should have pointed this out before, he hurriedly explains. 'You have to want to see, when you look,' is the best he can offer. Clearly it isn't enough. Turning the page upside down and this way and that, Fra Alessandro appears as perplexed as he has ever seen him. He takes pity. Leading his tutor to a mirror in an antechamber of the study, where his father would stop and fasten his cloak or adjust his hat, he holds up the page. The writing, which runs from right to left, now appears from left to right, entirely legible when the reader looks in the glass.

Fra Alessandro looks at Leonardo with a new expression. 'What is all this? How—' The tutor breathes deeply and corrects himself. '—why did you write this page backwards?'

'It's not just one page, see.' He returns Fra Alessandro to the desk. Fra Alessandro backs away. 'Possessed, possessed,' the tutor mutters. Then he does a strange thing: he clasps his hands together and begins to pray.

'Wait, stop,' Leonardo says. Fra Alessandro does not understand. But he will explain. 'It's not about the Ten Commandments, it's about the Great Flood. Look.' Wanting more than anything for Fra Alessandro to understand the connection between the shells and his notes, he produces the small bag of shells gathered from the cave and points to one of his sketches. The old man seems glad to see the shells. He takes out his spectacles and picks one up.

'You have been busy collecting things. Is this all you have collected?'

'There are more,' he says, eagerly. He pulls out the rest of his harvest. He spreads the shells on the table, their age set in stone. A wall of flesh, Fra Alessandro's wrinkled face looks down at them.

'See. They are shells, creatures of the sea.'

This startles Fra Alessandro. 'You've been to the sea? When?'

'No, no, no,' he smiles, thinking how it was that people seemed to become more stupid the older they get. 'The sea came to me.' Fra Alessandro points numbly to the open page where Leonardo left his father's book. Poseidon stands above turgid waters, his arm spanning great waves as they break and froth and churn.

He laughs in delight. 'The shells come from a cave in the mountains, beyond Prato Magno on Monte Albano.' He turns one of the pages of his notes over and shows strata of soil, where shells gleam like precious stones, row after row.

'B–but,' his tutor stutters, 'what does this have to do with the Great Flood?'

'Everything,' he says, carefully lining the shells up on the desk before him. 'The Bible, you see, has made a mistake.'

In the garden outside, the figure of Albiera walks past the window, humming. From the other side of the hill, the small church of Vinci sounds five o'clock mass. Fra Alessandro jumps. As though he has come to his senses after a period of blankness, his tutor picks up the teaching stick.

'Let's get this quite right.' Fra Alessandro gestures to the book where drawings stand out against lines of code. 'Your study says that the Book of God is wrong?'

'Well,' says Leonardo, looking up from the shells, 'there are often floods, but Noah's flood doesn't make sense.'

His tutor's face changes colour – from red to grey.

'Listen, child: knowledge is knowledge. You can't change it just because it pleases you. These things are written. And quite normally,' the tutor adds under his breath, although Leonardo knew that he was still expected to hear.

The voice inside his head takes over. 'But other things are also written,' he says. 'Are we not supposed to read them?'

'Written? Written where?'

He points to the drawings of the caves. 'In the land,' he says. 'I have read the land and the land tells another story than yours.'

'*God's*,' corrects his tutor in a thunderous voice, raising his finger in the air. '*God's* story.'

'But since God made the land,' he went on, 'then his story is written surely in the land, because the land is older than a book.' The teaching stick begins to wave to and fro.

'Older than a book . . .' says Fra Alessandro, '. . . makes no sense at all.' His voice booms and the stick waves. *No sense at all.*

Leonardo sits motionless in his chair. His tutor is angry. He thinks of the shells hidden in his room. Nobody will find those: they are his. He has found them. He shall keep them. They will not be thrown onto a fire.

Fra Alessandro looks at him, sighs and sits down. 'Say what you want to say, then the subject is closed,' he says.

'I've been up the mountain like Moses. That's where I found the shells. But these shells, they come from the sea. Now, this must mean that once, a long time ago—' he thinks of the wrinkled stone face of the shells '—the sea came as far as here and covered all the land.'

'Wouldn't that make it a flood?' Fra Alessandro interjects, then becomes more animated by the idea. 'If these shells are from water, there was water once where now there is none. A flood!' the tutor adds triumphantly.

'Yes,' Leonardo says patiently, 'and no. Your story sounds more like a sudden river flood.' Alessandro looks confused, so he continues. 'Look, these stones are complete. They're shells. They aren't from crags; they had creatures in them. And they lived in salt water, seawater. In which case, the Book of God just doesn't make sense. The book says it rained for forty days and forty nights then the water went away. If it all happened so quickly, why are there so many layers like there are in the caves?' He points to his drawings of the cave wall. He has not been to the ocean, but he has seen pictures. He imagines oceans lapping the shores of the mountains he climbed all summer; layers of mud like the mud of river beds, creatures trapped in mud, mud drying up and becoming rock. The slow work of time. 'The shells were in the rock, first one layer, then another, then another.'

'Well?' says his tutor.

'That must have taken more than forty days. The book has got it wrong.' The teaching stick rolls off the desk. He picks it up for his tutor. 'Anyway, how could all that water go down so quickly? Where would it go? If it did what water does after a big storm, if it all poured into rivers, and went down the mountain, then everything would be washed away, wouldn't it?'

This last question seems to drive his tutor beyond patience. Fra Alessandro shakes his head vigorously and stands up. His face has turned livid. The tutor grasps Leonardo's hand with a strong and painful grip. Propelling him towards the door, Fra Alessandro flings it open. To his great relief mixed with trepidation, the figure of a man bars the way. He swings off his cloak and strides into the study, removing his cap.

'What is all this commotion?' It is his father returned at last! Surely saved by the shield, his father towers over them both like Poseidon over the waves, his face like thunder.

The shadows creep in from the hills. Animals are stirring from the apathy of the day's heat and preparing for the onset of night. Rabbits have emerged to graze the open meadows between the thickets. Polecats seek the scent of the rabbits and will stalk them into the night. Martens will prowl the groves for fallen fledglings; while above them starlings are filling the trees, jostling as they roost. He sits listening from the open window of the small chamber where later at night he sleeps. He has snuffed his candle to better see and hear, but regrets it now, as the sense of unease that has dogged him since his father's return increases with the shadows that close in on him from every side. His mind heavy with anxiety, he slips out of his chamber, with the idea of returning to the study and the relative comfort of the books that line its shelves like sentinels standing guard over Fra Alessandro's knowledge.

Where is Fra Alessandro now? And where is his father? Both have retreated into his father's study while he has been instructed to return to his chamber. He creeps through the corridors past the lighted room where Albiera sleeps and, on reaching the study door, sees it slightly ajar, and the room still occupied. The voices of the two men float clearly through the silence of the night. He moves closer to listen. He remembers the night he heard his mother and father talking to the background of Antonio's brutal voice. There had been tears and the sound of sobbing. He blots out the sound that lingers in his memory and strains to listen to this one, dread rising in his throat.

'I have told you my opinion, Ser Piero – the boy is possessed. He's not normal; there's something, something . . . how can I say? Well, it goes against all I have ever seen of boys, and I have seen many. No flood, he says, no flood! Do you realise that if the Padre of Vinci were to hear that he would refuse Communion? Now if the Pope were to hear it . . .'

'Yes, all right, all right.' Footsteps cross the library floor. 'Nobody will hear it. Nobody has to hear it, now do they?'

'But what about this, this picture? Eh? I never saw such a thing! A painting without people, such savagery, such . . . such visions as I have never seen.' More footsteps. 'Yes, visions; the visions of a demon, the visions of . . .'

'Enough,' his father cries.

Among the notes he showed Fra Alessandro, there had been the picture he had drawn: the wind and the torrent of the river, wild water swirling into mud, while the rock of the mountain-side rose implacably beyond. He had drawn it with Lisa the last time he had seen her. Fra Alessandro had not liked it; where the tutor looked for people, he, Leonardo, saw nature; where the tutor looked for churches, he saw miracles. But still, it changed nothing: on the other side of the door, the conversation went on.

'The boy can draw; that much is certain.'

'Draw, yes – write also – see this.'

He understands that Fra Alessandro is showing his father his secret notes. He wishes more than anything that he had taken them with him and hidden them. Chastising himself for lessons not learnt since the day of the monster, he resolves to hide them the first chance he has.

There is a long silence. He hears the turning of pages, then more silence.

'And why did you not notice this sooner?'

'I . . . what do you mean, sooner?'

'You are his tutor. Why didn't you follow his work – correct it?'

Fra Alessandro is getting up. A chair scrapes the floor.

'Correct his work, I . . .'

'What about his mathematics?'

'The boy excels in figures, but—'

'If he excels, he can be taught.'

'Taught, perhaps. But governed – led? And there is his speed. He performs his calculations like some sort of wielder of magic.'

Another exclamation. 'A little ability – that's all. You go too far.'

'Too far?' There is a pause. 'This script of his – look at it.'

More silence.

'The words alone would be enough to put him on the stake. If I did not teach him this, who did?'

He leans his head against the wall, his mind struggling to make sense of this new Fra Alessandro. At length his father's voice speaks again, more subdued. 'Perhaps it would be best if you left. I shall find another tutor.'

'That may prove harder than you think. I have been indulgent with him – but he will grow up. As a child he is only in danger; but as a man he is, well, dangerous.' More silence, then the sound of chairs scraping. 'I see that you have your own ideas on the subject and have no wish to hear mine.' Another pause. 'I shall wish you good night.'

Footsteps push him back into the shadows. He presses himself into the wall behind the open door, while the figure of Fra Alessandro sweeps by, leaving a wake of crushing darkness which holds him in a grip of iron until the figure of Alessandro has moved away. His father pulls the study door shut. Now that there is nothing else to listen to, despair washes through him. Unable to think, he waits in the darkness for something to take away the misery. Nothing comes except pain: he cuts the head off the lizard – its body twists and shudders, then stops. A shadow is at the window – weak daylight illuminates a face, then it's gone. Albiera is praying because the cradle is empty. His father's face is a sad face. His father would like another child, but God will not grant him one. From inside the study, he hears the sound of footsteps and pushes the thoughts aside. Instead he imagines a big fire, burning with paper, sizzling with shells.

His feet come to life. He leaves the wall and takes the stairs three at a time. He pulls the door to the bedchamber shut behind him and scoops the pile of paper from the table. He takes the rest of his notes and rolls them up. The pile is thick but the paper is supple. He ties the bundle carefully with string. In an old tunic, which he lays out on the bed, he places a few of his best specimens of shells, as well as a few sketches, and carefully folds it up. He freezes, thinking he hears movement on the stairs. The wing of a bird brushes past the window opening. He goes to the wall and runs his hand against the stone. Pulling out a piece, he puts his hand into the cavity and feels around. It's dry, but as a precaution he puts the tunic in first and then the paper. There's just enough space. Hurriedly he replaces the stone, snuffs out the candle and looks out from the window opening onto the path that leads round the side of the house from the entrance. Cicadas croak from the long grasses that line the path. From the sea of green the stunted shapes of twisted olive trunks cover the hillside; their pale leaves will turn the moonlight silver. Into this picture steps the figure of his tutor. He wonders for a moment whether Fra Alessandro will turn back to look, and see his face at the window. But no; the tutor's dewlapped cloak billows out behind in the dark, and the night – devourer of people, bearer of evil news – quickly swallows the grey of his lonely silhouette, and in an instant he is gone.

V

He did not see his father the next day, or the one after that. He spent both days out on the mountain, but he didn't return to the cave. Nor did he sit by the river. Now he has found a viewpoint on the side of the eastern face of Mount Albano and busies himself with sketching, starting on one subject then abandoning it for another until he finally loses interest in everything but the horizon. When in the evening he returns to the candle in the window, he feels glad to see it, and wants more than anything to escape the dark and the sounds of night animals and find a fire and a welcome and a home.

Four days pass. He cleans out the stable. He sweeps the yard. He waits. It is late afternoon and a figure appears on the crest of the hill. He watches it descend into the valley and follow the course of the stream. A man on foot leading a horse.

He runs down the path. His father stops at the sight of him. The sky breaks up; a clap of thunder fills the valley. He takes the reins.

'Check her legs, Leonardo,' his father says. The clouds open. Sheets of rain lash the ground around them but the mare won't run. 'I've been walking her since the other side of the city.'

Once in the stable, he runs his hand down the mare's legs, one at a time. He feels her flinch. He tries to raise her fetlock but the mare won't let him.

'I think it's a sprain,' he says. 'If it is, then it's the other leg. She won't let me pull up this one because she doesn't want to put her weight on the other.'

His father looks worried. 'Poultice the leg.'

He is looking at the leg. 'Father, a knife.' He pushes his body against the side of the horse to give support and lifts the sprained foot. Taking the knife, he draws out a large thorn. 'By all the saints!' His father smiles. 'The thorn was here, beside the frog of the foot,' Leonardo says. 'She must have put the hoof down unevenly and pulled on this tendon.' He runs his hand over the tendon. The mare flinches again.

His father sits down beside the stall, removes his hat, smoothes back his hair and turns to him. 'Who taught you these things?'

'Nobody.'

'Then how do you know them?'

He shrugs his shoulders. 'By watching, mainly,' he says. 'And making notes,' he adds, cautiously waiting for a reaction. But his father doesn't want to give one. He takes a breath. 'Sometimes I go to the slaughterhouse. Once I saw the body of a horse that had died. I promised to cut ten sacks of herbs for the *patrone* if he let me cut open a leg.'

'Cut open a leg?'

His father leans his head in his hands. The walk from the city has made him tired. He offers to make him a tonic.

'That is kind of you, Leonardo, but not right now.' Then, after a long silence, 'It will have to stop, this ... this cutting things up ... this note-taking.'

He looks down at his hands, clasped together and hot. 'Stop?' Outside the barn the rain is still drenching the ground. He thinks of things that stop. Rain stops, for a while. Rivers don't; they go underground. 'Is it because of Fra Alessandro? You don't have to tell me anyway, I know it is.'

'Normally,' his father says sternly, throwing a cloth over the mare's back, 'boys do not go to slaughterhouses to cut things up; normally they do not disappear in the morning and return in the evening, unless they are the children of savages; normally,' he finishes, his voice flat, 'they write forwards, not backwards.'

'But I only did it to keep it safe,' he blurts out.

His father looks at him strangely. 'To keep what safe, Leonardo?'

He doesn't reply at once; but his father is waiting. 'Once there was a girl in the city who died,' he says, 'When she died everything she wore was burnt, all her clothes, even her playthings and her blanket.'

'She was sick,' his father replies. 'It was safer to burn her clothes because the sickness was on them too. But you are not sick, are you?' His father comes over to him and puts his arm around his shoulder. 'I understand that you are a ... curious child, and always were. But there are certain things you must understand. The world is made of people who fall into groups. There are princes and emperors; there are men of faith; there are merchants and noblemen; there are us. I am a notary like my father before me and his father before him. It is a respectable profession, but already it has its limitations. I have always tried to do my best for you, but,' his father says firmly, 'this cutting things up, this note-taking, this running wild in the hills must stop at once.'

It's more than unfair. His father agrees with Fra Alessandro. He thinks of the teaching stick and Fra Alessandro's pages of figures. His mind travels from the figures to Moses, then to the Ark, from the Ark to the calculations of mass and weight, from the calculations to the animals, from the animals to the horse's leg. From the leg to muscle, bone and blood; from blood to water, water to earth; the rivers of the body of nature and man, living, breathing as one, awaiting only the touch of his knife, his steady hand, his ready eye: his total understanding. 'I can't,' he says.

Night descends on Anchiano. The world is dark. The door is shut and locked. He has had no meal but he is not hungry. He does not need food. He listens for the call of the barn owl he heard again last night, but can hear only the churning of his stomach. On the other side of the door, a lighted candle approaches. His father unlocks the door and enters. The punishment is over. His father looks less angry, more tired.

Leonardo stands up. His father speaks. 'Albiera is waiting for you in the kitchen with soup.' He puts down the candle and sits on his bed. 'After you've eaten, I want you to pack your things. Then you must sleep, because tomorrow we have a long journey ahead of us and you will be tired.'

He follows his father down to the kitchen. He eats, packs a bag of clothes with Albiera's help. When Albiera has left the room, he goes to the hole in the wall and takes out the old tunic containing his notes. He hides the unfinished pages in the trunk at the bottom, beneath a heavy woollen cloak. The rest, together with the drawing of the rainbow and the butterfly board, he wedges carefully into the space between the stones of the wall. He lies awake for a while, thinking of the candle in the window downstairs, and closes his eyes.

He is riding the mare. Her leg is healed and she is galloping. Fields, trees and streams fly past and the wind is in his face. But fear seizes him. His hands slacken on the reins. This is no horse he's riding. He looks down at the body of a giant monster: part lizard, part dog. Scales and teeth and claw extend beneath him as the creature takes flight. He closes his eyes then looks a second time, doubting what he sees, but fear turns to horror. Rotting before his eyes, the monster breaks apart beneath him, shoulder, leg and back decomposing as he spurs it on – through verdant valleys, past silent caves, until they reach the highest peak of the tallest mountain – until he can see everything.

He has said goodbye to Albiera. She gave him food for the journey, then hugged him. 'Be careful,' she said. 'Florence is a big city. Don't get lost.'

'I never did,' he said. He looked at the valley, the forest and the hills and wondered when he would see them next.

He's riding on a gelding borrowed from the farm, with the pack containing his belongings. The lane runs past the pink villa by the river, with the wall where Lisa would lie in wait for him on his way to the mountain.

'I have to make a stop – notary business. Come with me,' his father says, dismounting and taking a hard look at him. 'Button your doublet.' Coming over to Leonardo and straightening his beret himself, his father says, 'Say nothing, just do as I tell you.'

The maid opens the door to admit them to the notary's office. They enter a room of miracles. Not natures, man's. The walls are hung with soft hangings: tapestries. On the parts of the wall not hidden by tapestries there are carvings: some stone, some wood. Elm, or birch. Every other space is filled with objects: vases and ornaments painted with fruit and leaves. Great, tall windows draped in a fabric that changes colour, from green to blue then back to green. Raised shapes of thistles and pomegranates with acanthus leaves around; he recognises oak leaves, pine cones and thistle heads. Fine gold threads shine here and there against a background of soft, deep scarlet. These are not the colours of the world he knows; they represent another, more intense one which makes him catch his breath.

He watches as another man enters the room and sits down in a large chair of carved wood. His father stands. The man examines some papers his father hands him. The man asks questions; his father must reply. This man is Lisa's father. He can see a family likeness: strong brow, strong stare. A mirror hangs on the wall to his right. He sees himself: more robust than he thought, thin but not fragile. Long arms, long fingers, long hair. Then he looks at his father; they could be strangers. But now, as he watches him, he becomes conscious of two things. *This is how the world works.* His father, bound by the demands of his profession and the status it has given him, is as different from Lisa's father as a rabbit is from a stoat. The rabbit is at the mercy of the stoat, while the stoat hides from the hawk. The boy in the mirror is neither rabbit nor stoat. Fra Alessandro said so himself.

The two men move into another room and he is left alone. His eyes fall upon a painting, a portrait of a young girl and her mother. The girl is young, perhaps seven or eight. The face is recognisable as Lisa's, but lacks something vital, as though there has been a misunderstanding, and the painter has got it wrong. He remembers Albiera's face before he liked it, then after. He furrows his brow and moves closer. Lisa stares back at him, willing him to find what's missing.

'Don't you like it?' A door closes softly and the subject of the painting crosses the empty room in living form. The green wool dress for out of doors has been replaced by one that whispers as she walks. He thinks of dry leaves, branches in the wind.

He turns from the Lisa on the wall to the one at his side. 'Not much.'

She holds out her hand and fills his empty one with petrified spirals: shells from the cave. 'I thought you might want them,' she says. He takes the peace offering graciously, stares at his palm and thinks how strange it is that things are only ever half-understood. Just the shells are complete.

'Well, why don't you – like it?'

He looks back at the portrait and smiles. 'I'll tell you when I find out.'

'Tomorrow?'

'Perhaps.'

He doesn't mention he is leaving. In any case, he knows he'll be back. He closes his fingers over the stone spiral in his hand, wondering if it's the shell that stays in the mountain, or the mountain that stays in the shell.

The men have finished their business. Their approaching voices drive Lisa out of the room. She slips through a far door, while to the right another opens to admit their fathers. 'Your apprentice?' asks Lisa's father, nodding his way.

'My son,' his father replies.

'Fine-looking boy you've been keeping to yourself.'

He passes his reflection in the mirror as they leave, sees himself as they do: worse off than both the rabbit and the stoat. If he's honest about it, according to the laws of this human world into which he was born out of wedlock, he does not even exist.

They walk the path beside the stone wall to the stable. A butterfly has landed on a patch of milk parsley at the base of the wall. Black on yellow, two orange spots, wings held vertically so it's not going anywhere – for the time being. *Papilio Macaone*. Once he would have leant across and seized it. Now he'll let it fly.

They drop out of the valley and he sees Antonio's house profiled against a blue slate sky. Somewhere within those walls is his mother. As the building becomes no more than a speck, he turns his face downhill and his body towards the wind, with the weight of all that he has left behind pressing on his back.

If the road is good, his father says, they will be in Florence by nightfall. It is the festival of the *brucatura*. The olive harvest is early and the groves are full of baskets. Less visible are the harvesters, their bodies concealed by clouds of grey-green leaves.

He knows that they are approaching the city. Disturbed by people, birds scatter; water voles stop playing in the brook; a suspicious crow goes cawing into the woods. It is late September. Antonio will be killing the pig. The harvest will be in; the land stripped of growth. Nature has filled their stomachs for another winter.

The first thing he sees is the cathedral. It rises above the rest of the buildings and stands out clearly in the sun. Its shape catches his attention.

'*Il Duomo,*' said his father, pointing it out. 'What do you think of it?'

If you cut the cathedral dome in half and drew it, he considers, it would make an octagon. A great wall surrounds the city, while within it, cutting through the middle, a river flows beneath bridges that join one bank to the other. The river is wide and deep, nothing like the brooks and streams he knows. He visualises the streams flowing into brooks and the brooks flowing into smaller rivers that join this larger one, like blood flows through living things. A bigger river means more people. More people mean more houses and more houses mean a cathedral. Like a grand structure, each section fits into place, and at the end of it Florence rises before him like the structure of all structures, and his eyes draw invisible lines through every shape and dome and tower, stamping a pattern in his mind so that he wishes he had a piece of charcoal and a scrap of paper.

'I like it,' he says.

The city walls are as high as many men, built to keep enemies out. Enormous doors hang at the side of the great arch. 'Porta al Prato,' says his father, 'At last.' At the gates men ask them their business. An old woman stretches out a hand. Someone throws a coin; she bends to pick it up. Behind her, rows of green vegetables grow in the furrows of square fields. Further ahead is a flash of water: his stream has become a river, and the water smells different, less green, more brown. There is other water too; it flows alongside the streets as they enter the city; he notices how it carries more than just sediment and wonders where it goes.

He watches people; there are so many. Each wears an expression different from the other; every face gives something away.

Men shout from street corners, their faces watchful. Others talk in groups, hands resting on the shoulders of others, or on their own chests. Women cradle babies that cry: their faces just born. Youths argue in the square, their eyes hot and their mouths hard.

They cross a square and he catches another glimpse of the dome of the cathedral. 'This will be your home,' says his father. 'You see this street? It is Via Ghibellina, and here is Via de' Macci. The Maestro lives here. Tomorrow, I will show you where I work, then you can come and visit me if you need anything.'

He dismounts and places two feet firmly on the ground. If he is neither rabbit nor stoat, then who or what, in the midst of so many city people, is he? The answer comes unpleasantly fast: nobody in particular – Leonardo da Vinci.

'And how do you find our city?'

'Big. Dirty.'

'Dirty you say? Big?' The Maestro wipes short, fat, grimy hands on an apron over a stomach to rival Fra Alessandro's and raises an eyebrow. 'Then you have not seen our cathedral, our churches, our palaces.'

'I've seen the river. And I saw a beggar woman crawl in the mud to pick up a coin.'

'Well, then she at least was satisfied.'

'Not nearly as satisfied as the man who threw the coin. He was on a horse and had a whole pouch of *soldi*.'

The Maestro laughs. 'It is human nature to want more than we have, and to have more than we need. But tell me, is there anything that does please your eye in this poor city of ours?'

He looks through the window opening at the cathedral with

its perfectly balanced dome, like smouldering ashes as the sun strikes it. 'That,' he says.

The Maestro turns to his father. 'Your Leonardo is an astute observer.' The man looks him up and down judgementally. 'He also has a fine build, worthy of sculpture. But has he a steady hand?' Placing a piece of paper in front of him, the Maestro says, 'Draw the cathedral.'

Leonardo from Vinci, neither rabbit nor stoat, takes up the charcoal and begins to draw. At first he draws nothing but lines, faint and thin. From the lines will emerge the perfect shape of the domed basilica. Then, beneath it, he makes his first sketch of the cathedral as he imagines it; shapes fill his mind and he transposes one upon the other until the picture looks right.

While he draws, the Maestro talks. 'Don't think he will do no more than paint here; he will learn how to sculpt bronze and marble, and how to fashion silver.' The big man turns back to the table. 'And if you listen to everything I tell you, then all of this beauty—' waving his hand at the city '—can be yours. All you have to do is reach out and take it – with your hand.' The Maestro looks down at his hands – long fingers, wide palms – then picks up the finished sketch and looks at it. Standing beside his chair, it is his father who speaks next, but not before the cathedral breaks the silence. From above the rooftops a bell chimes loud and strong.

His father looks up from the sketch. 'When does he start?'

Florence

I

'Vinci? Where in the name of God is that?'

'A *podere* in the hills somewhere.'

'I heard his father was a notary, here in Florence.'

'Then why isn't he a notary too?'

'Don't think he can do additions.'

'Andrea says he has the eye of Brunelleschi and the hand of Giotto. That he made a perfect sketch of the cathedral from memory in a matter of minutes, after seeing it only once.'

'Nothing but shit!'

'Have you seen his hands? They're huge.'

'Let's hope his head is smaller.'

'A few months of painting terracotta and it soon will be, don't worry.'

He moves behind the screen. On the other side of it, the group of boys that constitute the workforce of the *bottega* of Maestro Andrea del Verrocchio are busy discussing his merits. He tucks his hands beneath his armpits and leans against the wall. It has been less than a week since he arrived. He has spent three days chipping marble and learning how to solder. He tries to be pleased with the result: you need a steady hand to catch a butterfly; years of pulling pieces of paper from a pouch and sketching living things against the back of a tree or on the

77

curve of a knee have given him both a steady hand and the will to put it to use. Painting terracotta is good, especially if he can mix his own colours. He never wanted to be a notary.

'His flower was better than yours, Domenico. So I presume it is envy rather than scorn that makes you speak, and since neither are good, I suggest you stay quiet.'

'Those are wise words, Sandro.' The Maestro has come up behind the screen and propels him forward to face the others beyond it.

There were moments like this, and then there was his body. It seemed to be growing away from him, making demands that he did not understand and could not fulfil. He had taken to scraping hair off his face with a penknife and water, and found that sometimes he had the energy of ten men, and at other times the force of a snail. Once he stripped and stood in front of the mirror in his room at the side of the *bottega*. His body shocked him when he saw it. He had never seen himself in a large mirror before and noticed that his arms were long and lean, his shoulders straight, his back supple. His first impulse was to draw, and he sat in front of the mirror sketching his legs and genitals. When he had finished the drawing, he found that the drawing was not the result he had thought it might be, but the beginning of another quest that led on, inexorably to other details. If he could have, he would have even taken a knife to his own legs and cut them open, to see what was inside and drawn that too. In fact, drawing the leg on the outside was, he considered, only half of the interest: what really mattered was what lay within.

'I understand that the head of our new apprentice has become a subject of debate,' Maestro Andrea says, eyes wide, and then turns to him. 'Leonardo, take off your tunic.'

He wonders if the mirror has eyes too. But he takes the tunic off, pulling the coarse wool over his undershirt. 'That too.' Maestro Andrea stands back and stares at his abdomen, pushing forward the majestic proportions of his own. 'You have good muscle.' The great man places his hand beneath Leonardo's chin and surveys his face, turning to the others. 'Beauty,' the Maestro says, 'is a gift that some of us are fortunate enough to possess. But it is important to remember that it lies as much beneath the skin as upon it.' The Maestro pats the muscle of his abdomen, then harder until his hand bounces off. 'It is the muscle that lies beneath the skin that gives us the length of the curve here—' the Maestro points '—and here,' looking him straight in the eye. 'The contents of the head are also useful.' The great man throws him his tunic. 'David and Goliath: victory of small over large. You will be my David. We start tomorrow at first light.'

He nods, thinks of the gaps in his Bible studies and the gaps of the mouths of caves.

'David, the young boy who cut off the head of the giant. The boy who was smaller than his opponent and inferior in force, but who nevertheless—' the Maestro places a sword in Leonardo's right hand '—vanquished him.'

He becomes David, and spends the best part of the next few weeks as model, not apprentice. The Maestro works and forms the mould of clay from which a bronze cast will emerge: of him, Leonardo, sword in hand, with the severed head of the giant at his feet. His body takes this form of boy turned killer of giants, while his head thinks it over.

A thought crystallises; his mind races. Andrea, the Maestro, hovers around him like a hawk, his hands grey with clay. He thinks about what's inside his leg and wonders if Andrea does too. He thinks of the horse's leg in the slaughterhouse. He thinks of the horse. Small versus large. Large. His hands grey with clay, he sees himself building the structure of a giant horse. More enthralling than a giant, his horse soars many times higher. He wants to throw down his sword and hold up his hands and say: Look, I will use these – these long hands, these wide palms. He looks round at the others, some watching, some working, and defies them to build higher than the son of a notary from Vinci. Andrea wipes his hand on a rag. 'Time to eat.' The Maestro touches him on the shoulder, hands him the rag, smiles at him. 'Get the bread, Leonardo. All this thinking will make you hungry.'

He resumes work on his notebook, which he has barely touched since what he now calls the time of the Great Flood. He recommences in earnest, convinced that with painting as much as with sculpture, the key lies beneath the skin. One thing leads to another: as skin harbours blood vessels, veins and arteries lead to and from muscle, and muscle leads to movement. Movement leads to force and force leads to power. Power, he concludes, leads to growth, whether human, animal or vegetable. He does not need the Maestro to tell him the story of David, just as he did not need Fra Alessandro to tell him about God. God is everywhere: observation is enough.

When Andrea lets him go, he slips out before dawn like he

used to – discovers new hills, new valleys, new things to draw. He likes the Maestro; Andrea understands that his charge finds some things boring, and his manner of instruction is relaxed, far from the days of the teaching stick and the pages of arithmetic. Meanwhile, he works on other things: his notes, and a painting of his own that he has not yet shown to anyone. Andrea has not made him paint terracotta; has not in fact asked him to paint at all – until now.

The great man is working on the altarpiece commission for the church of San Salvi. The background is unfinished. The figures of John the Baptist and Jesus have progressed to painting stage, and Leonardo watches as Andrea and two senior students mix the tempera base together from the usual blend of egg yolk, water and vinegar. He dislikes painting with tempera. The mix dries too soon, leaving no time for depth, light or shadow; colour comes out flat.

Andrea has his back to him, but must have eyes in his head.

'You don't like the tempera?'

He looks at the palm tree and decides it doesn't work. He thinks of another landscape, far back in time, distant blue like far-off hills. The water is wrong. He says nothing. Andrea swings round.

'Sandro and Leonardo. Come here, closer.' The one they call Botticelli, little barrel, moves nearer. He looks at him with approval. He likes the fine features and pensive face. He calculates his age. Goldsmith work, apprenticeship almost done, ready for his first commission and guild. Ten years older than him? Not quite. Steady hand. His eyes flick over to Sandro's study on the other bench: egg tempera on wood. Too much light. Too much profile. Not enough life.

'I am giving you both the opportunity to make a contribution.'

He feels the eyes of others prickling on his back. He looks up at Sandro, who is showing the Maestro a sketch of an angel. Now Andrea is speaking to him. 'Domenico will help you with the tempera. The background has been prepared here.' Andrea points to the preliminary sketches for a river, with trees beyond.

'The river Jordan was a wilderness.'

The Maestro leans back, hands on stomach. 'Is that what you want to paint, Leonardo? A wilderness?'

He warms up. 'Yes, and then there's the figure of Jesus, and the water at his feet. And then of course there is the idea of baptism.'

Andrea looks startled. 'The idea of baptism?'

'Well,' he says, 'forgetting for a moment the concept of divinity ...'

'But not for too long,' Andrea puts in.

'... baptism means the cleansing of mortal sin, doesn't it?' Andrea nods, so he goes on. 'Therefore Jesus was, according to the philosophy of baptism, a mortal sinner.'

More eyes on his back. 'What do you suggest? That we paint him as a sinner?'

'I thought, Maestro, that perhaps we could paint him as a man?'

'Sinners like the rest of us ... You are asking too much, Leonardo.' The great man sits down and clasps his hands. 'And how do you suggest we achieve such a transformation?'

'By adding muscle here—' He points to the legs. 'And removing it there—' He indicates the shoulders. 'A man is both strong and weak; his body can be fragile as much as his will may be strong. Sometimes the body is strong but the will is weak. Perhaps the right combination of physical frailty, muscular strength and reflection would suggest both?'

Andrea considers him. 'So what do *you* think Jesus was, Leonardo, strong or weak?'

He thinks of the lizard, the maggoty dog and the sick child whose clothes were burnt. 'We are all weak,' he says, 'Because we are all going to die. Jesus died too – on the cross.'

'No, no, it is a good point,' Andrea says, holding up his hand to silence nervous laughter. 'I will allow you to finish work on the body and begin the angel, here at the side. Then you will complete the landscape,' he says to him. 'Sandro will paint the second angel, and the rest of you will attend to your own work.'

'Maestro?'

'Yes, Leonardo.'

'I also thought of something else: the paint. I would like to change it.'

'Change the paint?' enquires Andrea, running one hand over his face. 'What do you suggest we use?'

'Oil and pigment.'

'Yes, pigment of course, pigment. But oil? We always use tempera.'

'Oil will give me more time.'

Andrea hands the palette to him and removes his apron.

'Time is a point I also wish to make. You may stay if you wish, but it is late and I am tired – I am, after all, mortal.' The great man mutters something about baptism and leaves the *bottega*, providing him, Leonardo, with exactly what he wants: an opportunity.

He stuffs a piece of bread in his mouth with one hand and gathers pigments with the other. Then he begins the laborious process of mixing and blending until the consistency is perfect and the colour what he wants. The *bottega* clears. The noise of the day drops to nothing. Flies swim lazily the breadth of the room. He hears mice in the back room; a barn owl calls in the dark, silencing the mice, but he works on undisturbed into the night, lighting candles and lamps to see better. He needs the light of day but does not want to stop now, so he must make do. The oil works well. Pleased with the spectrum of shade he can apply, he uses finger and brush until he gets the right finish. Shadows speak of shape, form, dimension; his brush finds them in light where there is no colour, colour where there is no light; shadows in the dark. The lamp flickers. The Saviour's feet are steeped in water. Mortal sin, he thinks. Is that his face reflected? Beside it is another: she smiles; holds out her hand. 'Sea shells?' she enquires. He paints the ripples and she vanishes.

He does not make a conscious decision to stop. But it must have happened at some point in the early hours of dawn, because he feels a hand shake his shoulder and a voice in his ear. He looks up; it is day again.

Andrea is looking at his angel. They all are. It stands out from the other figures in the altarpiece painting on account of its face, which glows from the panel. 'From now onwards, Leonardo,' he says, 'you must paint the faces: all the faces.'

84

The Maestro packs away his brushes and says nothing else, returning to a sculpture not yet completed. 'Finish the background.' These comments seem to be all that Andrea can manage in the way of praise, and he, Leonardo, cannot help but feel a little disappointed that Andrea has not remarked on the body of Jesus or the water at his feet. Sandro offers consolation, observing his work with undisguised envy. 'I wish my angel looked more like yours. Next to yours the face of mine is sallow and dour.'

He glances at Sandro's angel and pushes the pot of sienna across the table in front of him. 'I think you're forgetting something,' he says. 'Blood.'

Andrea has them working on busts. A visitor comes to admire the Baptism of Christ. His name is Pollaiolo. The patron compares Leonardo with Andrea's David and draws his own conclusions, which have him looking from model to sculpture and beyond, to a future that Leonardo can already see: David vanquishes Goliath, but nobody understands how. Leonardo shrugs his shoulders and listens. Pollaiolo talks about muscle, sinew and flesh, but Sandro is not satisfied. 'There's no art in blood and guts,' the pale apprentice complains. 'On the contrary,' replies Pollaiolo, 'where is there life without blood?' In water, Leonardo thinks. The rivers of the body of the world. Pollaiolo points to the neck of a bust. 'Painting needs the depth of sculpture but does not have the space to provide it. Ways must be found to make that space,' the sculptor adds. 'Muscle is not flat.'

He hovers behind Sandro's back as the senior apprentice traces metal work, draws the lines of a preliminary sketch. He thinks, Sandro needs a monster on a plinth, body parts, the faint light of a dusky barn. He shakes his head. Those that are afraid of monsters are also scared of the dark. That night he changes Sandro's pigments for his own. Before the morning is over, Sandro has changed them back.

His father gives him the use of the mare. Now he can go further. He saddles her up and heads west. When it gets dark, he stops under a tree and watches the stars. They stretch above him in swirls, the glittering splinters of tiny shells thrown randomly at the sky. He holds up a piece of wood from the horizon to the North Star, moves it towards him and reckons its height. At dawn he waits for kestrels and hawks, larks and swallows, and sketches them on the wing as they climb higher. Wings are what he needs. With wings he is at the level of the rainbow, watching the world of men.

But now his feet are on the ground. He has scaled the wall of the Gherardini villa and is standing beneath a first-floor balcony. Taking a handful of gravelly dirt, he throws it up until it hits the stone. Lisa's face appears and beckons him away to wait on the other side of the wall. He waits, turning over the soil with a stick and wondering why he has come. After many moments she reappears, holding her dress and running alongside the wall to where he is waiting.

She looks different. Her hair has grown and her face is not the same shape as before. Her cheeks are higher and her skin is paler. She is taller, but so is he.

'Aren't you going to talk?'

'Yes, of course.' But he can think of nothing.

'I knew you went away. I saw you take the path to Florence. What are you doing here?'

'Studies,' he says vaguely. 'Geometry, Latin.'

The landscape between them has changed. Hills and streams are mountains and rivers. His mind races from sin to angels, wings to rainbows. He picks one.

'I've learnt how to fly.' He says this casually, as though he has completed a page of Alessandro's additions.

She looks him up and down and laughs. 'Have you grown wings then?'

'Of course not,' he says, his body tense. In truth, she is close. 'I've drawn them.'

'Drawing is easy. If you die and become an angel,' she says, 'then I suppose you may fly.'

'When I'm ready I will fly,' he says, walking off. 'But I should warn you,' he adds, 'that there is every chance I could die, since flight is a dangerous endeavour.'

She falls into step. 'You mean you intend to fly like a bird? How?'

'Well, you know,' he says, launching his stick into the hedge, 'there's no reason why man shouldn't fly. It's a process that can be learnt, mastered, like any other.'

'Some things you cannot teach. Birds can't talk.'

'They can sing.'

'That's not talking.'

'Why not? Birds sing because they have something to say.'

'Something such as what, exactly?'

'"This is my nest, this is my perch, this is my mate."'

He fixes his eyes up at the sky past her shoulder and watches the horizon. 'One day man will fly. It's a simple matter of observation and imitation.'

'Very well. At least if you die trying I will burn your body and throw your ashes in the air. Then you will fly well.'

She is laughing at him, a light, girlish laugh. His face burns. His body feels weak. Worse is yet to come: footsteps and the shape of a man in the shadows announce the arrival of Lisa's father. If he had ever wanted wings, it was now. Instead he has two badly shod feet, three soldi in his pouch and one unfinished painting.

Signor Gherardini, his face frowning like Alessandro's, walks over and stands between them, hands on hips.

'Now I see what this dawn absence means.' Lisa's father takes her by the arm and moves her round to his back. 'You – painter, by whose right do you talk to my daughter?'

He wonders how the man knows the true nature of his studies in Florence. Then he remembers his father's notary work – back bent over Gherardini's chair. His neck becomes hot; he wishes he had paid better attention to Latin, or studied Greek as Fra Alessandro had suggested.

'None but my own.'

Gherardini looks at him with a mixture of humour and irritation. 'Since that is the case, you can be sure that it will be the last time.'

'Father, you don't understand. He is not just a painter, Leonardo . . .'

'Leonardo!' Gherardini pronounces in disgust. 'I know you, but I expect not to know you from now onwards.'

'But Father, Leonardo is an inventor. He . . .'

The merchant moves with alacrity over to where he stands, rooted to the spot like a buffoon, and takes him by the doublet.

'You can be painter, sculptor or candle maker for all I care. One thing you can never be,' Gherardini says, nodding his head back towards his daughter, 'is suitor. Do you understand me?'

'A man cannot change what he is.'

'I'm glad we understand each other.' Gherardini slackens his grip.

'But he can change what he will become.'

Gherardini tightens his grip again, then lets go. 'What you will become is in the hands of God, until the day He casts you out. I know what you are. A no-name maker of trouble; an uneducated, illiterate unfortunate.' The merchant sends Lisa back indoors with a wave of his hand.

He backs away from Gherardini until he is up against a tree. His pride, already hurt, breaks like a wave in his chest. He imagines what he would be doing if he hadn't come, and wishes he was doing it, but the best thought he can muster is that perhaps, after all, the merchant is right. He jumps back in time to see the face at the window. Cloak flying in the night breeze, a dark shape recedes down a stony track. He looks down at his stained leather shoes, hardened by sun and rain and wandering. He is at Antonio's table in San Pantaleo; he doesn't eat meat, but the slaughtered pig hangs in the barn and that's all there is. His mother clears away his plate. Now Gherardini hands him another serving. The merchant points a finger into his chest. 'Rest assured, then, of one thing: if I see you here again, your destiny will be set in stone; and it will be neither God's doing nor your own – but mine. Good day to you.'

The merchant strides away, his daughter watching at the door. Leonardo walks up the path to the wall, grabs his father's mare and mounts. He turns the mare away. The air is swollen with thyme and oregano, cilantro heated by the sun. The wind stirs the trees; alder leaves flash silver and the mare becomes restless. She twists and bucks and he cannot stay her. He slackens the rein until she comes to an uncertain halt, her sides heaving. His father's house with its patch of russet land squats on the top of the next hill. Twenty minutes ride and he could be there. Anchiano and San Pantaleo: the bastions of his inherited condition, and the last place on earth he can bear to be. He turns back to Florence, runs his hand over the mare's neck and urges her on.

When he reaches the city he stables the mare and goes straight to the small room he occupies next to the *bottega*. He sits down on his bed and stares at his hands. He gets up and paces. He sees his face in the mirror beside his bed. Miserable fortune stares back. He thinks of the next state: Emilia Romagna, or better still, France. With a good night's rest and plenty of stops, the mare could make it in a few days. Then his eyes fall upon the unfinished painting in the corner of his room: the one he has kept to himself. He imagines building a fire and throwing it on; or picking it up and throwing it out onto the street. The Annunciation. His unfinished angel imparts the news to the Virgin of imminent birth: new life, new hope. The destiny of the chosen one. He picks the painting up. It's heavy. He covers it in a piece of fabric and opens the door. He will show the painting to Andrea, although now it looks far less interesting than the inside of Gherardini's villa. Then he will leave.

Andrea wipes his hands on a rag; Leonardo looks with distaste at his clay-smeared face and muddied hands, and at the general mess of the room, which in every crack and crevice harbours grime, clay, dust and sweat. 'What can I do for you, Messer Leonardo?'

He glances at the bust taking shape on the plinth. A face is emerging, a nose, eyes, a mouth. It is as though the face is straining to get out: the eyes to see, the mouth to speak. Grey lumps of clay litter the floor. Beside the plinth is a cask, beside that a half-empty cup. Andrea looks at the painting under his arm. He hauls it out and leans it against the wall. 'I have been meaning to show you this, but you are often busy and I have not wanted to bother you with it,' he begins. But Andrea brushes him aside and pulls off the cover, stands back and looks at it. Then the Maestro moves in close and begins to examine it. Shakes his head. '*Annunciation*. The Announcement,' he mutters. 'Yours, I presume?'

'Of course, if you don't think it's right, it really doesn't matter, because in any event . . .'

'Right? No I don't think it's right,' says Andrea, turning to face him. 'I think it's incredible. Astonishing.' The Maestro takes up his eyeglass. 'I would never have thought . . . such composure. And here the lily. And the folds of the gown, here and here.' Andrea puts down his eyeglass and looks at him. 'How long have you been working on this?'

'I'm not sure.' He remembers the sketch of a lily from a field near Anchiano. The draperies by candlelight. 'It must be a while.'

Andrea surprises him, taking him by the hand and clasping it. 'Beauty, grace, sharpness of mind and the hands of Giotto. What is there in the world that you do not have?'

The face of the bust strains in the clay. The mouth yearns for words that don't come. 'I don't know,' he replies. Andrea nods.

Stares through him. The Maestro is like Lisa, knowing without knowing. 'You are young, rather too young for commissions, but—' looking back at the painting '—I think that once Lorenzo sees this, there will be no need for hesitation. The perfection of colour, the expression. It would raise the spirits of the dead.' Andrea smiles and rubs his hands. 'Mortal sinner, you say! Leonardo, think no more of mortality. Immortality is what we seek. Immortality and all the glory that goes with it. Tomorrow we will pay a visit to the Magnificent Lorenzo. If it's glory you seek, nobody is better placed to sponsor it than he.'

II

While Florence sleeps, the world beyond the boundaries of the city walls engages in another kind of struggle. The stoat hunts the rabbit and the fox hunts the stoat. He puts pen to paper and in a few easy strokes adds the finishing touches to the sketch on his table. It's the body of a horse seen from several angles. On paper it is small, but in his head it rises to the height of four men standing. Then there is the lily. He would happily spend a week sketching flowers, but what he wants is the knowledge of the flower, not the sketch.

Too much to understand and never enough time. He looks at the angel in the painting he has promised to finish. He pulls on his weathered shoes, goes out and walks the streets, cutting through dark alleys past stone walls and buttresses, silent churches – il Duomo, Santa Maria Nuova – and he stops. From the tanneries he smells treated hide hung out for the night, and beyond that, the damp of a past autumn flood lingers at the base of stonework and wood, slow to dry out. A cart pulls up, drawn by a pony with two men driving. It is bearing a stretcher where a woman is laid out, her breathing heavy and raw. The men take the stretcher through the entrance on the right of the church. He follows.

The hospital of Santa Maria Nuova is full of the sick and the dying. The sound of movement and cries beyond the chapel carry on the air. He smells myrtle, laurel and pine: the aromatic herbs that cover the smell of the dead. But the dormitories are full; only the corridor has room for stretchers. The woman is put down on the floor, a blanket thrown over her. Seeing him there, one of the men says, 'Will you wait with her?' He nods. 'Keep your distance. We're busy enough tonight.'

He crouches down and listens to her breathing. Her chest rises and falls with the weight of fever. He takes her hand. She opens her eyes and looks past his shoulder. Before he can think of words her chest stops rising. Her eyes stare unseeing into the empty corridor of Santa Maria Nuova. He closes her eyelids and pulls a small mirror from his bag to see if there is breath. The heat from the fever is fading fast. Soon her body will be cold. He takes out his notebook and makes a fast sketch of her face with a piece of charcoal.

His hand lingers on paper; his mind races. If he could only see inside. If he could cut back the cover of flesh, pierce the mask of skin, and see with his own eyes. As the thought takes shape he feels the horror of it: the bloody floor of the slaughter-house, the pressing of knife on flesh. He stands up and his legs hurry him out, to the end of the empty corridor, through the door and onto the street. He breathes the fresh air again and passes his hand over his face, where the stubble of a new beard is forming. As though he takes the sweat on his hands for blood, he wipes them over his tunic, draws his cloak over his shoulders and walks away, stopping only once as the cart passes him by a second time, its wheels slow and laboured with the burden of the dead.

★

He has finished the angel. Gabriel kneels where meadow flowers grow: daisies, cornflowers, and a single lily. The Virgin's face is calm, bold.

'Now that he has seen what you can do,' says Andrea, 'it's you that interests him. Be sure to make a good impression. Don't address him first, and remember that the commission is important. It is a wedding portrait.' Andrea glances at him. 'But it is more important to you than it is to them: a fact worth remembering.'

They cross the Via Larga. The entrance to the Medici palazzo takes them through one of the loggias, where men sit waiting on the *banco* to give or receive money, past a fountain in the centre of a courtyard where a wide staircase leads to an upper-storey room. There they wait at the door.

'When dealing with the Medici,' Andrea whispers, 'one subject I prefer to avoid is money. Lorenzo is less concerned by it than you might expect, given that half the inhabitants of the city owe him some.' A pause while the Maestro considers. 'Although perhaps because. In any case, since this is your first portrait, better keep quiet. The price may not be fixed until the result has been achieved. And listen carefully to instructions. There will be preferences. The Venetian ambassador has just arrived in Florence and is commissioning the portrait as a wedding gift for Niccolini's beautiful young bride, although I suspect that the ambassador's interests lie elsewhere.'

'In matters of diplomacy?'

'I can see you're a beginner,' says Andrea, laughing. 'There's no diplomacy in sex.'

Lorenzo de' Medici is young and tall. The banker opens the

door himself, brushing past a herald, and looks at Leonardo with penetrating delicacy – eyes that weigh the value of everything. 'So, here is this pupil of yours, Andrea.' The voice is thin and musical.

He remembers to bow. 'I am honoured to offer my skills in your service.'

'Then I am pleased to use them.' They sit round a table.

'Signor Niccolini is keen to relay his preferences for the portrait, but first I should congratulate you. Your first painting is a fine one. Superbly original. The flowers were a nice touch; and the lily was particularly well drawn. I see you have an eye for plants. Is that where your interests lie? In nature?'

'The interest of any painter should lie in nature,' he replies. 'Where else should we look for inspiration?'

Lorenzo looks amused. 'I imagine that depends on who you are painting for. Some find faces more arresting than flowers. Particularly if the face is a pretty one.'

Signor Niccolini and his wife are sitting at the other end of the hall. 'What do you think, Leonardo?' the banker asks. 'Is she pretty?'

Niccolini's face is redder than the wine in his cup. His skin is coarse, his teeth twisted and grey. His bride offers stark contrast. She is young – half his age, with delicate hair and fine features set in porcelain skin. Fair and frail, she exudes an air of melancholy. In his hands she will break like china.

'Not pretty,' he replies. 'Fragile. Breakable.' Lorenzo sits back, smiles.

The Venetian ambassador arrives. Lorenzo goes to greet him.

'Bernardo, you have arrived just in time. You know Andrea of course. May I present our young painter, Leonardo from Vinci.'

They all stand. Niccolini sits first, thanks the ambassador for his gift. 'An excellent idea; I should have commissioned it myself, but you were faster than I, it seems.'

'I seek to please,' replies the Venetian. 'I only wish I could have attended the ceremony itself.'

Niccolini manages a grey, pinched smile. 'Shall we discuss the composition? I had in mind a colourful backdrop: a courtyard garden with an abundance of roses. Something gay, with reds and greens – the gown to be purple – or perhaps scarlet, with ermine cuffs.'

Such a combination of colour is starting to make him nauseous. He opens his mouth to speak but feels the pressure of Andrea's arm. He closes it.

Lorenzo puts the contract for the portrait on the table in front of the Venetian ambassador and calls for a new flask of wine. The Venetian ambassador is not looking at the contract – the diplomat's eyes have found their point of interest. Portraits are complicated, Leonardo thinks. There is the subject's portrait, the lover's portrait, the husband's portrait and the painter's portrait. One thing is certain: Lorenzo sees it all.

'Ah, wine,' says Signor Niccolini. 'Raises the spirits, calms the temperament. What do you think, Messer Leonardo?'

He watches the ambassador, notes the expression on his face, wishes he could draw that.

'More importantly,' Leonardo says, 'It strengthens the stomach, helps digestion, comforts the bowels, and is the best preservative against the plague.'

Niccolini smirks. 'He'll be telling me next that I should wash with it.'

'That too is possible. The ashes of burnt vine branches will, for example, whiten teeth with regular application.'

Lorenzo smiles. 'Physician as well?'

'My remedies are no more than common knowledge,' he replies. 'We need to look much further than superstition and guesswork if we are ever to make progress.'

Lorenzo slides the contract across the table, glances at him. 'Shall we begin with this?'

Andrea reads it and hands him a pen, but all he can think of is Niccolini's taste in colour. Another thing bothers him. He remembers Lorenzo's remark, wonders who he is painting for. Both the ambassador's leer and Niccolini's ignorance are abhorrent. That leaves the subject, and himself. He sits in his chair at the table with the strange sensation that everyone around him has missed the point. He slides the contract – unsigned – back to the ambassador. The Venetian stares at the sheet of paper before him in surprise.

'The colours you propose would not be right,' he says, replacing the pen in the ink pot. 'The lady's complexion is fine and delicate. Too much colour would detract from the main beauty of the portrait.'

'What do you suggest?' says Lorenzo, sitting forward.

'Gentler colours,' he offers.

'Gentler colours?' Niccolini turns an astonished face to Lorenzo. 'But I've already said what I want and I have no desire to change my mind.'

From the other side of town, the bells of the cathedral sound midday mass. 'In that case,' he says, 'I will be unable to take the commission.' Andrea shifts on his seat beside him.

'Well,' says Niccolini, 'Well, indeed.' The scarlet man turns to Lorenzo in annoyance. 'Can't someone else . . .'

'Everyone is busy,' Lorenzo replies, eyes fixed on Leonardo, weighing him up. 'It's almost Easter. There's nobody free until the Calends of July.' Andrea moves to speak, but Lorenzo stops him.

From his side of the table, the Venetian ambassador slides the contract back. 'I see no reason why we can't use gentler colours. I agree.'

'You agree? But wait. There's also the background to consider.' Niccolini pulls the contract away from the Venetian and towards himself.

Lorenzo observes him patiently. Leonardo wonders whether Medici can read minds as fast as letters of credit. He thinks of his shoes, sure that they too have been scrutinised – easy to see that he needs money. He searches for a background without red, and finds one. 'You mentioned the name of the lady?' he enquires.

'Ginevra,' says the ambassador quickly.

Ginevra, *ginepro*, juniper. 'I understand your preference was for roses,' he says, turning to Niccolini. 'But perhaps a juniper bush?'

'A spiky shrub with no flowers? You have something against roses? Don't they have any medicinal value?' Niccolini demands.

'Well?' Lorenzo says in amusement. 'Do they?'

'The juniper bush is known as a symbol of chastity,' he says.

'Ah, I see it! *Ginepro*, Ginevra. Ha!' says Niccolini, brightening up. 'That's not bad.'

'So,' says Lorenzo. 'Shall it be rose or juniper?'

The Venetian ambassador takes a piece of paper from inside his doublet and passes it to Leonardo. 'Juniper,' the Venetian says. 'And I would like you to paint this insignia on the back of the portrait. Together with your juniper, it should provide a happy resolution to the piece.'

Lorenzo amends the contract and slides it across the table.

He signs; the ambassador signs. Lorenzo offers a toast. 'To beauty, virtue and Leonardo's colour.' He raises his cup.

When they leave the hall and make their way back to the *bottega*, Andrea finds his voice.

'*Ginepro*,' his Maestro marvels. 'Whatever next? The wrong colours. How am I still in business? If he doesn't like the portrait, you realise that this could mean the end of immortality and the beginning of a very slow death. But why such a face after such a victory?'

'It doesn't seem much of a victory to me,' he says, adjusting his cloak. 'The idea of painting for the pleasure of an idiot like Niccolini brings a sense more of losing than winning.'

'An idiot perhaps. Although he does have the good sense not to drink their wine: Venetian poison. Bunch of fishermen. As for you, what a performance! Part of me would like to congratulate you for getting your way, but the other part would see more merit in putting you on the first mule I can find and walking it to Vinci myself.'

He is becoming indifferent to advice. The contract in his hand stipulates no more than thirty fiorini for the finished portrait, less if it proves unsatisfactory. The conditions are more favourable but the end result is less than he expected. It would barely pay for the trim on Gherardini's cuffs.

III

He wakes at five as he always does, and pulls on a woollen tunic. The first stage of creating the portrait took place at the palazzo, but now, nearly complete, the panel is back in the *bottega*, where varnishing has begun.

He lights the wood stove and wanders out into the silent *bottega*. Moonlight filters in through the glass panes above eye level, and he lights another lamp, treading carefully through wood shavings and pigment dust until he reaches the painting. He puts down the light. He prepares the varnish mixture, part egg white, part resin, while the face of the porcelain bride stares out at him, delicate, fragile – by his hand unchangeable. He thinks of Lisa. Dawn will be breaking on Monte Albano. The cave of marvels lies in shadow on the hill. Somewhere in the empty corridors of Santa Maria Nuova, someone is dying. He throws down his varnishing brush and paces before the panel. The woman on the stretcher would have neither known nor cared. The dead don't feel. He sees himself making the first incision. The knife presses against white, passive skin. His hand shakes. Her eyelids snap open. Logic banished by irrational visions. What are you afraid of? he thinks – God?

By the end of the month the ambassador has taken delivery of the portrait. He has painted the insignia on the reverse of the panel: a wreath of laurel and palm around a sprig of juniper, bearing the words 'Beauty adorns virtue'. He waits for settlement. 'The richer the man, the longer he takes to pay,' says Andrea.

After three flasks of wine Andrea is complaining of a fever. 'Leonardo, make me one of your tinctures.' The tinctures help but Andrea remains frantic. 'Plague begins with a great thirst,' the Maestro says. And what better victim than Andrea, since the sculptor has not paid a visit to confessional in three months and it is no more possible to confess to a lack of confession than it is to ask a cripple to dance – which brings him in mind of a pain in his foot. This is most certainly further demonstration of the design of the Almighty, whose aim it is to punish him with any means he has at his disposal. And what can be more innocuously hurtful than a toe? Sculpture must wait; Andrea must suffer the fate of the cripple. Nothing hurts like divine retribution. Leonardo fetches the physician, who declares a case of gout.

The physician draws blood from Andrea's leg, then leaves. Leonardo spends the next week at Andrea's bedside, administering his own cure. 'Lemon juice and garlic,' declares Andrea in disgust. 'If I'd wanted poison I'd have asked a Venetian.' Still, the sculptor drinks it, and within a few days he is back on his feet, prowling the *bottega* with a vengeance his students endure without complaint.

'God save us from plague,' says Andrea, taking a regretful look at the flask. 'But first He must save me from gout.'

'If you pay heed to my instructions, I will do that myself.'

He pores over books on anatomy. The only useful ones are in Greek. The words fill each page but he recognises only a few snatches. Latin and Greek have eluded him. He thinks of his tutor's departure. Too soon. He looks desperately at the page full of descriptions he can't read fast enough and pushes the book away in frustration. Anatomy. *Papilio Macaone*. If you want to see it up close, it has to be dead. He packs a bag: paper, pens, charcoal, knives — as many as he can find of varying size — disinfectant, and a wineskin of water. As he gathers his things, he catches sight of his face in the small mirror on his table. Dark grey eyes stare back. Furrowed brows: a history of fixation.

The corridors of Santa Maria are lit by torches. A trail of soot marks the wall above each flame: a concave of imaginary shadow. From the end of the corridor a man approaches. Calloused hands, empty eyes. The work of the *beccamorti* makes its mark. He follows the gravedigger beyond the dormitories of the living, to the room of the dead. A man not much older than himself lies without ceremony on a makeshift bed.

'And the relatives, family?'

The gravedigger shakes his head. 'They don't care.'

The response of the gravedigger stirs a distant memory of Antonio. His mouth hardens. Things will be done as they should be. 'I will pay for the burial,' he says, and closes the eyes of the corpse. 'See it's done at first light.' Taking the gravedigger's arm, he adds, 'I'll be back to check.'

He picks up the knife; he hesitates. In the end, curiosity, he sees, is stronger than fear. He makes the first incision quickly, at the top of the shoulder, and glances at the man's face. Nothing has changed. The mouth is open, the eyes are closed; the expression is peaceful. He breathes and cuts deeper, from shoulder to forearm, forearm to wrist. He will remember his first sight of human bone: whiter than he thought. He stands back, calm and cool, puts down the knife. He makes another, finer incision, draws back the layers of flesh on either side, marvels at the lack of blood. A surge of excitement hits him – a strange contrast: his own heart beating so loud, and there, nothing but silence.

He continues to cut away flesh either side of the bone until the interior of the arm is completely exposed, the skin spread out on either side like the wings of a butterfly. He puts down the knife, takes up his pen and begins to draw what he sees. He takes time on the complex sections where bone meets bone, moves the lamp the length of the arm, illuminates sections in turn, gazes in wonder at the array of bone, muscle, joint: the means for every movement, every gesture.

He, Leonardo from Vinci, must be twenty-two years of age. There was the big flood. There was the bad harvest. Then he was born: complications. Arrangements in the house on the hill; gossip in the city. His left hand moves over the paper as he makes notes beside every sketch. A further complication: when he writes, he writes with his left hand, in reverse – right to left. Means of protection, source of debate, now habit. As he unlocks the secrets of the arm he has cut, his hand puts them back into secrets on the page. His world is mystery, concealment. Shame.

He sews up the arm and shoulder and covers the wound. He leaves the way he came, past the black flames on the walls where soft-winged moths flutter round the mark of soot. With the reflex of second nature, he scoops one up as he passes. Outside, he opens a clenched fist. The moth is crushed; only dust flies off.

He sleeps until noon. Andrea comes and wakes him. 'I thought you had passed away,' the Maestro says. 'You look white as death. Are you sick?'

No, he tells him, not sick. 'Just tired.'

'I've work for you. A study of Saint Jerome, to be finished by Lent. Better get dressed. You must be ill to be sleeping so late.' Andrea throws him his doublet and comes over and peers into his eyes. 'A little red. I trust you don't have fever. Plague is marked by high fever. Influenza, perhaps? We start work tomorrow. Today you can take the day off. But wear nothing red. There are celebrations to honour the Venetians. In the piazza Santa Croce – lions and bulls.'

The prospect of something to sketch draws him out. The piazza is full. People stand around the edges of the arena, their feet hidden in sawdust. He turns away from the spectacle. A lioness roams the perimeter of the ring, the crowd drawing further back behind the barrier as it passes; two cautious bulls huddle against the open doors of a cage. A small boy from the crowd is poking a stick through the bars of the cage and into the thick hide of one of the bulls. He turns away in disgust and leaves Andrea to watch alone. Women sweep past, the hems of their dresses sandy. One of them turns back to look at him. From face to body to hands. He looks away, irritated. Her face is ordinary, nothing he would bring out charcoal for.

But now one comes into view that he does look at more closely. It's one he knows: one he has already painted in his head. Hair drawn back beneath a velvet band, Lisa Gherardini has taken her father's arm. He remembers Gherardini's hand on his doublet; the look of complete disdain he wore is probably contagious. He watches them pass. She barely glances at him. It will hang in his head for the rest of the day.

Andrea is at his shoulder. 'Someone you know?'

'Once,' he says. 'No more, on pain of death.' Andrea nods.

'Gherardini. You would be wise to avoid him. He banks in Rome, imports through Venice. Loyalties – Pazzi not Medici. Tastes – fine in everything.' Andrea looks at his badly stitched doublet and woollen hose. 'You can be as brilliant as Apelles,' the Maestro says, 'but if you sport the *palle* of the Medici and aren't wearing the right cut of silk, better give it up.'

He is asking himself what there is to give up. He has done his calculations. Soon men like Gherardini will be lining up for a word from his mouth, a brush of his hand, a stroke of his pen. When you take a knife to a body and make an incision, he thinks, notions of immortality fail at the sight of worn joints and stretched tendons. But glory he can manage, since it goes hand in hand with what he really wants.

So far he has only cut limbs, feet and arms. Something holds him back. He remembers a jolting tail and the head of a lizard beneath a knife and wants to laugh at his own childish fears. After all, what is there more natural than fear of the unknown? Ten years ago it was death. Today it is still death. As though if he took out another man's heart and held it in his hands, he might steal his soul.

The sun drifts behind a cloud and the light goes from amber warm to glassy cold. It is just how he likes it. In light like this, he can see. Expressions soften, profiles sharpen, objects bathe in sunless shadow. Four men wheel a cage through the crowd. They are taking the lion back to the menagerie of the Via de' Leoni. One of the bulls is dead. The barred gates of the serragli are pulled back and the lion passes from one cage to another. He sets himself before it and takes out his charcoal and paper. Saint Jerome, he tells Andrea, will need company.

★

It is ten days after Lent. Leonardo's new patron calls him in for the joint purposes of conversation and admonishment over late delivery – in fact, no delivery yet, since he has not finished the lion. He makes his way through the courtyard of the fountain, passes through the room with the canopy of stars, and is directed to private chambers. Here is Lorenzo's studio. One wall is covered by rows of books, leather bound with gold, another by tapestries run through with bright threads that pick up the firelight. Much of the space is taken up by sculpture. There is a fine bust of Plato, another of Aristotle. The slow texture of oil paintings lays depth and colour on smooth plastered walls: Dutch painters he recognises and loves. Lorenzo is discussing Plato with his brother. Surrounded by beauty, they sit on silk, drink from silver, ring a bell for service. A memory comes back: riding into the city behind his father's mare, while on the ground a beggar woman searches for coins in the mud. Mud and silk. He thinks of his room on the corner of the Via de' Macci. Even the mice prefer their own holes to his.

Lorenzo begins with conversation; that is his way. The way of his protégé is to listen rather than speak – he is not as he used to be, always ready with an idea or a solution. Now he hoards his knowledge like a squirrel hoards nuts.

Lorenzo turns to him. 'I have a story for you, if you are willing to hear it. It takes place in a cave. Have you ever been in one?'

Have *you*, he wonders. 'Yes,' he says.

'And what did you find?'

'A handful of shells,' he says. 'Darkness, dampness, bats.'

Lorenzo fills his cup. 'Then picture this. A community of people live out their lives in the darkness of a cave; their only light is fire. You could say they are trapped; their world is shadow and flame, the pattern of light on stone, an underworld of figures and forms. Bats too, if you like. Then one day, something happens. Perhaps by chance, or the will of God – although I think, Leonardo, that it is destiny – one of these cave dwellers finds a way up to the world beyond the walls of the cave. He steps outside, and sunshine strikes his face; the light is bright, so he shields his eyes. There is a period of adjustment, realisation, before our cave dweller looks for the first time on other things: trees, mountains, rivers – things he has never seen, nor even imagined.' Lorenzo pauses. He, Leonardo, remembers a handful of shells in the folds of a dress. The erudite banker goes on. 'Awed by the sight, and once he has taken his fill of it, he finds his way back to the cave and, in the thrall of excited revelation, recounts all that he has seen. Now what do you think is the reaction?'

Giuliano is the opposite of his brother. Where Lorenzo is tall, sallow faced and thin, Giuliano radiates energy. Lorenzo weighs his words; Giuliano glosses over.

'Disbelief,' the brother offers.

'Disinterest,' replies Lorenzo. 'Nobody wants to know.'

Giuliano laughs. 'That makes them a bunch of fools, then.'

'Not really,' Lorenzo says, picking up his cup. 'They have every reason not to be interested. The most important thing is that the returning cave dweller, having seen the sun, is no longer able to tolerate the dim light of the cave, and it is he who stumbles about like a fool, succeeding only in convincing others of his own ineptness.'

Turning to Leonardo. 'Have you read Plato? Let me lend you a volume.' Lorenzo rises and pulls a book from the shelf. He accepts it. 'I'm still a beginner in Greek. Latin too,' he admits.

Lorenzo nods. 'There is no shame in learning, only honour.' For Medici, the price of a book is a detail. Lorenzo instructs his brother to attend to business. The day is almost over. There are ledgers to check, and two Genoese dignitaries arriving by night-fall.

'No shame in learning?' Leonardo says. 'You contradict yourself. Would you not have me stay in the cave too?'

'No,' says Lorenzo, getting up and placing a small log on the fire in the grate of his hearth. 'But I would have you watch your step.' From a scrittoio beside the fireplace, a wreath of incense rises in slow spirals. Guiliano has left.

He says nothing. What does Lorenzo know about him? What does he know of the life of the son of a notary without a name? He weighs the odds. Watching his step is nothing new. He has made an art of concealment.

'We have spoken many times together, but you continue to puzzle me,' Lorenzo continues.

'In what way?'

'Little happens in this city that I do not know about,' the banker says, brushing specks from his robe with his manicured fingers. 'I guard the entrances and the exits of every cave that concerns me and in which I take an interest. Let us stop for a moment at yours.'

He thinks of caves; the shells of caves, drawings of shells; Noah and the Flood, the calculations of the Ark, and sips his wine.

'A young man, barely out of boyhood, comes to Florence from Vinci. His background is simple; he has had little formal instruction. The boy is exceptionally gifted, some might say precocious. He leaves his cave and ventures out. When he returns, nobody gives him credit. So what does he do?'

He wonders where this is leading. He thinks, this is how diplomats speak. With metaphor.

'The options are these: he can become bitter, even angry – difficult. He can forget about the world outside; he can leave the safety of the cave and, like Saint Jerome, lose himself in the wilderness. Or he can say to himself: this is my cave; those are my trees. I can come and go as I please, which is not only the most sensible solution, but the solution that will keep him alive.' The habitual smile returns. 'I am indulgent with you because I like you. But men like Niccolini and others will lose patience. Your reputation will suffer even before it is born.' He leans forward. 'I acknowledge that they are not like us. What is life without the ability to see art: to understand its secrets?' The log in the grate flares the colour of sulphur. 'Your problems are multiplying. I know that you are a visitor to the hospice of Santa Maria. I know what you do late at night, when you think the city sleeps. Word will get around.' Lorenzo holds up his hand. 'Yes, you are curious. You are not the first artist that has cut up a leg in order to better draw muscle and sinew. But it is a practice abhorrent to most and I cannot condone it openly. You know, Leonardo, I am Medici. You might think that is enough. A snap of the fingers and I can have things just the way I want. No. I am not Giuliano. I am more at home at mass than at the joust. Besides which, I only have so much influence. Florence is a city of accounts. Not a day goes by that my measure is not taken, my worth not assessed. I will tell you a confidence. For too long my desire has been to provide this city with the jewel in the crown of the state: the jewel that will give Florence the power she needs to be truly independent. And with a little more patience, I am certain it will come. A seat on the papal throne: a native-born cardinal. Pope Sixtus watches Florence closely. I will not give him a reason to turn us down.'

The banker stands up. 'You, Leonardo, can change your name. Leonardo the Florentine can eclipse Leonardo da Vinci. But to become that man, you must remember that Florence is a city of beauty. Beauty is the measure of her greatness. For that, I need you. But while I acknowledge that you are exceptional in your talents, I believe that the destiny of any man is governed by the limits he places on his impulses. I say this because you show a tendency to leave work unfinished. The lion, for instance?'

He has not finished the lion. It has been three months since the dissection of the old man. In that time he has done two further dissections: a woman, and a man of some forty years. He has redrawn the internal structure of the foot and elaborated on his written notes. He has designed levers, pulleys and winches. He has read Latin and begun Greek. He has found Pliny's book and used all his remaining money to purchase it. He has asked Andrea for an advance. He has devised a dam and revised his construction of a canal.

'I suppose I have been a little preoccupied,' he replies. He knows it is the wrong answer, that his time is Lorenzo's time – that Lorenzo's preoccupations must be his; that this is how the world works. Whether he wants it that way or not.

It is time to go. The banker gets up and they leave the intimacy of the studio. Once outside, the banker is in demand. A herald here, a servant there. The loggia is closed, but tomorrow the benches will be full again.

'Tell me,' Lorenzo says, taking his shoulder, 'do you play music?'

'A little. I like to make my own instruments.'

'Then bring one tomorrow. What have you ready?'

'A lyre,' he says, 'fashioned from the skull of a horse.'

'A curious thing,' Lorenzo says. 'You don't like horses?'

'Quite the opposite,' he says, 'I love them.'

'Ah. And will you finish the lion by Easter?'

'Of course.'

IV

His father stands before him. Older, more tired: smaller in stature than before. Now his father is observing Saint Jerome, standing against the background of wilderness and rock, and becoming a part of the painting, his figure filling the space in the foreground beside the lion.

He asks his father if he likes the painting. He has never asked before.

'When will you finish it?' his father says.

'Soon,' he replies. He changes the subject and brings out drawings of his canal, sketches of a dam. Control water, he tells his father, and you control everything. He shows him the Archimedean screw and begins to explain. It raises and lowers water levels. He waits for a reaction, but it is not the one he expects.

'I want you to start out on your own: your own workshop. There could be a place, along the river. Ideal for deliveries – used as a storehouse, but empty most of the time. There is a good market for Madonna statues, crucifixes. You could make a comfortable living. Then there would be commissions. With work like this, and the introductions you have already.'

He pictures himself making a single mould for fifty bronze effigies of the Virgin, and shudders. But he does not say no straight away. The prospect of choosing his own subjects seems a good one at first. But he has more sense than Lorenzo imagines. He would have even less room for manoeuvre without the backing of the power house.

'No,' he says. 'I can't.'

'Why not?' exclaims his father. Only a fool would say no. What does he have to lose?

'Time,' he says.

'Time for what?' his father asks.

Plans crowd his mind and make him dizzy. Sometimes he feels his body fall away beneath him, while his mind rushes on to the next thing, and the one after that. It happens that he forgets to eat. Time runs away and he runs to catch it. It goes too fast for him. A man only has one lifetime, and he must spend his quota wisely.

His father leaves, asking him to think about it. I will, he promises. He remembers to thank him. Alone at last, he sits at his desk. He pulls a piece of paper towards him and drags a lighted candle closer.

Choose your subject.

He takes a piece of charcoal, a small one, and stares into the empty page. His left hand draws without his head. A triangle in a square. A square in a triangle. Then another. Now he is drawing a spiral; now a vortex. An eddy in the Arno River. Beside it he draws a flower. The petals of a rose overlap in ever-decreasing circles. Leaves twist around a bud, twigs around a branch. He finishes another spiral. Always the same shape, he thinks. The shape is important but he doesn't know why. Not knowing why frustrates him.

He draws other shapes: an arbelos, Archimedean circles, a pentagon, a trapezium; the curve of a rainbow. He remembers the day he saw the rainbow on Mount Albano. He goes to his trunk, pulls out his notes and leafs through old pages until he gets to the entry. Amused, he sees another spiral at the top of the same page. He puts down his notes and thinks. The rainbow is deceptive. Sometimes you see it, sometimes not. Move a few feet and it disappears.

He takes a fresh sheet of paper and writes the word *perspective*. He writes without stopping for what must be a few more minutes. He looks up and it is dark. He marks out a border and draws a circle. Then he draws two arcs that touch it. Then two more until they each touch the circle at four points. The other shapes are in his head. He continues to draw. A face emerges from the page: a body. He works on it until the outline is complete. Then he stops; leans back; shakes his head. *Papilio Macaone*. You have to catch a butterfly before you can draw it. Draw what you see. Anything else is a lie. He remembers the lion and bull in the piazza, then remembers the boy with the stick – thinks of the boy with the sword. The thought has never left his mind: Goliath and David, the boy who vanquishes giants. Tomorrow he will pay a call on Gherardini. There are more important things than the right cut of silk. Besides, in this Lorenzo can't help him. There is no Niccolini – no husband, no lover. Gherardini has already made it clear that there is no suitor either – and in any event, he considers as he snuffs out his candle, there is no contract for a painter's portrait.

Tomorrow arrives. He pulls out his best clothes: a green velvet doublet and a cloak with no holes. He smooths back his hair.

He glances in the mirror and softens a preoccupied expression. Unfurrows his brow. Smiles more. Once he makes a decision, there never is any going back.

Domenico asks him where he's going all trussed up like a Milanese. Andrea looks worried and suggests that wherever he is going he'd better be back by noon. He will be. He heads for the stables at Santa Croce and asks for directions. They can't tell him, but the blacksmith will know.

Antonio Gherardini arrives in time for Lent and stays until the warm weather, he learns. Rooms at the back of the Via Larga, past the fish market. Second alley, first house. He heads off again.

He is ready for a cold reception. The servant opens the door and enquires as to his business. He is here about a commission and would like to see the Master. She leads him through a small courtyard, where an area is laid out to shrub: myrtle, laurel, small herbaceous borders and a stone table beside. From the loggia a staircase leads up to a salon, which he enters. Two wooden benches run the length of two facing walls, and a long table occupies the central space of the room, which is a perfect square. There is a fireplace – not lit – carved with family arms he doesn't recognise. On the opposite wall to the fireplace is an *acquaio*. The basin is filled with water. Beside it a table bears a piece of linen neatly folded. His forehead is prickling with heat and the temptation to plunge his hands in the water is strong, so he sits instead on the bench and counts the number of times the pattern is repeated in the cornice.

'You wish to see me?'

He almost jumps up. 'I do.' He looks curiously at Antonio Gherardini: less threatening than he remembers, but still the same measure of disdain. He wonders whether he, Leonardo, will still be in the room on his feet moments from now, then reminds himself that this is another kind of Antonio.

Gherardini crosses the room, scrutinising as he approaches: his face, his body, inevitably his hands. 'What can I do for you, then? I hope you have a good reason for knocking on my door.'

'I do. If you are willing to hear it.'

Gherardini nods. 'State your business, since you have come this far to do so.'

'I would like to make a proposition – an offer.'

'Oh, really? What sort of offer?' Gheradini's face darkens.

'I would like to offer you my services as portrait painter,' he says. 'Without payment,' he adds hurriedly.

'Indeed.' Gherardini sits. He stands. 'And why would you want to do that?'

He is not sure how to answer. He chooses the explanation a silk merchant is most likely to understand. 'If you remember, a number of years ago I once accompanied my father inside your home. While I was there waiting, I caught sight of a portrait of your daughter which I felt was—' here he struggles '—lacking in the qualities that a portrait ought to display. I feel that I could do much better, and would like to prove it to you.' He meets Gherardini squarely eye to eye, thinking that if he cannot elicit a positive response, then at least he can go out with dignity. To his surprise, Gherardini does not refuse.

'Very well. Come back in seven days. If my daughter agrees, you can start after Easter.' He raises a hand. 'But I say yes for one reason only, and that reason is del Verrocchio. If Andrea has taken you on, then I suppose there must be some redeeming feature about you besides your looks, which may go some way towards pleasing the women, but which have little effect on me.'

He reminds himself to take a closer look in the mirror next time. He must have missed something. Gherardini certainly has. Even now, as he walks out of the room and back down the staircase to the loggia, Gherardini is thinking: he is infatuated. He shakes his head. There is nothing extraordinary about Lisa Gherardini. Her face is plain, although well proportioned. Her eyes are neither particularly green, nor particularly blue. Nor are they brown. Her looks, like Leonardo's own, interest him as a view interests him, or a shell. He doesn't want the drawing of the shell, just the knowledge of it: discovery, not beauty. But if you asked him what there was to discover – at this particular moment, walking through the loggia out of the alley and into the piazza crowded as ever, the noon sun streaming down on his face – he would have to say, quite simply, that the answer was in the rainbow.

V

'You have a private commission? Is that what you're telling me?'

'Yes and no.'

'Ah, yes and no. Of course there are far more interesting things to do than give explanations to the ignorant.'

He slows his lathe and brushes off his hands.

'A little information on what you are in the process of constructing would not be unwelcome either.'

'Certainly. It has never been my intention to . . .'

'Yes, yes. We can dispense with all that. Get to the point, for the love of Mary Madonna.'

He smiles. There are men who stand out from others. Andrea has spent his life fostering children barely able to handle a soldering iron and somehow made them into artisans. The Maestro looks for meaning wherever he can find it: a lump of clay, a block of marble.

'A portrait. Although at the moment I am constructing a sighting box. Its purpose is . . .'

Andrea interrupts. 'Congratulations. And who is the lucky subject . . . the portrait?'

'The Gherardini family.'

'The entire family?' Andrea asks. 'Greyhounds included?'

'I was not aware they had dogs.'

Andrea sits down. 'Would it be too much to ask a budding physician for a cup of wine? Or must I take a tincture?'

He fetches the flask and serves Andrea a cup. He pours one for himself. 'You know, I have made a study of gout, and in my view ...'

'So, the commission is for the girl.'

'Yes.'

'Well,' the great man places his hands on his stomach and stretches out his back, 'I am glad to hear it. Surprised, but glad. I realise that you will need either an advance or materials. I will therefore express a preference for materials – before things become any more complicated than they are already. I do this, of course, with the expectation of pleasure in mind, since a wedding feast has always been a favourite occasion of mine, and ...'

'It's a commission, not an engagement,' he says hurriedly. 'Furthermore, I have every intention of paying you for the use of materials.'

Andrea looks disappointed. 'If you insist. But check your accountancy first. I've not yet had settlement for Saint Jerome. Although, of course, you don't need me to tell you the reason for that.'

He does not. Unfinished lions. The consequences of it present themselves to him the following morning, with alacrity. On returning to Santa Maria Nuova to see what money he has, he is confronted with the full extent of his savings: less than ten florins. If it lasts him the month, he will be doing well.

To pay for the burial of his last subject of study, he spends part of the morning sketching the gravedigger's dog. 'I'll be back before Passover,' he says. A few steps away from Santa Maria Nuova, he comes across a group of actors rehearsing the harrowing of Hell. The church wall fresco comes to life as Jesus enters the underworld and rescues its souls from the clutches of Satan. One of their number spots him. 'Make us a costume, Messer Leonardo,' he calls. He holds up his arms. 'Look what they have *me* wear!'

He pays a visit to Sandro's *bottega*. Sandro has done what he himself could not – he has taken some premises. Now they meet at the Tre Rane and he talks Sandro through Plato to Aristotle to compensate for the time that the boy had his head in clouds instead of books. Sandro says he needs to borrow this hammer, that lathe, as an excuse to come back to Via de' Macci. Now as he arrives at his *bottega*, he sees the artist clothed in his leather apron, bathed in dusty sunlight, apprentices at his feet. Sandro was never the son of a tanner; will always be the goldsmith's apprentice. The boy would have fled his father's shop and the hides of beasts hung out to dry in the heat to get to here, where the apprentice wants to be, in this light, tracing his golden lines like a poet puts pen to paper. He has given up trying to tell Sandro to read between the lines. You can't tell an angel there is no such thing as paradise.

He wanders around the workbenches and stops to admire Fortitude – the dreamlike face of Sandro's Madonna. But for all the activity, it is not enough. He leaves the dusty sunlight and tells himself that he has made the right decision. He is willing to paint a portrait, but only for his own purposes – and not even for a Medici.

*

He pours Andrea's wine into a pitcher. With saltpetre, charcoal and sulphur, it forms a noxious paste.

'Is this really going to work,' asks Andrea, 'your smoke?'

'Gunpowder without the firearm,' he corrects. He moistens the mixture and shapes handfuls of it into patties. 'Once these have been lit, the smoke shall be fanned and the lighted candles will appear to be floating on a sea of mist.'

'Holy smoke?'

'Smoke.'

Careggi is the stage for Lorenzo's Easter pageant. They work for four days on costumes, flags and Leonardo's smoke. Once the bulk of the preparations are complete, he returns to Santa Maria, and the *beccamorti*'s latest offering: a man, not too old. Maybe thirty. He imagines the life this man has led, people met, sights seen. He thinks about this for a moment, then puts it aside and sets his mind on one thing only. He adopts this attitude at such moments: the detached observer. He turns the head of the subject on its side. Placing his fingers over the eye opening, he slowly and carefully eases the eye from its socket and lays it gently on a piece of lint beside the subject of study. He notes the thread-like connections to the inside of the head and takes out his pen. It is delicate work and his hand must be steady. He notes the point of connection, the muscles around the pupil, the shape of the lens. He draws what he sees, and struggles with an incomplete analysis. Light comes in here, like a pinhole in a box. He follows where it goes, but the rest of the picture is incomplete. The threads from the eye run to hundreds, transferring the final picture of vision to the mind. What then?

He draws what he sees. Daylight already. Forever fighting time.

The *beccamorti* wants him done by dawn, or they start asking questions. He packs up his things and cleans the subject's face with water. He gently closes the eyelids, covers the body with a clean cloth, and leaves. Before he can close the door, the *beccamorti* steps out of the shadows and closes it for him. It is late, the gravedigger tells him. Dangerously late. This must be the last time. An instruction is an instruction. The sketch of the dog is good, but even a dog has to be fed. Messer Leonardo is a good man. Why doesn't he paint more instead?

He walks back along the Via Cavour in frustrated anger. This is Lorenzo's instruction. So close to understanding the mysteries of sight, now he must be satisfied with the blindness of others. The town is full of foreigners. A scuffle has started in a corner of Santa Croce. An onlooker steps in and pulls the youths apart, one by his hair, the other by his shirt. He feels tension everywhere – in himself and in others. The town has filled up for Easter, every-one preoccupied with the business of their neighbour. Tonight is the night of holy fire. Torches will flare; the procession will move from door to door, lighting the candles of the dead.

A garden stage is set in the grounds of Careggi. Beneath the wood his gentle gunpowder waits to smoulder. Lorenzo has what he wants: smoke without fire, light without flame – a show of beauty to impress Cardinal Riario. For this, the banker has emp-tied his purse. Leonardo observes the damask tablecloths, the silverware. Servants bring out the usual delicacies. It is not for him. Give him bread, cheese and olives after a day at his scrittoio. He will leave Andrea to make the conversation he doesn't want. As the Cardinal arrives with his entourage of purple-cloaked bodyguards, he slips away. The other side of the hedge, Archbishop Salviati blocks his path.

'Messer Leonardo, isn't it? Have we said something to upset you, that you are so ready to leave?' The archbishop's face is level with the top of the hedge. The balding cleric watches the row of bodyguards as he speaks, not happy until he locates his cardinal, and Lorenzo. 'Tell me,' he says, without turning his face, 'where is Giuliano?'

He explains what he knows: an eye infection, he believes. Lorenzo's brother is indisposed. He watches a shadow of irritation cross the cleric's face and takes his leave, thinking of Giuliano's eye and reminding himself to look for chickweed.

The gardens of the villa spread over the hill, part cultivated, part wild. He wanders through woodlands of oak, poplar and plane. He notices pine and cedar, a growth of frankincense against the side of the hill: a small ragged tree more like a large weed. He takes out his knife, cuts away a little bark and spills the sweet resin into a small pouch. Herbs and spice plants lay here and there: he harvests myrrh and myrtle, admires wild rose and feels the freshness of cilantro in shady ditches – but finds no chickweed.

Two hours later Andrea has nobody left to talk to but Leonardo. The Cardinal and Salviati have left early. 'It seems that your gunpowder is going to be wasted. Dinner is at the Via Larga. Cardinal Riario appears to have developed an interest in art.'

He points out that even a Riario can appreciate a painting.

'That is not a word I would have chosen: *appreciate*. Besides,' continues Andrea, 'the Riario brothers are more likely to be evaluating the extent of Lorenzo's personal fortune on behalf of the Pope than they are to be appreciating paintings and tapestries.' He looks at Leonardo's bag of spices. 'But I see you have better things to do than court a cardinal?'

'If Lorenzo wants me, I'm sure he will send word.'

'He already has,' says Andrea, handing him a sprig of rosemary. 'Your presence is requested, and I imagine Lorenzo would prefer it to be accompanied by speech this time – if you could stretch to that?'

He rides with Andrea to the Via Larga. A servant brings him a jug of water to wash, a fine linen cloth to dry his face. He crosses the familiar courtyard. On the late-afternoon breeze, his cloak billows out like the tail feathers of a bird. His feet ring hollow on stone. Lorenzo is busy with preparations in the great hall. On seeing Leonardo, the banker beckons him over.

Various paintings have been brought in to add to the tapestries and sculptures which already fill the hall. There are two paintings of his own: *The Annunciation* and a painting he has recently completed of the Virgin and child.

'Leonardo, I am pleased to see you,' says Lorenzo, taking him by the arm. 'I did not want you to miss the opportunity. Commissions rarely come without conversation, you know.' The banker looks across the room at Leonardo's paintings – says lightly, 'Rome does not have the talent of Florence. Sixtus must feel it. If the Cardinal is not impressed by these, then the meaning of divine must be lost on him.'

'Commissions in Rome may be good for some,' he says, 'but not for me.'

'Why do you make things so hard for yourself, when they

could be so easy? Why not think on what I said to you – a reputation is made only once?'

Frustration he has felt ever since his return from the hospital rises to the surface. That and the crowds have made him uneasy. Nothing, however, will ruffle Lorenzo; the man has the smile of a diplomat and more charm than anyone he has met; Lorenzo is like metal point, essence of steel. Precise, brilliant – but incomplete. He would like to ask the banker: how is your Florence great without science? But knowing you don't question a Medici, he exercises restraint, feels it drain his will. So instead he thinks of holy fire, of the purple entourage of the Cardinal, and Salviati's impatience. Then another thought: where is Giuliano? He puts his hand to his pouch and remembers there was no chickweed. Something else worries him but he cannot put words to it.

The Cardinal is announced. Lorenzo signals the herald and turns back to him. 'I know you feel held back, that I have put an end to your work at the hospital, but you must understand how things are. I cannot back the ideas of one man against the needs of a city. Especially now.' Guests begin to file in. The Cardinal removes his cloak. 'The shadow of the gallows is longer from Rome,' Lorenzo says, 'and Sixtus only too ready to open the door to accusations of heresy. I know what you are – don't imagine otherwise. You think the city needs you – and perhaps it does,' he adds, quietly, 'but it needs a cardinal more.' Archbishop Salviati and the rest of the entourage follow the Cardinal, move towards their host. Lorenzo touches his arm. 'There is only one to fear more than God,' the banker mutters, 'and that is His servants.'

★

Giuliano is showing the young cardinal a collection of silver armoury for jousting. Lorenzo is deep in conversation with Francesco Salviati. He, Leonardo, stands on the edge of the crowd, looking in.

He takes out his sketchpad and begins to draw, his hand brushing over the small piece of paper in soft, fast strokes. 'You'd do better to talk,' says Andrea in his ear. But something has grabbed his attention. The pose of the Cardinal, or perhaps his expression. He leans against a wall discreetly and continues to draw.

'A fine likeness.' Francesco Salviati is looking curiously over his shoulder. 'No surprise then that you are responsible for some of the finest paintings in this room, Messer Leonardo, but I have heard that your talents do not stop there.'

'Many things interest me,' he replies, putting away his sketch.

'Including anatomy, it would appear. The Cardinal and myself have been admiring your Saint Jerome. Lorenzo was gracious enough to take us as far as his private chambers and store rooms.' Having left the armoury, the Cardinal thanks Giuliano for sharing his passion for sports but appears dissatisfied. With a nod at Poliziano, the restless man makes his way back to Salviati.

'We have been speaking about anatomy,' Francesco says, then, turning to him, 'The Cardinal finds your study of Saint Jerome a little overworked.'

'I'm sorry you think so,' he replies. 'One man's inspiration does not necessarily accommodate the tastes of another.'

'Inspiration is not one man's work, it is God's,' replies Cardinal Riario. His robes have the stature the man himself lacks. His body is lost in the gown, his profile hard, pinched and – he notices –

incredibly tense. 'But you seem to have supplanted a saint with a study.'

'My inspiration comes from what I see around me. Saint Jerome is a figure of suffering, and there is plenty of that to be found. A brief visit to any hospice in Florence, Pisa or Rome will provide it in abundance.'

Salviati looks over at Lorenzo, who is trying to finish a conversation with the Ferrarese ambassador's wife. 'And is that where your inspiration for anatomy comes from, Messer Leonardo? A hospice?' Lorenzo is walking over. 'So it is that Florence is becoming a city of heretics,' the Cardinal mutters. 'In the event—'

'Lorenzo, your brother is no longer sick. I am glad to see him up and well,' Salviati cuts in.

'A small matter of an eye infection, but nothing serious. Thank you for your concern.' Lorenzo is wearing a metaphor in a smile.

'And I hope he will be well enough to attend the celebrations tomorrow?'

'I hope so. He has seen a physician, although of course it is not serious, but still, where would we be without our sight?'

Where indeed, he thinks.

The Cardinal turns back to Giuliano, who is holding up a finely wrought golden chest plate to a group of admiring Ferrarese, and says to him, 'That is a fine collection. I hear that your brother puts it to good use. And such wonderful paintings ...' On Lorenzo's face, politics gives way to passion. 'I see that you have also been enjoying the work of my favourite, Messer Leonardo.'

Poliziano draws Leonardo away. 'Don't make an enemy of the

Cardinal. Ever since Volterra, Lorenzo has been searching for a way to provide Florence with a seat on the Holy See. But the Pope sees to it every time that a member of his own family gets there first.'

Lorenzo is taking the Cardinal's arm and leading him to the feast.

'Then he is already too late.'

'Perhaps. Although there are few who can resist Lorenzo's charm when he's making an effort.'

'Yes,' he says. The Cardinal's entourage moves into the dining room. 'But I am not altogether certain that the effort is flowing in the direction you suppose.'

'What do you mean?'

'Only that I feel it to be the Cardinal who wants something rather than Lorenzo. And if it is the case, then whatever the Cardinal wants, it must be more problematic than a seat on the papal throne.'

'What makes you say that?'

He takes out the sketch from inside his doublet and shows it to Poliziano. He has captured a fleeting expression on the face of the cleric. His face is pinched; his eyes stare wide and restless beneath a heavy brow. 'The cleric's preoccupations outweigh Lorenzo's,' he says. He thinks, even a Cardinal can fear God.

He takes his leave before long while Andrea remains behind. An armed guard leads him out. He passes children bearing torches and candles, their faces full of holy light. This night of silent Saturday, scripture holds open the door between the dead and the living. But he has already slipped through and back. If scripture holds any mystery for him, it is not the mystery of resurrection, more likely the miracle of faith. For once, he lies down early. In any case, he has run out of candle wax. But once on his bed, he can't sleep. He dozes intermittently, disturbed by childish dreams. His thoughts return to the preliminary sketch he has prepared in his mind. Another two days and he will call again at the house behind the fish market. He closes his eyes, and before long he is standing, barefoot and bare-chested, on the shore of a great ocean.

The wind touches his body and face. Around him waves are breaking. The mounts of Poseidon rush towards him, only to dissolve in a mass of foam and shingle at his feet. He looks ahead at the horizon, where a bloated crimson sun hangs low in the sky. He looks down. At his feet is a perfect spiral shell the colour of old olive wood. He bends down to pick it up, but the wave is quicker. It washes under his hand and takes the shell away on the current of the water. His hand is empty. The sun dips below the horizon line and he opens his eyes a third time, once again in darkness.

He spends the following day at his desk. Andrea returns before noon, throwing open the door of his room and pushing it shut behind him. It is Easter day; the bells of the Duomo are ringing. 'Mass already over?' he asks Andrea.

Andrea is not a fragile man. The Maestro falls into a chair, head in hands. It is a sacred day, and a cursed one. Christ has risen from the tomb and all of Christendom gives praise. But here in Florence, the city of Mars, Giuliano de' Medici has been struck down, slaughtered in the aisle of the city's beloved cathedral by the hand of a cardinal, an archbishop: Riario, Salviati. Only Lorenzo has been spared. Although he sustained one near-fatal stab wound to the neck, the magnificent man is still safe. Now they must mourn the body of his brother, which is lying even now not three braccia from the altar of the cathedral, in a pool of blood.

Andrea holds him back. Everyone is on the streets. The road to the piazza is blocked with upturned carts, but the murderers have fled. Now the crowd will not rest until they find them.

They pack away; put away knives and lathes, hammers and axes. They pile up crates and wrap tools in cloth. He takes up his cloak and thinks of his father. He brushes off Andrea's concerns and strikes out through the back streets, avoiding the piazzas. He stops at the Via del Montecomune and learns with relief that his father is at Anchiano. He pictures Lorenzo, wounded and grieving. But the Via Larga is seething with people. A large crowd has gathered at the gates of the palazzo. He pushes aside a woman, her four children and a group of shouting youths who shove him back in turn, frightened and angry. The banco where men sit and wait on days of business has become the focus of accounts settled. On three spikes are three heads, their faces grey and bloody. Each one wears the expression he has died with. It is more than he can bear. One of the youths takes up a spike and thrusts it forward, pushing the ghastly face in his. The crowd roars approval. He backs away in horror and ducks beneath the fray of bodies heaving for a view. His hand shaking, he pulls aside a passing soldier. 'What news of Lorenzo? Does he live?'

'He lives, yes. But not his brother. Where are you from?' the soldier enquires, suspiciously. 'Nowhere,' he replies. And then, 'The studio del Verrocchio.'

He strikes out again, retracing his journey of five days past. He dives into back alleys. A cart is stuck down one side alley, its horse on the edge of panic. Frightened passengers dismount and push the cart forwards. A man struggles past, pursued by three others. One is holding a *spada*, the other a lance head. He flattens against the wall to let them pass, and has a sudden flashback of himself a small boy, holding a wooden shield. The image clouds, as a trailing mass of jeering men elbows past him, two of them stained red with somebody else's blood. Sick and disgusted, he at last reaches the great wooden door of the Gherardini house, thankful to be alive. The servant is putting the last of the trunks onto an already full cart. The previous one is already long gone. Messer Antonio and his daughter left as the riots began, she says. Back to Vinci? he enquires. No, she says, the villa was sold the previous year. Ser Piero did the transaction, the notary by the abbey. Such horror. And poor Giuliano: a prince in his gold armour on the day of the festival. But now even princes can be killed, and even a cleric can be a murderer. What is there to do but leave?

He nods. He turns away and heads back to the Via de' Macci, taking the longest detour he can think of. Angry voices and the sound of chanting drive him further out towards the river. He walks along the bank until the city walls push him back inside. As he watches the river pass beyond the fortifications of the city, to become meandering tributaries and hidden streams, he wonders why he is surprised at all – Lisa has done what she has always done. She has disappeared.

VI

He steadies his hand. He writes as normal: left hand, right to left. Andrea watches without a word. He completes the entry in his journal: this day, the thirteenth day of the calends of June. On another page, unfinished, is a sketch of a man hanging from a gibbet.

They have barely left the rooms of Andrea's villa. His home is simple but comfortable – full of sculpture at various stages of completion. Arms without bodies, a bust here, a torso there. 'Salviati's body is already in pieces,' says Andrea. 'The others are in hiding but before long, Lorenzo will find them and they too will hang. But your way of writing may get you to the end of a rope faster.'

He puts down his pen and looks up at Andrea. He wonders, which is worse, accusation or concern? He dismisses both. 'I will not change the way I write in order to stave off a bunch of murdering clerics.'

He picks up the manuscript and gives it to the sculptor. It is now a thick wedge of paper, held together by a leather strap. Long years of observation and study, the source of his elation and his trials, his very reason for living. Looking at the pile of pages as he hands it over, he can barely imagine where, in all those words and images, Leonardo ended and Leonardo da Vinci began. His life seeps from worn pages: an echo from a time when monsters could be created and destroyed, dreams woven, unravelled, remade again. But what will Andrea see? He hands him a mirror. 'This is what I need?' The sculptor moves the mirror horizontally along the drawings and notes he has made in the small back room of Santa Maria Nuova. To see better, he moves into the daylight that streams in through the window.

It is almost full summer. Lorenzo has recovered from his wounds but Florence is still hurting. War has broken out with Rome and Naples, as they knew it would. Of Giuliano's murderers, only one remains alive. The palazzo was roped like the mast of a ship with the corpses of Salviati and Pazzi and those of their family. Only Riario has been spared. No crowd will hang a cardinal. A diplomat to the end, Lorenzo stands back quietly and lets the Signoria inflame the mob.

Andrea places the manuscript on the desk. 'What you have written and drawn is astonishing,' the Maestro says.

It has been a long time since David. He looks at Andrea: past his prime, too much gout, too little patience, and knows that a man only lives so long before he loses the will to challenge Goliath. He waits for the words he knows will come next. 'What you have done is more than dangerous, it is foolhardy.' The most recent drawing shows the workings of the human eye. On the corner of a page, a smear of dried blood has flaked to nothing.

'I wonder how you can do such a thing, it's, it's . . .'

'Barbaric?' he enquires, quietly.

'Yes. Since you say the word yourself. It is.'

As a boy of eleven, he worked because he couldn't stop. Now

he works because he knows he mustn't stop. He could be tethered to his desk. On either side shadows close in.

'Very well. If that is what you think, then I'll leave. Here. Florence.' He thinks of his first day at the *bottega*, his drawing of the cathedral, Andrea emerging from the dust of six hours of chiselling. Everything has its history. There was the face at the window, the figure on the stony track that left in the night. The weight of Anchiano at his back, and before him, Brunelleschi's dome – Florence. Lisa. His life is full of the precedent of departure. What is one more?

Andrea shakes his head. 'Leonardo, your mind has been set on its own path ever since the day I met you and from the moment I first took you into my employ. I know too well there's no point in arguing with you or even in trying to persuade you to listen to me. You have become my son in all but name; that is how I think of you. I know you're stubborn: perhaps not even stubborn, something more uncommon than stubborn, but the thought of this manuscript in the hands of someone like Riario, who would bribe his brother to murder his mother if it paid him to do so, makes me tremble. Even if Lorenzo were in a position to help you, now he may choose not to.' The Maestro reaches out and touches him on the shoulder. His reaction is to back off, so he stands rigid instead.

'There are other powerful men who would be glad of my talents.'

'Undoubtedly. But if you want to do battle with the Church you will need friends of a different kind to Lorenzo de' Medici. The Medici will pay your bread and board, but they will *not* have the stomach for dissections.'

'My battle is not with the Church,' he says. 'It's with the minds of men, of everyone around me.' He turns away. Andrea, of all people, should have understood. 'Even you.' He feels his voice trembling and regulates it. 'Men who think that to cut off a man's head and impale it on a spike is less barbaric than cutting open his chest and examining his heart.'

'That,' says the sculptor, 'may well be true. But let me offer you some advice. What there is in the heart of a man is one thing. What there is in your own is another. Cutting one up won't tell you that.' The sculptor holds up his hand. 'Let's say no more for now. I have a friend I want you to meet. Speak with him; then make your decision. That's all I'll say. If then you still want to pack up and leave, at least you may have direction. This man has watched your progress with keen interest. *The Baptism of Christ*, you remember – the angel you painted first drew his attention, but it was your work on the figure of Christ that struck him most.'

'Fine,' he says, 'But there is no person I can imagine who can help me better than I can help myself.'

He returns to his rooms and looks at his trunk, his modest collection of brushes, pigments and books, the bronze sundial on the corner of his desk, the assortment of plans, diagrams, his unfinished sighting box, and other models he has devised. There are piles of fabric, paper and various pots of oils, powders and mixtures, labelled and dated. This room is his home, but never has he felt so ready to leave. He knows that Andrea is right about Lorenzo, but does not want to hear it. He is tired of other people and their limited perspective. Their rigidity binds his hands and closes his eyes. Is it heresy to seek the truth? Does God not want them to understand His world, to decipher His mysteries? Can none of them stand back and see the full picture: man, God and nature as one?

He moves to his desk, takes up a piece of chalk and several sheets of paper. He will sketch as he writes. He will write what he chooses. This is how he is: his hand moves from right to left, his mind performs the calculation before his hand can commit it to paper. He casts aside Andrea's rulers and compass and lets the picture fall out of his head onto the page. His next commission will be his last. They have given him the subject, but the form and style will be his. Head to hand, the pen cannot keep pace. Dissatisfied, he takes a second sheet, then a third. Iconic Virgin becomes living mother; Son of God becomes son of man. The mother is holding the child on her lap. In her hand is a cardamine flower, at which the curious child clutches with inquisitive fingers. They give him scripture; he will give them truth.

In the full sunshine of a Florentine spring, he takes off his leather clogs and dips his feet into the cold water that flows over rock and stone in tiny eddies of gurgling meltwater. He is sitting beside a mountain stream which has its origins high up in the mountains they call the Apennines. Above him, the Futa Pass forms a ridge between two peaks. Below him, on the plain to the west, is Florence. The stream, in which he now washes his hands, will take this water and deposit it, along with its minerals, sediments and stones, into the Arno River and on to the coast. Like the body of a vast creature, the mountain is veined with the blood vessels of rivers and streams. But how that vast body of folds, ridges and peaks came into being is not something he can draw, observe or document with eyes or hands. The mountains, old as they are, have grown out of the land spontaneously. They are ancient folds in a rocky fabric. As cloth moves over skin and folds into pleats, likewise, the surface of the land has been pushed upwards. This is what he believes. He no longer makes reference to floods, arks or the gods of antiquity, but looks for the simplest explanation: the one most visible, or most logical.

He notes the composition of the soil: clay and sandstone. He rubs clean the stone he is holding. Around and below him, forests of chestnut and oak provide nesting for ravens. Kestrels use the wind in the valley to hover over rocky outcrops, searching for shrews. He has found little in the way of herbs, but the ancient stone in his hand is full of crystals, and provides the compensation for the distance he has travelled. He has been walking for many hours, his feet are sore, his shoes badly made. He calculates the time it will take him to get back and begins walking, suddenly feeling that the mountain is no longer high enough, the horizon too small, and that if he were to turn around and look over his shoulder, he would catch a glimpse of a girl in a green dress hiding behind a rock or a bush, ready to tell him he has got it all wrong: that whatever it is he thinks he has in his bag, it is only half the story.

In sight of the city walls, he sees the figure of a man walking out to meet him. Tall and of Saxon descent, he is fair and fine featured. The stranger addresses him by name.

'It is better for you that you do not know mine, so I would ask you to call me John: John of Wittenberg is all you need to know.

I have been waiting for you. There are few who take the trouble to walk through the mountains only to return the way they came, so I imagine you must be Leonardo di Ser Piero da Vinci?'

'I am that man. Although you are the first to call me by my full name.'

'The legacy of illegitimate birth is a burden,' says the stranger. 'But heresy is a heavier one.'

'*The Baptism of Christ*?' he says. This is Andrea's friend. A passing interest in his painting seems to have developed into something more than curiosity. He weighs the stranger up. Sober dress, patience, frankness. Northern coldness is new to him. He notices the cross round his neck: cross, not crucifix. 'I'm used to burdens,' he goes on, 'I have carried them for many years. I see no reason why I should falter now.'

They enter the Porta al Prato, make their way through the city. Disorder is everywhere. Trade has all but stopped. The price of wool or silk is immaterial. The scene in the cathedral still fresh, the blood not dried. He leads the stranger through the workshop. Domenico stops soldering. Sandro has come in to borrow pigments. He leads the way through to the back room beside the yard. He boils water over the stove and adds a handful of herbs: sage and lime.

'If you want to leave Florence,' the stranger says, 'I have come to offer you an alternative.'

'Thank you,' he replies, 'but I've no intention of leaving Italy.'

'My principal aim in coming to see you is to warn you. You may not yet be aware, but you are gathering enemies just as surely as your patron Lorenzo has done. You need new friends.'

He takes a cloth and picks up the pot. 'I have no enemies here,' he says. Sandro enters the room. 'Domenico needs a steady hand. Will you come?'

'I'll be out in a moment.'

'Tell me,' says the stranger, accepting a cup, 'your reasons for walking out today into the hills of Prato.'

'I have always walked,' he says, simply. 'I study nature, like any artist.'

'Ah, but you are not just any artist. Andrea has told me about the drawings you have made on anatomy, your studies of plants and alchemy . . .'

'I am no alchemist,' he says. 'Or physician. Simply an observer.'

'But there are some who object to scrutiny,' the stranger says. 'The Church of Rome, for instance.'

'I have no argument with the Church.'

'You have an argument with the Church whether you want one or not,' replies John of Wittenberg. 'Even now those responsible for the murder of Giuliano de' Medici have dispatched a letter to Lorenzo warning him that if Florence continues to shelter heretics, then he will suffer the consequences of excommunication, as will the entire city. Lorenzo will be forced to make concessions. Perhaps not today, or tomorrow, but the threats to the Holy Roman Empire grow greater every day. You are one. The Church is another.'

'The Church threatens itself?'

'I'm sorry. I have not yet mastered your language. What I am saying is that there are those in the Church who do not share Rome's lust for power and wealth. There are those of us who believe that simony is a crime, that holy office cannot be bought and indulgences cannot be sold; that true heresy lies in corruption, not knowledge; that true knowledge is old. Older than Rome and even Greece. It came from the plains of Egypt, where the Nile flows through landscape unchanged since the days of legend. At that time Isis, Mother of the fertile Nile Delta, venerated for her power over life and death, guarded against sickness and drought. The sun worshippers, ancestors of those pagan believers who watched Jesus preach his word from the slopes of Mount Zion, were the Esseni – the keepers of Torah, the inheritors of ancient knowledge. They believed in the power of nature to change, heal and govern, and so they made their homes along the shores of the Dead Sea – water rich with the strength of minerals. From these waters they devised their cures and became healers of the sick: miracle workers. From among their number came one whose name you know well; like others of his kind, the Baptist venerated the water for its spiritual, cleansing power. He saw clearly how the world was made up: some followed God's message as Moses had proclaimed it, but others came who used it for their own purposes. They were the pretenders to the Kingdom of Heaven: the inheritors of Rome, who wore the mantle of Babylon. *For behold, I will give the land of Egypt unto Nebuchadnezzar, King of Babylon; and he shall take her multitude, and take her spoil, and take her prey; and it shall be the wages for his army.* And so it came to pass. The seat of their power lies in the Holy City: the Vatican. Now the task has fallen to other believers to put right the mistakes of the past. The conspiracy that killed Lorenzo's brother is but one small part of a rotten whole: a body of corruption and vice.'

'Tell me,' he says, 'are you asking me to renounce the Catholic Church and use my work to bring it down?'

'You have already renounced it,' the stranger replies, 'through your work.'

He stands up. 'If I am to be cast out by one church, it shall not be to seek protection from another.'

'Then who shall protect you?' John says. 'Florence, Rome?'

'Myself.'

'There, if you will permit me to say it, you are wrong. Out on your own, you would not last the month. I think you will find that we all need people, Leonardo, even you.'

'I know what I need,' he says. 'I always have. Earlier you asked me why I walk so far only to return. The simple explanation is always the more accurate: freedom, space.' He takes up his cloak. 'Andrea should be back soon. As for me, don't expect me to leave Florence. And it will take more than heresy to drive me out of Italy.'

He finds a soldering iron for Domenico and holds it in his broad palm. 'Tell me,' he says, 'you think your church better than Rome's – but who are your heretics?'

'An easy question to answer,' John says. 'Giuliano's killers. Those who wear the robe of Cardinal, but fail to understand that an unshod monk is closer to God than they. Our inspiration comes from Saint Augustine. We are ready to embrace what the Catholic Church fears most.'

'Which is?'

'The thing you want most: freedom and space. The freedom to think; the space to find God.'

On a corner of the table is his pile of sketches. 'I see you like horses. So do I. Noble creatures: graceful, beautiful. Before you go – a word of advice. If you insist on staying in Italy, then you may be safe in Milan. The House of Sforza has the power to withstand the Pope, but do not look for freedom. In Italy there is no such thing: only power and those who have it.'

Three days later, he receives word from Lorenzo. He is required to leave the services of Medici and present himself at the court of Ludovico Sforza by the end of the month. He packs his trunk and all of his possessions. Andrea gives him new brushes, a servant and a cart, money he has not made. He thinks of the sunset on the Arno, the distant blue of Prato Magno, goodbyes he has not said, others he isn't ready for. He tells himself there will be other hills, other rivers. As he takes the eastern door out, he feels the ties that bind him to other people stretch and weaken. They give way to freedom. It is a summer's day and the Arno is at its lowest level. He goes against a weakened current, following the river as it bends away from Emilia Romagna and forces him north.

Milan

I

The walls of the Sforza castle cannot be breached. On either side of the castle gate is a broad portal splayed with archivolts. The wall runs in a straight line, appearing to diminish in proportion to distance, as is the way with perspective. Inside the castle walls, well-planted gardens provide a much-needed contrast to what is essentially a building of hard symmetry. There is not the beauty of a Florentine garden. The shrubs and borders have no roses, no laurel bushes. Rectangular buildings enclose an imposing courtyard. From the parapets, flocks of starlings perch like tiny archers. They take flight in an orderly mass, like shoals of small fish. He slips from his horse and feels beneath the saddle. It is soaked. He finds a stable boy. 'Rub her down with straw,' he says.

'Your letter of introduction reached me just this day. You are hot on its heels, Leonardo from Florence. Tell me, what are you running from?'

Ludovico Sforza reclines in state in the centre of the hall, in the heart of the fortress at the gates of the city: his yet not his. Soon Galeazzo, nephew of Sforza, will be dead. Then, the Duchy of Milan will fall into the uncle's lap, like fruit from a tree.

'That is a good question, Messer,' he replies. 'How indeed can it be possible to judge, once a man is mobile, whether he runs towards one object or away from another?'

His host throws back his head and laughs. Robust and strong in body, the man is as solid as his fortifications. 'Lorenzo is not wrong – this time. He says you have the intuition of five men and the wit to outsmart a thousand. What do you say?'

Before he answers, someone else does. 'That would be well, since his tailor is clearly lacking in both.' Sforza's entourage are noblemen, wives, mistresses and merchants. They are richly dressed, in colours he has rarely seen on the backs of either sex: some wear scarlet, others gold and even purple. The hands of Sforza are decked with gold; his cloak is edged with ermine. He, Leonardo, is wearing wool.

The Sforza household has given him lodgings. He now has three rooms and a private courtyard. The workshop has windows that let in the light. He stands in the middle of the Corte Vecchio and pictures how he can fill it. This is light for sculpture. He hates the dirt and the dust, but knows that Sforza craves greatness, and greatness needs sculpture. He has already worked it out, the weight of the statue, the quantity of bronze and the logistics of sectional casting. He will give Milan what Florence could not give him: stature. Then they will see whether silk matters more than wool. As he looks at Ludovico Sforza he sees his history: a family of *condottieri*. Mercenary soldiers, sons of Generals, masters of destiny. He can do this.

He clears his throat. 'I claim neither intuition nor wit. Nor even elegance, since Florence is a city of simple refinements.'

Ludovico speaks. 'Tell me, what is your evaluation of Lorenzo's position, in the wake of the cruel and barbaric act committed against him with the murder of his brother?'

He is not prepared for such a direct question. What, he wonders, does the son of a *condottiere* want? The answer comes fast: strategy. 'Florence is at war. Lorenzo faces two choices – attack his enemy head on and face the consequences, or back down and wave the flag of peace.'

'And what, if you were he, would you choose to do?'

Strategy. 'The greatness of a man is measured by his choices, not by his abilities. I would advocate a display of both. The choice of peace over war becomes all the more significant if it is counter-balanced by a display of strength.'

Ludovico moves his great figure forward in the chair. 'And this display you suggest . . . what form would it take?'

'People need greatness. Sometimes it must be conjured for them.' He wonders at his own words, his and not his. 'I would erect a statue of bronze to the glory of my fathers,' he says. 'But not just any statue.'

'Go on,' says Sforza.

'From the impossible, I would create the possible. While everyone around me would say that the thing cannot be done, I would prove them wrong.'

Ludovico looks at him with penetrating interest. 'So Lorenzo has sent me a worker of miracles?'

'Only God can make miracles,' he replies. 'I merely put them into effect. If the wind is a miracle, I can harness it. If the power of rivers, oceans and water is a miracle, then I will make it serve a purpose. Where others create problems, I provide calculations. That is all.' He thinks, you can't argue with mathematics.

Sforza stands up. The court rises. 'We will discuss this at greater length, alone,' the Regent says to him quietly. 'But now' –

turning to the crowd – 'it is entertainment we require. My Florentine ally tells me you are also a musician.' Again quietly, 'Well, are you?'

He thinks of the lyre fashioned from the skull of a horse, which he has in his trunk. If they criticise his tailor, what will they make of that? 'I play a little,' he says.

'What is your instrument?' the sartorial nobleman calls out.

'I couldn't say really that I have any particular preference. What would give you pleasure?'

The nobleman seizes a wooden flute from the hands of a nearby troubadour, but Sforza raises his hand. 'Bring a lute,' Sforza says. 'Let us see what he makes of it.'

'What shall I play for you?' he asks, politely.

'Something of your own composition,' says the Regent.

He takes up the lute. The owner of the instrument passes him a quill, but he declines, preferring to play with his fingers. He checks the strings, sounds a few notes, and plays. He chooses a passamezzo: a plaintive twelve-bar composition that he varies often for his own pleasure. The ravishing notes of the instrument fill the room as his fingers pluck the strings delicately, at times lingering, at times fast. He glances up as he plays; his familiarity with the strings gives him the pleasure of detachment.

Ludovico Sforza appears reflective, absent; his mind fixed on private thoughts. On a chair to one side he notices that a lady watches the Sforza Regent with unwavering attention. When the tune comes to a natural close, Leonardo stops. There is loud applause. Ludovico leans back in his chair, the spell broken, and raises his glass. 'Welcome to Milan,' he says.

★

'My name,' says the man at his door, 'is Francesco da Melzo. And if you will have me, I wish to offer my services as your apprentice.'

He has unpacked a few volumes of books, his tools and the contents of his trunk. He has arranged everything in order. Now he is making fresh labels for those damaged in transit. Pigments must be tidied, brushes washed. He enlists the help of Francesco, who watches in bewilderment as he classes plans, diagrams and rolls of sketches. Lines things up, stacks them.

'You may find yourself better suited elsewhere.'

'I would like to work with you.'

'Why?'

'Because you're from Florence. Because I know who you are.'

'But perhaps if I told you what work I had in mind, you may change yours.'

Francesco stands straight, head raised. 'Well, I don't know . . . I am keen to learn.'

'Do you like sculpture?'

'I love sculpture . . . I am . . .'

'Good,' he says, glancing at his arms, which he sees are strong. 'Then you can stay.'

'Thank you.' Francesco puts down his bag.

'Not here, there.'

'Sorry.'

'What . . . if I might ask, with respect of course . . . did you have in mind to build?'

The man is not much more than a boy. Must be ten years younger than him. But that doesn't mean he can stand the pace: his pace. He takes the young man's hands and looks at them.

They are white and soft, small and square. He could crush them in a second. He draws out a single sketch from a roll of papers and lays it on the table.

Francesco looks at the drawing of the horse, then back to him. 'A sculpture?' He nods. 'Bronze,' Francesco mutters, looks up. 'No man can cast seventy tons of bronze.' Francesco gazes at the sketch and the dimensions beside it as though someone has asked him to walk on water. 'How will you do such a thing? It's impossible.'

'Mathematics,' he says. 'There is always a calculation.' He glances at the young apprentice. 'Changing your mind?'

Francesco opens his bag. 'No.'

He smiles. Fair enough. The boy has guts. 'Good; I need a strong pair of hands and a steady eye. A strong back wouldn't hurt either.' They walk together into the courtyard at the back of the *bottega*. 'The model will fill this space completely,' he says. They stand and stare. His eyes wander upwards, tracing the invisible dimensions of the final cast until he finds that he is looking, head tilted, at blue sky and diaphanous cloud. A bell tower looms high on one side. On the roof builders are constructing a dome on the church.

Francesco says Milan is bursting with projects. The Regent is busy arranging marriages and building an army – which amount to one and the same thing. Sforza spends big. If a project takes his fancy, Sforza must see it done.

'Must?' he enquires. *Must*, he thinks – at any cost. He nods. That is one way of doing it. He rolls up the plan and puts it back in place.

'He must be enthusiastic about this one,' says Francesco, watching.

'He will be, in time. I will see you're paid well. If necessary I'll pay you myself.'

'I don't mind waiting for money,' Francesco says, setting out his tools. 'A task like this will be spectacle enough – as long as we have the means to carry it out.'

'Yes, although even a sculptor must eat from time to time,' he says, 'or he will cut too fine a profile.' He takes up Francesco's chisel and weighs it in his hand. Too light for him.

Francesco says, 'I can see from your hands that you've five times my strength.' The young man picks out a knife, beautifully wrought with a carved wooden handle. 'Try this. The name of Sforza has a sharp edge. Perhaps I should watch your back.'

He has things as he wants them. Except that he misses Andrea and his gout. He sits in a chair and thinks of Florence. Domenico will be doing the varnishing on the altarpiece. Sandro will be in and out because he can't stay away. Andrea will be worrying about his leg or a non-existent fever, which he is not there to cure. The rest he pushes back.

Milanese autumns announce themselves hard. Life fades away fast. The trees are already half-bare. The swallows are gone. A kind of loneliness accompanies the rhythm of work he picks up as though he has never stopped. This is Plinius country. He finds his copy of *Natural History* and looks for Padus: river of amber banks and thunderbolts. The next morning he takes out his leather clogs and his thick brown tunic and has a look at what the Po valley has to offer.

Mountain lakes feed the river. But he needs the horse to get there. His father's mare is getting old. He examines her and feeds her oatmeal mash, but the muscle will not build. She loses it instead and there is nothing he can do. He fixes on a cure of barley and spends time he doesn't have rubbing her down. The stable boy doesn't have a clue. He gives instructions. If she gets any worse, he will have to take her to the slaughterhouse. He can't bear the thought. The day before he left Florence, he stopped at Via Montecomune. But the visit was short. His father said too much, he too little. Between the two of them he imagines they had a conversation. He straps the mare's legs, puts her out to pasture, and thinks he must ask Sforza for the use of one of his horses.

Francesco has gone out in search of fabric. The Regent has warned of impending festivities. Leonardo senses that the costumes and flags of Florence will not do. Sforza wants spectacle. He will have to supply it. It frustrates him, but there is always the prospect of mechanics. He has designed a new pulley; he wonders whether Francesco will be able to make it, or if he will have to waste more time showing him. Then he remembers Andrea's patience and soaks in a little humility. He hears someone outside and opens the door, expecting Francesco. Instead, a herald who barely has time to do his job announces the arrival of the Regent. Sforza waves him aside and enters as though he's in a hurry.

'Well then, is everything as you want it? I hear da Melzo has placed himself in your service. That is good news. There will be others, no doubt. You will have no trouble keeping them occupied, nor trouble settling their wage. I shall see to that.' Sforza puts his hand on Leonardo's shoulder. 'I am expecting great things from you, Leonardo. Great things. Lorenzo speaks very highly of you, although of course with things as they are he doesn't have the liberty to sponsor every project he would like. I, on the other hand, do.' The Regent places his gloves and hat on the table and walks round, glancing at a pile of books without comment, then stops at the rows of paper. 'You must show me what you have here.'

He is not in the habit of showing. Ingrained reticence holds him back from even opening his trunk, never mind displaying its contents. But he has baited the bear and is in no mind to turn back. In any case, for the time being, there is no back. He runs his finger along the rolls, pulls out his sketches of horses, followed by his drawings for the construction of a canal. Another time, another place. His design to link Florence to the coast might as well have been a journey to the stars. Sforza leafs through his sketches. The Regent, who is more interested in rider than horse, in admiring the thrust of a lance, the fluid movement of a lancer's shoulder, turns to him. 'I have for many months been desiring a steam chamber, such as those they have in Genoa. This would be easy for you to arrange, I think?'

He swallows. 'Yes. Of course.' *Must.* He waits for the next thing.

'Good, good.' Then, 'As for any personal projects you may have, you will find me a liberal benefactor. Use whatever materials you want. Order what you need. I have heard that your interests are broad. Isn't that so?'

'That is true.' This he was not expecting.

Sforza looks amused. 'You don't talk much, do you? I know, for instance, that you are interested in anatomy.' Francesco's knife is where he left it. Sforza picks it up and examines it. 'Fine blade.' He puts it down. 'Well, are you?'

'I am.'

Ludovico Sforza: warrior, fighter. Strong name, strong will. The man must have his answer. He takes a breath. 'I have carried out a number of dissections, and have made significant progress in many areas in the understanding of—'

Sforza cuts in. 'Dissections? With or without permission?' The man already knows the answer.

'Without.'

'In that case, from now on you can do them with. The Ospedale Maggiore should be able to oblige. I will see that arrangements are made.' Sforza removes the gloves and hat from the table beside the knife, and with a nod and glance, takes his leave.

He sits for a while in a chair in the corner, thinking about the unpredictability of princes. Francesco arrives. He sets him to work cutting the fabric he has brought: rolls of black crepe. He shows him how to make a pulley. Vary the wheel dimensions, he says. Carpentry is not his thing. He will perform the calculations but dislikes the dust and dirt they create. He leaves Francesco to it and roams through the Sforza stables to avoid thinking about the steam chamber, admiring each horse in turn. The stable boy asks him a question about poultices. Clay and eucalyptus, he says. He shows him how to do it. It's easy to get what he wants. Filippo makes ready a black mare. He rides out of the castle gates; the sun is warm on his back and the wind is in his face. If the mare had wings, she would fly.

He crosses the plain of Lombardy. Springs water the soft clay ground, flowing down from the mountains beyond Bergamo like the veins that feed a body. He follows the trickling tributaries counter flow, heading up towards flashes of clean blue between tall trees. A vast stretch of water fills a bowl between mountains. At one end the land flattens, and the lake drains into the valley. From there, wind funnels in, providing lift for birds of prey high above the lake. Now he is at their level. He slips off the back of the mare, hangs the rein over a branch and watches the flight of the birds high above the water. How high? To find out he would need to walk down to the lake then up. That can be done later. A sudden gust of wind brings a white feather floating to his feet. He doesn't pick it up. Feathers are one solution, but there are others: flight is a mathematical calculation. He has known it from the first moment he watched a hawk in mid-air, or a flock of starlings in formation. You can't argue with mathematics. Every problem has its solution. And since Sforza has given him freedom to find one, then he will do so, even if it means building Sforza's steam chamber. Wings for steam: a fair trade, he thinks.

There is only one difficulty he can think of as he pulls himself back into the saddle: weight. He makes a note in his mind that starvation is necessary. Then he turns Sforza's sure-footed black mare back down the hill, and lets her have her head.

By the time he gets back, Francesco has made the pulleys. He counts the days to the date of the festival. Enough time. He takes out two rolls of paper and sits at his desk. He has already drafted the sketches of the Sforza monument as he sees it in his head: a mounted cavalier holding a spear, at his feet the vanquished figure of his enemy, while larger than both – larger than any statue in any state of Italy – the figure of the rearing horse. Next to it, there are three other unfinished sketches: the figure of a woman: no face, no background. Just shapes. Some paintings are complete before they are finished, while others will never be over. The painting of Lisa Gherardini, he tells himself, is not meant to happen. All the same, he wonders whether, if he had drawn her eyes to see, she would have looked across at his drawings of the Sforza statue and offered encouragement. No, he thinks. Laughter; the sound of a stream in hidden green groves; the brush of a bat wing in the depths of a cave.

He pushes aside the sketch of the Sforza monument and grabs a piece of charcoal. The concept is simple; surprisingly, beautifully simple. He shakes his head as he draws the thing out. Skins: light and strong, stretched like the wings of a bat onto an extendable wooden frame. Bat wings. Feathers are one solution, but there are others. Chastising himself for not having thought of it sooner, he draws until the room is cold and dark. He forgets to light the lamp. Francesco comes to find him. His gentle apprentice has prepared food. He must come and eat. 'Not now,' he says, 'later.' To make Francesco leave, he agrees to eat. Bread and olives, but not cheese. Starvation is necessary, but difficult since this new apprentice of his has other ideas. Does he sound like Andrea, he wonders? Soon he will be asking Francesco for tinctures.

Alone again, he opens Andrea's letter: ... *have returned now from Venice, back to our familiar bottega of Florence, in dust and disorder as a result of my absence and despite the efforts of Domenico who, like Sandro, now has his own place of work and precious little time to spare listening to the complaints and exhortations of an ageing Maestro. For information, the friar I mentioned in my previous letter has returned to Florence and has been seen preaching at San Marco. His sermons worry me. It seems that greed is a greater sin than I had previously imagined, although if the day should come that I moderate myself accordingly, then I will thank the man personally for his efforts. Florence becomes a dangerous place, revolts on every street corner and rumours that Lorenzo grows weak and tired of conflict. The Signori of Venice request my collaboration for a commission in honour of their murdering condottiere and I have sent them to the Devil several times already. Still, one more time will do no further harm, and will serve only to appease my own spirit and compensate for the inferior quality of their most rancid vines, whose fruit holds a faint torch to the warm glow of our own Tuscan fermentations . . .*

As though Andrea were here with him, he pours himself a cup of wine, and drinks a toast to moderation and the end of gout. The letter has been much delayed. He already knows that Lorenzo has left Florence to broker a dangerous peace with Rome. The diplomacy of metaphor will win the day, but not until enough blood has been spilled to flood a nave. His last memories of Florence are red. Tomorrow he will put Sforza to test and pay a visit to the Ospedale Maggiore. If the man is as good as his word, then perhaps there is still hope for princes.

He sleeps fully dressed. The nights are cold now. He takes a last look at his Greek before he closes his eyes. He knows what dream will come. He is standing above the lake. Around him is free air, beneath him, open water. His body is made of skin and wood. His arms stretch out beside him, touching space. He takes a breath and runs towards the edge of the cliff. But the cliff comes to him, sweeping him off his feet and into the air. He looks down; the lake is passing beneath him at speed, but he is rising, not falling. As he moves through the air, his wooden arms become wings, his skin grows feathers. Like a giant bird he feels the current of the air and controls it, tilting his body to make the turn, embracing the wind like a lover.

But now something dazzles his eyes. The sun, more powerful than the wind and stronger than the current, draws him on. Blinded by the light, he cannot hold back. Waves of heat scorch his face. Sparks singe his feathers, then rays of fire start to rain down on him, devouring his feathers until he becomes an airborne torch. His skin blisters; his wings are now wood batons that crackle and flare in the sun. As he flies, streaming flames into the heart of the fire, he has a terrible recollection. He must go back. Through the dying embers of the skeleton of the bird, he glimpses his father.

'Come back,' calls his father. 'You have to stop.'

His father's face is stricken, his hand outstretched. In the confusion of the moment, he remembers a conversation. But the bird is in ashes, and there is nothing more to say.

I can't, he thinks, and closes his eyes.

It is the longest night of winter. Putting on his cloak, he leaves the Corte Vecchio and walks out of the castle gates towards the city. Faint voices carry on cold air, babies cry, servants chatter in courtyards. From one house he hears breaking crockery; in another, someone is playing a clavichord.

He passes the cathedral. Its vertiginous structure stirs the darkness. Vertical lines of masonry rise up beside the portals and windows of the facade, where the vaulted apertures of the building cast an empty shadow, like the closed eyes of a sleeping stone giant. On the steps, a group of men – some youths, some older –

stand talking in groups. One in particular he notices as the youngest. He is strikingly beautiful; his face delicate and sharp, his hair a pile of loose curls. He walks past; the group follows further back behind him, then vanishes, swallowed by another dark alley.

He stops, leans against the wall. Cold air meets colder stone. Voices echo from alleys behind him, gentle at first, then forceful, then silent. His fingers touch the stone. He presses his back against it. He knows what he hears, the sound of men and boys taking their turn. Disgusted, he fights against instinct, draws away from the wall and walks on, until panicked shouts and turmoil send him running back to the alley. The group of youths is holding the youngest locked against the wall while the others jostle for position.

Without stopping to think, he plants himself before them. He has not struck a blow in his life, but there's no time to worry about it. He takes one of the youths by the neck and thrusts him aside. Another he grips by the doublet. His grip at least is strong, that much he knows. It is easier than he thought, the youths struggle fruitlessly.

'What shall I do with you filth?' he cries. 'Do you wish yourselves on the gibbet?' He calls to the others. 'I have your faces, if not your names, but your names are only one word away from his mouth.' He points to the curly-haired boy who stands shaking in his shadow. 'And I say he'll be ready enough to reveal them.' To his relief, they turn and run. One hangs back. 'Not me,' the youth calls, 'I did nothing ...'

'Then take yourself home,' he says calmly.

He turns to the boy. 'Are you all right?'

He says he is cold; his rescuer gives him his cloak. 'Where do you live?'

The boy shakes his head.

'Then what is your name?'

'Giacomo.'

'Come,' he says. They walk on as far as the great entrance of the Ospedale Maggiore.

From behind the grill of the hospital door a withered face peers out. 'What do you want?'

'I am looking for Bonafù.'

He is admitted without delay. He turns back to the boy. 'I have business here, which will last until dawn. If you wish to wait for me, when I have finished, I'll come back for you.'

Bonafù steps aside to admit him. He thrusts a number of coins into the guardian's hand. 'The boy there outside,' he says, 'see that he eats.'

Bonafù shakes the coins. 'You're in luck. Tonight's came straight from prison. Even if a relative turned up for the corpse, as far as the padre is concerned they would have more chance of burying their dog. So he is all yours, *Dottore* – compliments of *il Principe*.'

He does not like Bonafù. The hospital guardian has no respect for anyone, either dead or living. 'How did he die?'

'Like I said the last time, what does it matter? I'm alive, and nobody cares how.'

They reach the room where the corpse has been laid. As they enter, the smell of death hits him. Trapped within moist walls, it forms a vaporous odour. The body of a man lies on a stone table. The face is invisible – matted blood conceals the features, with the exception of the mouth, which gapes slightly open. Bonafù takes a piece of cloth to his mouth. The guardian hands one to him, surprised that he declines.

'What was his crime?' he asks Bonafù.

'Murderer,' says the guardian in a muffled voice, nodding at the corpse in distaste.

The man's body is covered with a lint cloth, which he removes at once. He closes the mouth and, taking the only lighted candle in the room, opens a closed eyelid and peers into it. Bonafù hangs at his back.

'I need more candles,' he says quickly. 'And a jug of water.'

'What do you want to . . .'

'No questions!' He swings round, taking the candle with him. 'Understand?'

Bonafù withdraws silently, returning with more candles and a jug.

'Leave me now. I can't work with you here.'

With Bonafù gone, he stands there a moment, knife in hand, conscious of a need to clear his mind. He makes his first incision. There is little blood. He cuts through the flesh of the chest until he touches bone. Then he cuts away the flesh from the middle of the chest, going side to side, until he has exposed most of the ribs. If he can only get through the rows of ribs without damaging anything, then he will get what he wants: a clear view of the heart as it lies in the body. It is not easy. He uses a tooth-edged blade and saws as gently as he can, terrified that the blade will slip and cut through the organs protected by their cage of bone. After what seems like a long time, he has broken through four ribs on each side. He puts down the blade and washes his hands in the small pitcher by the grime-stained window through which the moon strains to shine. He wipes his face with a damp cloth and flexes his hands. He takes a breath and notes the moment in his journal. *The human heart.* So often talked about, so little understood. He leans over the open cage and wipes particles of bone and clotted blood from the surface of the heart. Then he begins to draw. When the drawing is complete he takes up his pen and writes, his thoughts returning to the last observations he has made, now locked away in the depths of his trunk, but always in his head:

The surface of the heart is divided into three parts by three veins, which lead from the base. Two of these are on the far side of the right ventricle beneath which two arteries run in close contact. For the third vein, I have not yet noticed if it is accompanied by another artery and am therefore preparing to remove more flesh from the surface, in order to satisfy my curiosity.

He takes up his knife and makes a further incision, cutting across to reveal the inner chambers of the heart. He stands back and takes in the whole picture. He thinks: the beat of his heart has changed for ever. He will never feel it the same. One of the candles burns down; the arm beside it is scorching. He snuffs it out with his finger. Dawn is breaking. He begins a new line.

The heart is not the principle of life; it is a vessel formed from dense muscle nourished by arteries and veins. The heart beats spontaneously without stopping unless it stops for good.

Unless it stops for good. Death is reduced to these few words. He remembers the spike that bore the head of Lorenzo's conspirator. More than a few words, he thinks, and he blocks out the image. He tidies up, packing bone and sewing skin, conscious that the guardian will be back soon. He tells himself it does not matter, but respect and a sense of privacy drive him on until the body of the man looks as it did. He rolls up the paper, stashing that and his journal away just before Bonafù makes another appearance at the window.

He watches as they carry the corpse to the fire. Out of sight of God and men in a purgatory fashioned by Dante.

When he returns to the main door Giacomo is where he left him, curled up on a stone bench. They walk back as night moves to dawn, and the streets fill with people. Giacomo knows, as he does, that quiet alleys, grime-soaked walls and purgatory are revelations of the night. Night stalks the shadows of the mind. Bearer of evil news, devourer of men. It feeds the curiosity of those who cannot sleep. And they steal the peace of those who have no choice.

He throws open the door of the *bottega* and finds Francesco in a state of agitation.

'Where were you?' says Francesco, looking at his white face and red hands.

'Working,' he answers.

Francesco nods, worried. Then, brandishing a preliminary drawing of the Sforza monument, 'I've been thinking . . . Does the statue need to be . . .'

'Not now, Francesco.' He pushes Giacomo forward. 'We have a helper. He should learn about pigments first. Can you show him?' He throws down his cloak and bag. 'Oh, and we will need more rope than you have there.' He gestures to a pile in the corner.

'Of course,' Francesco says, looking with horror at Giacomo's rags.

'And see that he wears something decent.' Francesco doesn't like the look of Giacomo, but it can't be helped.

'But first . . .'

'First find more rope, more wood, leather strapping, and I need some phosphorous.'

'But shouldn't you get some sleep? You look half dead. What are you planning that can't wait?' Francesco looks with regretful confusion at the sketch of the statue. 'A new wing for the cathedral?'

'No.' His eyes follow Giacomo as he wanders through the *bottega*, touching this, feeling that. 'Sorry. Didn't I tell you?' He pours water over his hands and rubs off the grime and the blood. 'We're going to banish the night.'

II

He would not get out charcoal for Beatrice, Duchess of Bari. Fortunately Sforza has not asked him to. There is no beauty without fragility, and the wife of Ludovico Sforza is too robust to paint. Her reactions interest him most, and from what he can tell they are dependent on two people: her husband, who is seated within easy eyeshot, and just a little further away, a woman of carefully tended beauty, who gazes into space with the innocent air of a girl.

'Lucrezia Crivelli,' says Francesco. 'And all of Milan is talking about her, as you can see, with good reason.'

'I can see that the Regent has not taken his eyes off her during the time that we've been in this room,' he replies. 'And I'm not alone in my observation.' He looks over again at Beatrice; her expression has turned sour. She rises to leave.

But Sforza retains her with a word, and she returns to her seat beside him, her face set.

'Tell me, Francesco,' he says, turning to his apprentice discretely, 'how to judge a man who, while loving his nephew would take the Duchy from him, and while asking his wife to sit beside him would at the same time wish her gone?'

'It is a good point,' says Francesco, 'but there is another here who also presents a different face to the one appearances suggest.'

He points to Giacomo, who is swiftly pulling his hand out of the purse of a nobleman. The nobleman, the same who had remarked on his tailor on the day of his arrival, is deep in conversation, and thankfully oblivious to the theft. He skirts round the back of the crowd, but too late. The nobleman feels the sudden movement and, seeing his purse open, cries out. 'Five florins gone!' The nobleman's hand emerges from an empty purse. 'How can this be – thief!' the man calls, turning about.

He delves into his own purse and hastily finds five florins. He waves his hand in the air and moves forward through the crowd. 'Who has lost this?' he says, in a loud voice. 'Signor Crivelli!' comes a shout. Crivelli turns and sees him, coins in hand. 'I found them on the ground,' he says hurriedly. 'Yours?'

Crivelli looks at him doubtfully. 'I suppose it must be. Ah, it is our Florentine painter again. Tell me,' says the nobleman, 'You seem a man of common sense – in every way, and since you have the sense to return lost goods, perhaps you also have the sense to fetch me a cup of wine.' There is a ripple of laughter.

'I can do better,' he says, 'I can bring you wine and entertain you with a fable at the same time.'

Crivelli hesitates. 'If you have a story, then we would all be pleased to hear it, I am sure, especially since you have already displayed a talent for punctuality. Although we can't expect too much from a painter, can we?'

From the other side of the hall, Sforza has stopped looking at Crivelli's daughter and has turned his attention to the father. 'Your cups everyone. More wine!' Sforza raises his glass, then says, 'Let's all hear your story,' glancing at Crivelli with a smile.

Leonardo takes up a cup. 'Wine, divine liqueur of the grape, finding itself on Mohammed's table in a richly wrought goblet, was transported by the pride of such an honour until, all at once agitated by contrary sentiments, it said:

'*What am I doing here? Why do I rejoice? Do I not see that I am at the very edge of death: that I am destined to leave this golden goblet in which I now find myself, to enter into the vulgar and fetid chamber of the human body where I will be transformed from an elegant, perfumed liquid into an ignoble and disgusting fluid?*'

He hands Crivelli a goblet. '*And as if such disgrace were not enough, I must then dwell in the hideous recesses, alongside obscene and corrupt matter emptied from the entrails of men.*'

He looks directly at Crivelli and bows slightly to the sounds of stifled laughter around him. 'Thus the wine implored the Heavens for vengeance from such an insult; that there might be an end to this degeneracy. And so it was that at this time, when the country we speak of yielded the most beautiful and the best grapes on earth, they were spared from becoming wine. Jupiter made the wine drunk by Mohammed ascend to his brain, where it rendered him mad. He committed so many follies that, on coming to his senses, he proclaimed a decree forbidding the drinking of wine to all peoples of Asia. Thus the vine and its fruits were left in peace. And so it is that as soon as wine enters the stomach of men, it begins to ferment and boil; the spirit leaves the mantle of the flesh and rises towards the Heavens, relinquishing its hold on the body and seizing the brain. There it works its intoxication, demonising he that drinks it, rendering him capable of irreparable crimes – of which few are more serious than the vilification of his own person and the wanton defamation of others.'

There is silence, then applause. The roar of Sforza laughter. Francesco has stepped up beside him. 'Giacomo has disappeared,' his apprentice murmers.

Crivelli leans forward. 'Your apprentice surpasses your quick tongue with his sharp eyes. But tell me, does your love of fables extend to other things? Do you read Homer?'

'I enjoy Petrarca,' he replies.

'Ah, as I thought,' says Crivelli, 'Latin but no Greek. But then, with no tutor, what can a man do but paint?'

Face cold and blood scorching, he turns away. From his seat, Sforza makes his way across. 'Well delivered. Very well delivered,' says the Regent. 'It puts me in mind, Leonardo, that I would like to suggest to Signor Crivelli that you offer him your hand as an artist, at my expense naturally, in the faithful rendition of a portrait of his daughter.' Sforza smiles and glances at Crivelli, who acquiesces with a bow.

He would like to refuse, but no opportunity is given and he does not make one. Strong name, strong will. Sforza continues. 'Let's take a walk outside, for I believe there is a spectacle waiting.'

The moon is full. Noblemen, ladies and merchants make their way down the perpendicular walkways of the upper section of the gardens. On either side of the path, dwarf lemon trees in pots form a perimeter. The path ends at a marble basin where carp make iridescent ripples. Further ahead, stone walls enclose a second garden, with radial paths as far as the eye can see. Orange and cedar trees run along walls. The crowd reaches the furthest end of the garden, where all walkways converge at a raised bed of cypresses, laurel and myrtle.

Ahead is the tented enclosure he has erected. A swathe of black fabric covers the entrance. Francesco directs them in, then joins him round the back.

All around is dark, but not quite. The glow that fills the enclosure comes from above. In a few seconds the attention of the crowd is drawn upwards. There, on the ceiling, the phosphorous stars of his night sky shine like fireflies. A new moon hangs suspended in stationary orbit. But the gaze of the crowd is drawn yet further. Far back into the reaches of this illusory night sky, planets glow: great Jupiter, beautiful Venus and bright Mars. The perspective of near and far, larger and smaller planets and stars has the desired effect: heads turn upwards in wonder. But then, the dark veil of the world slides back. On all sides of his tented space shadows fall away. From nowhere a hundred lighted chandeliers encircle the night, making it day.

From the edge of the enclosure, he watches the cogs of the gear turn as the weight of the canopy is drawn aside. He motions to Francesco, who switches position deftly to turn the wheel on one side, while he takes the other. The rope coils around the wooden shaft. The first of the wire appears, while above them on the other side of the screen, the planets are drawn upwards. The scene changes.

The night sky has gone. In its place the sun shines bright and gold. In the midst of the enclosure, a loggia with Ionic columns decorated with golden cherubs enshrines a fountain of marble. As the crowd watches, it bursts into life. Birdsong fills the air; water surges up and forms a shooting cascade. Angels emerge from every lighted corner: small children, oblivious to the beauty, or too much a part of it to notice, throw cut flowers at the feet of the crowd.

'That just about does it,' says Francesco at his shoulder. 'Anything more and they'll think they're in paradise.'

'It seems a pity to raise their expectations,' he says. Francesco smiles.

He steps into the enclosure.

'Brilliant,' Sforza exclaims, clasping his shoulder, 'This I call magic.' The Regent lowers his voice. 'I shall want to see more of this . . . this magic of yours.'

He bows and returns to Francesco. 'What did he say?' Francesco asks.

'Something about magic.' He looks at the wheels and pulleys, thinks of the pumping system and the sound box at the base of the fountain and recalls the phosphorus in the pigment of the paint. 'Give them science,' he says, 'and they see magic; give them answers and they call it heresy.' The thought strikes him – perhaps this is all they will ever want from me: a night of fake stars.

'As far as I'm concerned, the real miracle is how we managed to finish on time,' says Francesco. 'You only started on the planets last night.'

It is done. Sforza has had his first taste of spectacle. The steam chamber will be finished by the end of the month: all that is left to build is the cistern. He has ordered the materials for the bird; the only thing he can do now is wait. Wings for steam. The portrait of Crivelli's daughter is a distraction he could do without, but it cannot be helped. He hopes she's a good sitter. He runs through the rest of his current projects. His visits to the hospital have yielded more than he could have hoped. A threshold has been crossed. His first dissection of a human heart has been completed. To Sforza he has promised greatness, and he knows he will have to deliver. Greatness or the illusion of it. The Sforza monument: the impossible made possible. Magic. If that is what men want, then he will give it to them. The fountain has stopped; Francesco is packing away the night sky. He goes over to help.

'I suppose I should congratulate you.' Crivelli says, coming up.

'If it pleases you.'

'Tell me, what will it be next? Rumour says a great sculpture?'

'If it pleases the Duke.'

'Duke in all but name,' says Crivelli. 'But then, not everyone is what they seem.'

III

In his hands he holds a letter from Florence. Andrea's journey to Venice was his last. Maestro del Verrocchio did not have his slow, painful death from plague or gout. *The heart beats spontaneously without stopping unless it stops for good*. The great man is gone. Sandro tells him it was sudden, but Venetians with their talent for secrecy will never say much. He thinks of their hasty goodbye in the workshop and closes his eyes. Outside, the day is already warm. By noon, the city will be sweltering in early summer. He holds his head in his hands. Solitude, forever a friend, cuts into him. His reply to Sandro's letter will have to wait. Now a picture of Andrea in his apron comes into his mind, chalky hands and dust. *What there is in the heart of a man is one thing. What there is in your own is another.*

The dust settles. Death is for everyone, he reasons. Andrea's glory and immortality are seductive but illusory. Only truth matters. You cannot argue with a calculation. How many years does he have left? How many good years? You cannot save everyone, he thinks. Not even God will do that. The sculptor must become a sculpture: frozen, immobile. He thinks of the *bottega* on the Via de' Macci closed down, or worse, a building like any other. One day a warehouse, another a shop selling rolls of fabric, or pieces of furniture. He must push the image back. He pulls himself up from the chair. There is work to do. There is no point, he tells himself, in crying over the dead. He imagines himself in a mirror: older, mortal, tired and stiff. Sudden is best.

Summer brings its count of festivities. He and Francesco are kept busy by the needs of a Milanese court, which outweigh those of Florence because of the Sforza taste for magic. Lorenzo gave a show of elegance; Sforza gives a show of strength. Francesco is complaining that Giacomo eats too much. The boy wants to live for three men, he says, but he does the job of less than one. And now this. He points to the half-used paper that Giacomo has made use of, together with charcoal, to make his mess: a half-drawn horse, a series of faces. Ignoring the waste of precious paper, he tells Francesco that if they turn him out, the boy will not last the month. I know he is a thief, a *Salai*, he admits, but there are worse things than thieving.

He returns to his desk, spending most of the night altering the position of a lamp and noting the subsequent effects on the illumination of fabric and skin and on the reflection of light on metal. He sees that he is almost out of oil for burning. He must buy candle wax. He brings out the rapid sketch he made of Crivelli's daughter in court. Oval face, large almond eyes. Half-captured on paper is something less tangible, which he struggles to develop to scale. It is a fleeting expression, which lasted only an instant. In court, he had taken out a scrap from his notes and sketched it out in a second. But it is not enough. Now it eludes him. He loses interest, glances over at his notebooks and sighs. Once Fra Alessandro and his simple arithmetic had kept him from his work. Now it is people he does not want to paint, or people who do not want to be painted.

Lucrezia Crivelli sits with her hands folded in her lap, facing him. He moves away from the panel, wondering what it is he has to say to make her sit the right way.

'Just turn again and face the window, over there.'

'But you said you would not paint a profile. I thought . . .'

'I know, and I won't. But nevertheless, I would like you to turn to the side and face the window.'

She slowly shifts round. 'That's fine. Now, I would like you to look at me.'

She turns her head to face him, while her body at last is where he wants it to be: facing away. 'Good enough. Now stay like that.'

'If I am in the position you want, why don't you paint?' she says. It's a valid question. He would like to say: If you will let me know you, then I might stand a chance of painting you. For a moment something strikes him. His mind races. He is standing on a hilltop on Monte Albano. Then he sees it, an explosion of colour, a shimmering arch. He takes a step and it vanishes. His hand is suspended over the paper. He closes his eyes. Is there something he is missing?

All his life he has known things. Known the answers to Fra Alessandro's arithmetic, known that mountains are old, that the sun does not move, that the soul of a man is not in his heart. But one thing he has never known: when you look at a rainbow, what do you see? Is it the rainbow, or is it the illusion of the rainbow? He does not know why, but the question is important. What do we see? Perspective. He needs to go back outside. He looks at the placid eyes of Crivelli's daughter in irritation. Perhaps he had seen something that was never there.

Lucrezia Crivelli shifts in her seat. Somewhere behind him, a door creaks open. He should ask the servant to bring musicians, perhaps some dogs, as a distraction. But in an instant, illumination arrives. Her expression is transfigured. In too much of a hurry to be surprised, he begins to sketch with new energy, his eye moving from subject to hand. At last he has it, a face that needs and fears, yields and possesses. He looks round and discovers the reason. 'So, Leonardo – is it so hard to paint a vision, or was your star-filled canopy easier to fathom?' At his shoulder, Sforza is looking directly at Crivelli's daughter and he, Leonardo, is drawing the result.

Beatrice is sitting beside her husband. Sforza, by all appearances, is weary from days spent in the company of visiting dignitaries. Diplomacy bores him. He prefers action, making the point, taking the chance. He listens attentively to his wife. Leonardo is refusing food. His target weight, if he is to stand any chance of getting airborne, is achievable in a month. In the face of Francesco's reasonable objections, he has altered starvation to moderation. At the Sforza table, it is easily done.

'No meat,' he says.

'Why not? Are you ill?' Donato Bramante serves himself several slices of meat.

'There are other reasons for not eating meat,' he says. The architect has just taken a seat beside him and appears to have the appetite of three men.

'Such as?'

'There are other foods,' he says, 'vegetables, bread, fruits.'

'Ha,' snorts Bramante. 'You'll be telling me to eat berries next.'

'There is virtue in berries,' he says.

'Virtue!' The architect slaps the table in delight. 'If it's virtue you seek, then you're at the wrong table, my friend.' The architect is evidently amused. Built like a mausoleum, he is thick, strong, angular. 'But you have the face of an angel.'

'I have heard it said.'

'In which case, that makes you the only one in court. Because, you can take it from me—' he waves his knife '—there is no other here.'

'So you built a choir out of stone, voices of angels fallen silent?'

'Mmm, Santa Maria presso San Satiro. I fashioned the choir in stone relief because there was no room for a real choir. He insisted on a choir; I complied. That is all,' Bramante says, glancing at Sforza over a mouthful of meat. 'As must everyone in his service.' The sturdy architect pours a cupful of wine and pushes it in front of him. 'You see him surrounded by family. Yet he was born a bastard. He wears the cloak of a prince but tradition is a stranger to him; his father and his before him were mercenaries, the *condottieri*. They forced their way up to the rank of general, now he is Regent and soon will be a duke. Prince of Milan. He has no need of providence, for he makes his own luck. The title will pass into his hands and then he will stop at nothing until he has what he wants. I thank God he liked my choir of stone. Otherwise the transept would be a pile of rubble and I would be somewhere beneath it.'

'Stop at nothing?' he says. Bramante drinks like a Roman. He notices that the man also smells like one.

'The politics of Italy are like nowhere else, but the politics of Milan are spectacularly incompetent. You know how it is. There is disagreement over land, the position of a boundary. A lunch is arranged. They talk, they talk.' Bramante spears a piece of meat. 'Everyone takes his leave as though he has just taken the other to bed, then they all go home and prepare for war. Then' – he wipes his knife on the tablecloth – 'comes the big battle.' The architect takes a swig of his wine and waves his hand. 'Both sides make a go of it. There are a few casualties. Perhaps one or two dead, but on the whole they keep it to a minimum. Then, one side decides that enough is enough and everybody goes home.' Leonardo leans back in his chair and glances at the top table, where the smiling Regent has taken his wife's hand. 'But not Ludovico Sforza,' continues the architect. 'He'll fight to the last man – the last dog.'

'I have no interest in politics,' he says. In truth he finds it hard not to admire Sforza. The Regent is no philosopher, but the man has guts.

'No, of course, of course you don't. As I don't. We care for art, but without politics there is no art. You are the sculptor who talks of casting the giant horse?'

'Yes.'

'Then better hope he likes it. You may have the face of an angel, but not, I fear, the heart of a warrior.'

He is thinking: my father had a shield. But what was his father? A notary. He had no more need of a shield than his son would have need of a lance. He often wonders what became of the shield and the monster he had drawn upon it. Perhaps his father didn't burn it. Perhaps he gave it away or perhaps even now he kept it hidden somewhere in a trunk or in the bottom of an old chest, out of sight, just in case. He remembers the departure of his tutor, the stony track and the receding figure. He struggles to remember his mother.

Bramante has stopped talking. From the other table, Sforza imposes silence.

'Now that you have dined and drunk your fill, let me say a few words. We live in difficult times: dangerous times. My duty to you, to the duchy, is one of protection. I watch over you as a father over his children, or as a noble creature of hill and plain that risks life and limb to safeguard the litter. In such times we must surround ourselves with friends, and that is my intention.' Sforza moves away from the table and stands in the centre of the hall. 'We must surround ourselves with friends, but also we must surround ourselves with the most beautiful women, the most talented artists, the most gifted musicians and the most brilliant minds. To give satisfaction to this last requirement, I have chosen to endow Leonardo the Florentine with the title of Engineer to my court.' Sforza turns to him and smiles. 'Does the Maestro accept?'

He stands and bows his thanks. He wants to sit down, but the crowd will not let him. 'Give us another story!'

At his side Bramante mutters, 'Try to find a different subject from wine, won't you? Your last story affected my humours.'

He looks round at the court and begins. 'In Hyrcania there lives a noble beast. His name is Tiger. He is strong of limb, swift of foot and when he casts his eye upon you, the brightness of his gaze will fix you where you stand and stem your flight.' He moves across the room towards the far table, where Lucrezia

Crivelli is sitting. 'He is a hunter but he is also hunted. As hunter he is the big cat: fierce and fast. But the hunter that seeks him out is a wily creature, and will win the day by trickery. Rumours tell of one such hunter, whose intention it was to steal away the tiger's cubs, of which there were six. One by one he took them away by stealth, and placed in their stead a mirror in the ground. Thus, when the tiger returned and looked into the mirror, he saw a tiger's face. At first, believing it to belong to one of his cubs, he was calm. Until, after a while, he scratched the image with his claw and saw it was a fake. He sniffed the wind and off he sped in pursuit of the hunter. Long and hard he searched, following scent and marker. Some say the tiger found the hunter and took his life, returning to his lair with all six cubs. Others say the tiger left the plains of Hyrcania and moved south, searching long and far without success; that when he grew thirsty and sought to quench his thirst at a lake, he saw again the reflection that had fooled him and could not take a drink. Thirsty in the wilderness he roamed, forever searching. And so it was that he became a solitary spirit, best abroad by night, when the sun is away and the day's thirsty heat has abated.'

The crowd applauds. Musicians take up their instruments. Sforza beckons him over.

'Your fables are instructive. But do not concern yourself on my account. My judgement has never been wrong. That is why I am sitting here, in this room on this chair. Tell me – your portrait . . . is it finished?'

'It is.'

The portrait has been delivered to Sforza's private chambers. They go there together. Sforza likes to talk, about war, men, ambition. 'Milan will be greater than even Florence or Venice,' the Regent says. 'They imagine themselves free, but they have misunderstood the meaning of the word. A state is only as strong as the man who leads it. There is no freedom without power.' Leonardo removes the cover and they stand before it silently for a few moments.

Sforza stands back admiringly. 'Your talent exceeds expectations. Lorenzo said you had great skill, and I can see that you have captured her likeness perfectly. Tell me,' the Regent says, pointing to the shading around the face, 'how do you do this?'

'Degrees of colour,' he says simply. 'Where there is light, there is also colour. One exists through the other. On a bright day, colour is stronger. On a dull day, it is weaker. Therefore, if you remove the colour, you create darkness; if you add colour, the effect is that of light.'

'I see. Very well done. Beautiful indeed. But what pleases me more than anything is the expression. Those eyes,' the Regent murmurs, 'enough to die for, or kill for.' Sforza places a hand on his shoulder. 'All it will take is a word in the ear of a servant and she will be in my chamber this night or any other night.' Sforza glances at him, smiling. 'You see, Leonardo, how easy it is? Tell me, there must be someone in court. A favourite, a preference?'

He looks at the expression of desire in the eyes of Lucrezia Crivelli. It doesn't move him one way or another. He has captured it; now it is over. If Sforza lined up twenty women, the effect would be the same. 'Not really,' he says.

'Well then, let me know if you change your mind. In the meantime, take what you need, order what you want.'

'I have another project, if you remember,' he says. 'The monument I spoke of: the statue to honour your father.'

'The bronze horse. Yes.'

'Shall I make the preparations?'

'Make them. Build it.'

'I'll begin with the model of course, in clay.'

'Naturally.' They walk back towards the hall. 'There will be other things I shall need from you,' says Sforza. 'But all in good time. Finish my steam chamber. Then we'll talk again.'

Some paintings are never over; others are finished but never complete. As he follows Sforza out, the eyes of Crivelli's daughter do not leave him in peace. Perspective will not let him rest. He spends the rest of the night making changes to an old sighting box, a camera obscura he had begun building years before. By the time dawn comes, he has perfected it. Now all he needs is good visibility and the sense to use it well. But days of rain and wind break his plans. Storms peal through the sky, crashing thunder over the fortifications of Sforza's castle, lighting up the clouds and rolling sulphurous chiaroscuro into a smoky horizon. It matters not. He has work to do. He finds his way to the hospital through driving rain and soaking streets. Bonafù has set aside a room for him with a stove and a larger table. Now he has hot water to wash and a place to put his things. It feels like coming home.

He picks up the eye and places it in the palm of his hand. Then he places it on a dish and takes up his pen. He writes in his journal: 'Dissection is impossible. When cut, the eye does not keep its form. Will try boiling.' He places the eye into a pot of water on the stove. *Papilio Macaone*, he thinks. But this is no butterfly. What he wants is what lies behind the retina. He fishes out the eye and places it, gently steaming, back on the dish. Now other things happen. The eye splits apart unevenly, becoming distorted and effectively altered from its natural state. He discards it in frustration.

The sounds of the hospital are the sounds of women torn by childbirth, of missing limbs and choleric children. Sisters of the Holy Order float like spirits from room to room, administering their mercy where they can cure, waiting for God's where they cannot. He waits for Bonafù.

Dissections, when they come, are arduous. Despite improvements, the room is badly lit. He has brought his own glass lamp, which he lights as night comes on. A new candle in the window. It makes him think of Albiera. Bonafù arrives with a companion and a corpse. They heave it onto the table. He watches the gestures of the guardian with distaste. He draws back the sheet to reveal the body of a woman.

She is young; her face is peaceful, her body strong and robust even in death. He looks at her abdomen and with a surge of dread sees the hidden reality.

'She's pregnant,' he says.

'Has to be,' replies Bonafù, proudly. 'Rare, these are.'

'Leave us then,' he says. He forces the words. 'Thank you.'

Us. We are three, he thinks: himself, the woman and the unborn child. He had not expected this. He could have her buried before Bonafù returns. He places his hand on her abdomen. Any child will surely be dead; is of course dead. The uterus is still and hard. All too aware of the opportunity he faces, he steadies his hand and begins to cut. He stops. This is not right, he thinks. There must be something more. Lowering his head he says a silent prayer. It is the first time he has felt the need. Heart thumping and his mouth dry, he opens the abdomen and draws back the lining of the uterus as carefully as he can. Once his hand slips. *Mother of God*. He takes a step back. The foetus is fully formed. It lies curled up in the open womb, its head resting on hands and knees, the cord wrapped at its feet. The skin of the unborn is waxy and white and there is no sign of life. He retreats into the shadow of the room, his face damp with sweat; his eyes hot with tears.

'Children,' he whispers, 'like a seed in a pod.' He waits a moment, then takes a cloth and wipes his face and hands. He reaches for his notes and pen and now begins to sketch, feeling at every stage that if there were ever a time he needed something more than a calculation, a knife, a page of paper, it is now. But prayer is not enough. He stares at the unborn child, imagines the unlived life. Death is the only problem that does not have a solution. He thinks, the best we can manage is understanding.

As work progresses, one revelation leads to another: the gestation of the foetus in the womb; the way the child would leave the body of the mother. The complexity of the female reproductive system opens before him like a book of knowledge from which he reads until dawn. When all is done, he closes up her body and sews up the cuts he has made. Then he draws the sheet back up to her collarbone and imagines her looking back at him behind closed lids, as though nothing but understanding has passed between them, and all is well.

He returns home to find Francesco waiting for him at the door.

'There is a woman here in the house,' Francesco says.

For a moment he thinks of Sforza. A favourite, a preference? 'Well? Who is she?'

'I don't know,' Francesco replies, awkwardly. 'She says she's your mother.'

Francesco pushes open the door to reveal the hunched frame of a woman, a grey shadow of himself. She is of medium height and build, but bent by age. Her hair is silver, and pulled back from her face to reveal fine features like bone china, formed like a landscape by the elements into smooth ridges and hollows. It is Caterina.

It is hard to collect the thoughts that race through his mind. They follow each other in succession, flashes of memory from long ago. A space of more than twenty years stands between them, and the dread of time strikes him: passing like the water of a river through an open hand. He realises that he has not moved a muscle and that Francesco is waiting. Caterina has been waiting longer. It is he who has not moved.

IV

He takes a seat at their square wooden table opposite his mother. He glances at Francesco, who nods and passes a dish of bread across the table to Caterina. She does not take the bread but stares at it as though it is a familiar food altered by circumstance.

'Why don't you eat?' he says.

He passes her the plate and the bread and the cheese.

'Eat,' he says. He stares miserably at the food.

'You still don't eat meat,' she says. 'You're too thin.'

There is a reason for everything, he thinks, remembering the bird and his target weight. But not everything can be reasoned. She turns up at his door after years of absence and stares at his bread. They sit across the table like strangers. He is wondering why she let him leave; she is wondering why he didn't come back. He wonders if the answers can be found; if there are any.

'Do you want meat?' He jumps up from his seat. 'Francesco, go and ...'

'No, please, no, not for me,' she says.

Francesco has poured wine into a cup and places it before him. It is the flask they had been saving for when the statue is finished. 'I never have eaten meat,' he says. 'Not since – a long time.'

'Is your father well?'

'Yes, very well.' He remembers a conversation. His father listening without hearing, him speaking without talking.

'Your sisters are married. Violante last summer. Your brother Giuliano has left for Pisa.'

He nods. He does not know them, nor they him. They are the ghosts of a family he does not have, and never wanted.

'Antonio is dead,' she says. Can she still tell what he is thinking? 'You are my eldest. Now I have nowhere else to go.' He stands up from the table. 'You can have my bed. I'll sleep on the floor.' But when Caterina stands it is not for long. She is running a fever. Francesco helps him put her to bed.

'Should we fetch a physician?'

'What, listen to Galen and have her bleeding everywhere?' he replies. 'No. I shall make her well.'

He takes a jar from the shelf. Sambucus flower: for fever and headaches. He keeps a running supply, as the shrub is hard to find. He makes a tincture and throws an extra cover on the bed. He pulls up a chair. 'Get some sleep,' he orders Francesco. 'There is no need for two of us.'

He gives Caterina the tincture. She passes the night in a fit of sweats, in and out of sleep. He works late, but produces little, save a couple of mediocre sketches. Outside, the storm has stopped. He thinks of his mother making her journey in the foul weather. Damp like that would have been enough to bring on the fever. He feels for her heartbeat. It is faint, but present. He administers more of his cure, taking out the last root end from the jar, then burns cedar wood to clear the air. After checking her pulse a third time, he drifts off to sleep. *The heart beats spontaneously without stopping unless it stops for good.*

Outside the barn, the sky is low and dark. The lizard nestles within his grip, its heart beating. He takes out the knife and feels the blade: it is sharp. It is his father's blade. The lizard moves in his grip, its pulse quick and warm. He brings the knife down. He has to do it in one fast stroke. As the knife begins to cut, he wavers. The pulse quickens; the lizard flinches. Panic rising, he presses it down hard, so hard he almost cuts through the wood beneath. Drenched with perspiration, he drops the knife. The lizard lies quiet and still.

There is pressure as someone takes his arm.

He opens his eyes. Francesco is at his side. 'It's morning.' The sound of regular breathing tells him Caterina is sleeping peacefully. 'I think she's out of danger.'

He stands before a roughly square block of clay larger than his own height and many times as wide as he is. Francesco watches beside him. He runs his hand over the slab.

'Too dry,' he says. Francesco passes him a brush and together they douse the block with water.

'Every piece of clay is different,' he says. 'The first thing is to become familiar with it, like dipping your hand in a river to tell how cold the water is. The clay will tell you everything you need to know. If it's thirsty,' he adds, reaching for a fresh jug of water, 'you must let it drink. If it's too fat, you must thin it out. As you shape the clay, you can think of your work as a conversation between you and the block.' He takes up a knife and begins to carve off chunks like giant slugs. 'Like a conversation between two people, sculpture is an exchange between yourself and the subject you create, whether your medium is clay, wood or stone.

Sometimes you talk to the subject,' he says, taking another section of the block out in one clear cut, 'sometimes the subject talks to you.'

He points with his knife. 'You take out here, and you put back there. But never repeat yourself, or the clay will become disinterested in the conversation and break off. Then you will need to moisten, question and start again; and all the while that you are talking an understanding grows between you and it. After a while, your subject becomes an object: one that has developed a life of its own. From that time onwards, it is the object that tells you how to sculpt, as this horse will tell me the slope of the shoulder and the position of the muscle. Then it becomes a test: how well do you really know your subject, and how much has been no more than conjecture?'

Caterina is watching from a chair in the cleanest part of the *bottega*. She is well enough to get up, but he suspects that inside her body she is weak. Yesterday he found her standing at the stove, stirring a pot of soup as though contemplating what she would find in it: the body of a butterfly, the boiled skin of a furry caterpillar. He cannot say how things have changed, only that it seems an old weight has lifted. He remembers Lorenzo's account of the cave dweller. He has emerged into another kind of daylight, and stands there in the warmth: rays on his back. It's not the light of knowledge; he wonders if it's the light of peace.

During the days that preceded work on the clay model of the Sforza horse, he spent his time at the Duke's stables observing the horses and their movements. Old observations grow fat with time. Memory is lazy. Draw what you see, then more than you see. Now as he stands at the slab, carving off chunks here and there, he is conscious that the Milanese winter is almost over. Before long there will be clear skies and clear views. He will be able to get out again, see things. Sculpture is not painting. He can carve it, mould it and shape it, but it is never unfinished. It is always over. Every night the model takes another form, a new shape. The conversation is over. The next day it starts again. Only perspective draws him on like nothing else: the mystery of the eye.

He throws another slice of clay onto the ground, where Francesco collects these discarded pieces and returns them to the basin. As the chunks leave hollows, he shapes them here and there without stopping, his hand moving from hollow to promontory and back again, pushing and plying the clay.

'You have the strongest hands,' Francesco says, tossing pieces of clay aside. He can't keep pace.

'The clay is hardening.'

Francesco passes him a water brush. He hands it back without looking. He does not like to admit to Francesco that this is his first large sculpture. Working alongside Andrea, the sorry sight of the Maestro after several hours of dust and sweat had always dissuaded him from the business of sculpture. Now he shapes the body of the horse instinctively, deciding not to stand back and check until he has reached a certain stage. The structure, in any case, is in his head, while the dimensions are in his hands. He feels the drip of perspiration down his back and on his brow and dislikes it immensely, but not enough to stop. They work through the night. The dry air does not help. For the final casting they will have to work outside, and he thinks as he works about ways in which they might compensate for the effects of air and sunlight: a moistened sheet of course, perhaps also a canopy like the one he created for the festival.

The final bronze statue will be the height of four men or more; the model is no larger than one. Once the model is right, the rest will be a simple transfer of proportion. The result: an inverted mould held together by armature to be cast in sections, then welded together. As winter gives way to spring the model progresses, until he feels that a fundamental stage has been reached. Now they possess the body of the horse; that of its rider must wait a little longer.

He takes on two more apprentices, youngsters for mundane tasks, but good clean workers. They fall upon a stash of fabrics and food that Giacomo, or Salai the little thief, as he calls him now, has made in a wall cavity. He remembers an old butterfly board hidden within the walls of his father's house and says nothing.

The *bottega* has expanded to fill part of the courtyard. With Francesco's help, he erects a shelter and they bring out more worktops. After considerable delay, the cistern is complete. Sforza complains, 'A man must wash.' Leonardo finishes what is left to do of the steam chamber in haste, putting everyone to work on the final stages of its plumbing.

The model of the Sforza horse towers above them. Francesco is at his side and together they contemplate it.

'The angle of the spear ...' he murmurs.

'... is right,' replies Francesco.

Even at this size the model is imposing. When the time comes for seventy tons of bronze to give it substance, it will fill the night sky, eclipse the night stars. The ditch has been dug already; delivery of the bronze will, according to Sforza, be a matter of weeks. In the meantime, the model is to be unveiled on the occasion of the wedding of Sforza's niece. He covers it with a sheet of cloth. He has been summoned to Sforza's chambers at noon. He will take the opportunity to try to settle accounts. If he does not obtain means for payment soon, both he and Francesco will have to inspect the rubbish heaps of Milan, or join the sick at the doors of the hospice to wait for the plates of the dead.

When he reaches the Sforza chambers, he finds no sign of the Regent. Beatrice is sitting beside the fireplace, repairing the shreds of a torn tapestry. She asks him to sit. 'I am with child, Leonardo. Did you know?' He did not. He glances down at her abdomen hidden beneath folds of fabric. He imagines the stage of gestation; fully formed, knees drawn up, head tucked down. 'Then you must rest,' he says. 'Your energy is needed by the foetus.'

She seems surprised. 'I did not know you had knowledge of medicine. But then, these days I am kept in the dark about everything I want to know. Only those things I don't want to know are thrown into my face.' She fiddles with the threads of the tapestry on her lap, stares beyond him at the window. 'But first let me say how sad I was to hear of the death of Lorenzo. Ludovico has sent his condolences of course, and I can only add my own to you personally, as I know he was your patron.'

He says that he did not know this news; this is the first he has heard of it. With Andrea gone, word from Florence has been sporadic. He asks, 'How did Lorenzo die?'

'I believe it was gout,' Beatrice replies.

He shakes his head, thinks of Andrea and his tinctures, has a memory of Lorenzo drinking over silver, sitting on silk. Not enough walking, he thinks. Too much wine. He says, 'Lorenzo was a fine man, and a learned one.' He wonders at the fate of Florence. Sforza's wife reads his mind.

'Piero of course will take over business, but he was always a lazy child, nothing like his father. But then, there is always the Republic. Florence is more than just one man. And that is a good thing, since the false judgement of one man makes a heavy burden, while the false judgement of many can at least be called politics. Ludovico is a great man, but he has his faults. He is quick to give friendship to others. Too quick.' She may not have Crivelli beauty, but her mind is sharp. It rests on something, makes the sum of it, and passes on. 'He has entered into an alliance with the French king and I am afraid for him, but not only for him – for us and for the whole of Milan. He thinks the King will bring security to our borders, but he is blind.' Her face hardens. 'You are not blind, are you?'

A chill passes down his back. He says, 'You fear the alliance will not hold?'

'I do not trust the French. Ludovico sees the danger from one side only. But I am a woman. I see danger on every side. Every day I pray for him. But it is not enough.' He feels her eyes on his hands. Sculpture has made them raw. 'I see you have been busy. The wedding?' she says. He nods. 'Before long all of Milan will be his. Even now it is as good as his.' She crosses her hands in her lap. 'I have been his many times over, but there is no safety in ownership.'

If he wants to find Ludovico, she says, he should try the apartments in the other wing: the wing where his portrait hangs in the hall, the portrait with the eyes that take away the peace of those who pass before them, and open up the doors to dangerous intimacy.

He emerges into the courtyard of the castle beneath bright sunshine. He crosses to the opposite wing through the gardens. He re-enters through a small wooden door and makes his way up two flights of stairs. Lucrezia Crivelli looks at him from the panel on the wall as he passes; her eyes follow him through the hall. He announces himself to the guard and gains admittance without delay. On the table the remains of a feast are spread out: half-eaten meat and empty cups fill the table.

'Leonardo,' Sforza growls, 'why are you late?'

A small matter of the wrong apartments, he says. A door opens from one of the opposite rooms and the figure of Lucrezia Crivelli appears. Sforza's eyes follow her across the hall. 'There is a wedding in two weeks, the dowry for which has cost me a small fortune. What have you arranged? Crowds are the lifeblood of a city, Leonardo. They must be entertained.'

'The model of the Sforza monument will be ready and awaits your approval. The statue of your father . . .'

'The horse. Yes; of course. Good. It can be unveiled. But now, there are other matters with which I require your help. Come with me.'

Sforza leads him out through the door he entered earlier, and they cross the courtyard to the Regent's private chambers. Maps are spread upon a table.

'You are aware of the threat we face from Naples?'

'I am aware of a threat,' he replies, 'but as to where it comes from, I cannot say.'

Sforza motions to a chair. 'Then let me explain. The French need a southern port.' The Regent points to the map. 'Naples. From there, the Holy Land is nearer by half. They can pass by the west and south coasts of Greece. Athens in two or three days. Across the Bay of Salamis, then Constantinople in another two or three. An easy journey if the wind is right.'

'You feel then that if the French take Naples . . .'

'Better the Franks than the Neopolitans. Alfonso talks too much. Soon he will follow it up with action. He needs a lesson, and he will have it. That is all.' Sforza points to the map. 'Our borders here at Modena and Mantua need reinforcing, strengthening. Men are not enough.' Sforza turns to him directly. 'This is where I need you and your magic. I need something; something more . . .'

'I can divert rivers, I can build portable bridges to give power of passage over the enemy. I can cause damage to enemy arms, however large or small.'

'You can damage arms — but can you build them?'

'Build them?' he says. 'My skill lies in invention, in the creation of diversions. But not in weaponry.' He wonders at which point Sforza has misunderstood him. 'I am an engineer, not a man of war,' he explains.

Sforza nods in agreement. 'Of course. I understand. Who does not seek peace? But peace has its price, as I'm sure you know already.' The Regent places both hands on the table and leans forward. 'You have had everything you need, everything you wanted,' Sforza says smoothly. 'There is nothing I have refused you. Even at considerable risk to my own popularity.' Then, looking up at him from the map, 'Your activities at the hospital would turn the stomach of even a learned man. As for the Church ... I can wield more freedom than most, but you have asked me to risk my own soul, Leonardo. Do you know what that means? You of all people must surely know that?'

Does he? He tries to remember a time when he asked about souls. *The soul of a man is in his heart.* Dissection has the effect of a lighted candle in a dark room. The function of the heart is the delivery of blood. What does Sforza think he is risking? What is really at risk? 'The soul of a man is a mystery,' he says, simply. 'The Church has always used the fact to its advantage. There is more to fear in this world than in the next.'

'Quite right,' says Sforza. 'And that is why I need you.'

He bows and turns to leave, wondering at the unpredictability of princes.

'Wait. I have not forgotten that I owe you payment.' Sforza places a bag on the table, beside the border of Ferrara. 'For the portrait,' the Regent says. 'If I've calculated wrongly, let me know.'

He gives the money to Francesco without counting. 'Pay the accounts,' he says. 'Make sure you pay yourself; buy what we need.' When he returns to his room at the hospital, he finds that Bonafù is too busy for him. 'Four children admitted in one night,' the guardian says. 'Some think it's the sweating sickness come over by boat. But I heard the physician in the hospital, so I can tell you, *Dottore*, that it's the influenza.' Even if he had the heart for it, Bonafù shakes his head. 'The parents are alive. What do you want me to tell them? That I sent them to the slaughter-house?'

He leaves the hospital, feeling tired as never before. His mind is clouded; he wonders about Sforza's calculations. Franks or Neopolitans. Sforza's other calculation weighs on the generous side. When he returns to the *bottega*, Francesco shows him the jar of soldi. 'I've put the change in here,' he says.

'What about the accounts?'

'Everything paid,' says Francesco, pleased. He agrees with an enthusiasm he doesn't feel.

The structure of his bird is taking shape on paper. The materials arrive. By the time Francesco unloads them from the cart he is ready for answers. 'What are we doing with all this silk taffeta?

Where will we need cane wood? Leather is always useful of course, but . . .'

He sits Francesco down and shows him the plan. Francesco's eyes register shock. 'What are you going to do?' his worried apprentice asks. 'Jump off the roof?'

'More or less,' he replies. As Francesco crosses himself, he has a memory of his father doing the same. 'Don't worry. I have it all worked out.' Francesco is not convinced, but that is normal. The conviction of one man is enough.

They go out into the courtyard and he looks up at the roof. 'At first I was thinking of that.' He points to the bell tower of San Gottardo. 'If you launch from there, nobody will see. But then I found the lake. Safer to land in water than on land.'

'Yes, safer to drown than hit the ground,' says Francesco. 'But even if it works, then what happens?'

'What do you mean?'

'If it flies, what will you do with it?'

He laughs inside at the limits of other people. 'Tell me,' he says, his arm around Francesco's shoulder, 'why were boats devised?'

The architect Bramante comes to see him. 'The Regent keeps you busy. Soon he will be keeping the whole of Italy busy. Let us hope that the French armies reach Naples quickly. Twenty-five thousand men heading south, and many of them Swiss soldiers using culverins and bombards. The sight of their artillery, so they say it, has driven even the fiercest *condottiere* off the battlefield. Sforza spends half of every day reviewing his men and the other half surveying every move and turn of the French king. That is to say, when he's not in bed with Lucrezia Crivelli.'

'Swiss mercenaries?' he asks.

'There are no finer crusaders. Nor soldiers happier to reap the fruits of their labour then return promptly to their valleys to enjoy them. Which brings me to the subject of labour. I have heard that Sforza will soon be commissioning your skills for a mural on the refectory wall of Santa Maria delle Grazie. Since I am working on the apse, perhaps you will be so good as to allow me to watch you draw? I used to be quite good, you know, at one time, until I discovered buildings.'

He is listening to Bramante but observing Caterina. Her face is pinched and pale, her step unsteady. She is complaining that she is hot. He thinks of the bodies of children lined up in Bonafû's back room. He turns suddenly to the architect. 'Forgive me. Can you fetch a physician? I think she has influenza.'

The physician arrives quickly. There are some advantages to being the Engineer of Sforza. Caterina is floating between scorching and frozen, her pulse is irregular and her breathing laboured.

'What can you do for her?' he asks. 'Bleeding will make her weak.'

'What has she eaten?' asks the physician, peering into her face. 'The balance of her humours is wrong. Without bleeding, you cannot correct it.'

He thinks of the arteries and veins around the heart, and the flow of blood from there to the rest of the body. 'No,' he says. Then he thinks of her lungs. He brings his head closer to Caterina. She is as she was last time, in and out of sleep. Only her breathing is worse. It comes in gasps: a hoarse, desperate rattle. 'Listen to her breathing,' he says, turning to the physician. 'She's drowning.' He feels her pulse. 'Peripneumonia,' he says.

The physician looks from Caterina's pale face to his, and says, 'Very well. Remove her to the hospital.'

He thinks of the room with the grimy window, the table and the unlit stove. 'No,' he tells the physician. 'But thank you for your time.'

The physician leaves him lungwort, but he gives her Sambucus. It is his last clump of the flowering herb. Cursing his lack of foresight, he wonders whether to take the mare and ride out for more. But the day is already half over. He opens the door, airs the room and burns cedar wood. He makes the tincture and covers her with as many blankets as he can find, in the hope that sweating will do the rest. Then he sits and waits, thinking about the causes of sickness and disease and running over what he knows already, and what he does not. There are remedies, more or less effective, but what bothers him is cause. Francesco takes over, tries to make him rest, but Caterina continues to drown in her sleep. He sits her up and makes her drink. As he lies her back down, it occurs to him that she is slipping away like a leaf on a stream, that there is nothing in the world that he can do about it.

Dawn comes. He tells Francesco that he is riding out for Sambucus. 'Black elder. It worked before,' he says, 'it will work again.' It grows near rivers in the shade. 'I know where to find it; I'll be back before noon.'

He takes his father's mare rather than Sforza's black horse. The mare has gained weight from months of rest. He knows she will go well for him. Besides, the payment for the Crivelli portrait has given him an aversion to favours. He heads south to the Po River, thinking as he rides how much easier it would be if he could bring the river to the city. He thinks of Caterina and pushes the mare on. The first spot he tries yields no elder. He remembers that black elder needs moist ground. It will be on the edge of woodland, where the birds can see it and where the soil is rich. Luck is on his side. He finds an abundance of dark-fruited branches and woody stalks. The shrub is small but there is plenty to harvest. He cuts what he can carry and packs it into his bag on the back of the saddle. He jumps on the mare and she runs without slowing, sensing his urgency.

The angle of the sun tells him how much time has passed. As he enters the city, there is the smell of food cooking. He thinks of Caterina well and standing, leaning over her stove. *If that's another one of your flying creatures I don't want to see it in the soup later.*

Francesco is waiting for him at the door. 'How is she?' he says, throwing down his bag.

'I'm sorry,' Francesco answers. Behind him the room is dark and smells of cedar. 'You were gone too long.'

The Milanese winter is over. Beyond the walls of the Corte Vecchio, beyond the walls of the city, rivers swollen with Apennine snow will surge into lakes. Lichen will take the place of ice. Primroses will bloom between the rocks. Lower down, the groundwater will rise. New reeds will push up in place of old ones. Creatures will stir again. There will be renewal everywhere but here, in this chair. He looks at his aching hands. Runs them over his bony face and rough beard. A pain in his right hand has been bothering him since the sculpture, but as he writes with his left, it doesn't stop him working. He wonders how long before the left goes the way of the right. How long before his body gives up. And when it does, what of it? He thinks, if I stop now, what will happen? Will I live more? What is more? More of what?

He makes the entry in his diary: *Caterina died this day. Arrangements for burial:* and he lists the detail and cost beside the words, in neat rows, right to left. He rubs his hands over his hair and pushes back emotion. The room is closing in on him. He needs answers. He throws down his pen.

The sky above Vigevano is a mass of layered cloud brushed by wind. He enters the courtyard and wagers to himself on the location of Sforza. East wing, west wing. A guard directs him to private chambers. Map room. He requests an audience and is granted one at once.

'Leonardo. I am glad to see you. Galeazzo and I are discussing strategy. You couldn't have come at a better moment.'

He says he is glad to hear it. But he has a need he would like to discuss in private, if possible. They leave the room. He says to Sforza, 'The last time we spoke, you told me I could ask for what I needed. So, if you are still willing to help, I have come to ask.'

'Tell me what you need.'

'Time,' he replies. 'More apprentices, more funds, more freedom.'

'You have it,' says Sforza without hesitation. 'Now tell me what you have in mind? Cannons? A culverin to rival the French? Yes. That is what we need.'

'No, you misunderstand,' he says. 'The hours I spend at the hospital must be increased. There is work to be done.' He must explain. Patience is necessary. He tells Sforza that every sickness has a cause, but to find out the cause, what is needed is a different kind of dissection. There is dissection for anatomy, and dissection for disease. Only by understanding the causes of disease after they have occurred is treatment possible. There must be cooperation: a chain of understanding, from observation of symptoms to observation of cause. Post mortem. One man is not enough.

Sforza stiffens. 'Very well. You have the time and the freedom to make enquiries. Start with the court physician. But first, I have my own stake on time. Come.' They return to the chambers where Galeazzo Sanseverino, commander of the Milanese armies, is drawing lines on maps. 'You are not the only one in need of foresight. Protection is necessary, even among friends. Thirty thousand French on Italian soil. I brought them in because I needed them. But one place I do not need them is Milan. As I said before, what I want from you now, Leonardo' – the Regent takes him by the shoulders with both hands – 'is a little magic.'

He buries Caterina. He finishes the model of the horse and its rider: father of Sforza. He completes the preparations for the wedding festivities. The rhythm of work settles into him like a machine. The model keeps Sforza fixed to the spot as he contemplates it. The feet of the horse strike out, driven by the power of muscle. The eye stares down, petrified and fearless, from a great head, where strands of mane are thrown by an absent wind. Mounted upon it, the intrepid figure of Sforza, arm drawn back, eye fixed on target, brandishing a lance.

'Astonishing,' says Sforza. 'The body of a horse, but more besides.' He runs his hand over the muscle of the shoulder.

'The spirit of the horse,' adds Francesco. Leonardo's apprentice is wiping clay from worktops and cleaning tools, knowing his dislike of dirt.

The font is ready: the ditch that will hold the bronze. The pit, many braccia deep, is a brick-lined furnace. There, the bronze will turn molten for casting. The mouldings for the full-size statue are ready and occupy most of the *bottega* on account of their size. Now he must wait for Sforza to pay for the bronze. One month, perhaps two, he had said. Patience is necessary. He returns to his study and shuts the door, feeling anything but patient.

He sits at his desk and stares at the trunk containing his notebooks. Not yet, he thinks. He focuses his mind on the task at hand: Sforza's battlefield. His mind wanders from the Sforza horse to the wooden horse of the battle of Troy: a structure that could save lives. Like a shield, such a device could advance on the enemy, leading infantry into battle and dispersing soldiers before it. A 'Trojan horse' would hide cannons, but its main function – that of surprise – would be sufficient to give the required advantage.

By dawn he has conceived of an armoured machine that can travel overland. The car would be shielded by a conical cover, with sighting turret. Cannons set around a circular platform. He spends hours pouring over various techniques for moving the car. By lodging several men inside the structure, a system of cranks and toothed wheels could provide the mechanism for displacement. He writes:

The armoured cars, safe and unassailable, will then enter the close ranks of the enemy with their artillery, and no company of soldiers is so great that they will not break through them. And behind these, the infantry of soldiers will be able to follow quite unharmed and without any opposition.

Once he has put the ideas on paper, he considers the scene in his mind. Soldiers on horses startled and fleeing before the sight; cannons providing coverage from all angles, enough to deter infantry on all sides. Prevention; protection. If battle is a human disease, the only way to deal with it is to use a deterrent.

'A deterrent?' Sforza examines the plans and nods. Then he walks around the *bottega*, glancing at the rows of paper and books. 'Ingenious, quite brilliant.' He smiles. 'You are a man unique in his talents, Leonardo. But you forget that as you live by your art, so I must live by my sword. You understand this?'

'I understand that men must fight, but I don't condone war,' he says.

Sforza nods. 'You are not a military man. I know. But see things another way: on the battlefield one man's death means another man's life, does it not?'

'If you say it that way, but . . .'

'So then is it not simply a question of saving the right soldier?'

'Perhaps, but then who is the right soldier?' He has said too much. Sforza's face darkens.

'The right soldier, Leonardo, is the one that lets you do the things you want: live, eat, paint, sculpt and cut up cadavers.'

His mouth is dry. *The things I want.* People pass before him: Fra Alessandro, his father, Lorenzo, even Andrea. Now Sforza. *Tempus revenio*: time comes back, but the future is always out of reach. He wonders what it will take for people to understand. A voice tells him: they never will. He is wasting his time. He has travelled to the surface of the unknown world and seen the light; when he returns to the cave, nobody wants to know.

Sforza hears his silence and picks up the plans. 'This is good work, but I need more from you. Forget about your Trojan horse and consider this: the greatest surprise that awaits a man is death. You of all people should know it. It is a fair exchange for freedom. Men lay down their lives in battle for no less.' He gestures to the courtyard, where the model of the statue stands waiting. 'Unless,' Sforza says, 'I use the bronze elsewhere.'

Mixed right, serpentine gunpowder can wreak great havoc. Placed well, it can shatter metal and scatter men limb from body. It can tear a man's heart from his chest and make a hole in his skull bigger than a walnut. He takes his charcoal from willow. If it is smoke alone he wants, he needs more sulphur, less saltpetre. But destruction requires a different ratio.

Through the smoke of battle a victor emerges. Sometimes, when he weighs up the odds, it is Sforza. Other times, the smoke clears and he is alone on a hilltop of Monte Albano, and all the revolutions of the planets, the waning of the moon and the slipping of the sun beneath the horizon tell another story. They say you are one man. What difference will you make?

He runs his hands through the mixture that only needs one spark and sits down to draw. But all he can think of is the swoop of a swallow or a day in early spring when nature will push out new life. He touches the ripples of streams, feels the perspective of far mountains, sees the shape of the wind in groves, and the flash of alder leaves in the sun.

He pushes the images back, and his mind forwards. Nature –

the laws of nature: movement, strength, weight and percussion. The laws of physical movement, for man and machine. Each governed by the same force; the same energy gives life to each. Why not death? Water can flow through a stream as easily as it can flood a dike. He draws a blade, then a scythe. Gears will make it turn. The transfer from wheel to gear to blade. But it needs power: the strength of many men. The strength of horses. He draws a chariot. The blades rotate on spiked wheels. He continues to draw. When he has finished his brow is damp with sweat.

Drawn by horses, the chariots flash over field and heath, the blades on their wheels spinning like giant knives. He pays particular attention to the horses as he draws. Eyes wide, their hooves strike out in terror as they draw the weapon on. Like Hermes with his winged sandals, they tread the path of destruction. Unable to flee the carnage, they bear it with them, and the doors to the Underworld open without hindrance as they pass, for they are the messengers of death.

The Sforza flag depicts a crowned serpent devouring a man. On a stage erected in the centre of the courtyard, musicians stand ready. Sforza, the Emperor Maximilian and his new wife, Sforza's niece, have taken their seats under a pergola draped with flowering plants and banners painted with the portraits of the married couple and decorated with laurel, palm and rose. Maidens representing the seven virtues scatter petals at their feet. Lights shine out from billowing white sheets and make shadows run like phantoms across the stone paving. In the centre of the stage the statue is hidden beneath a vast cover. Francesco turns the gears that raise the sheet. He is standing in a sea of people; hands clap his back and words of praise find his ear.

From the back of the crowd Donato Bramante weaves urgently through people towards him, his expression grim. 'What is it?' he asks.

'It seems the new duke must change his robes for armour,' says Bramante, grabbing his arm and drawing him away from the crowd. 'The French king has taken Naples. That much is not news. But now he has turned his armies north.'

'How long?'

'Until he reaches Milan? Weeks; perhaps not many. But I suspect he will be delayed. First he has set his sights on Florence.'

VI

They are dining in the refectory of Santa Maria delle Grazie. It is a Tuesday. Sforza dines in the refectory two times every week. Now he is seated on the right hand side of the prior. Before them is a large empty wall, which is covered with string like a giant cobweb.

'The great Leonardo weaves his web,' Bramante is saying at his left. He looks at the vast wall as they all do, in between mouthfuls of soup. 'Where will you start?'

'The lunettes,' he says.

'And the layout?'

He taps his head. 'Mathematics,' he says. 'Calculations.'

'It's a hard task for any man, made all the harder by the inevitable prospect of the Duke's comments twice weekly,' Bramante says, raising his cup. 'I salute you. As for me, I suspect that it will be many long months or even years before I am finished.' The architect drains his cup with customary skill. 'Picture this: a man, faced with the prospect of war, and having limited means with which to fight it, orders the construction of his mausoleum, a construction that will cost him dear in men and materials, or let us at least say materials, since no man I have yet met, other than you of course, is willing to ask him for settlement. Where he should be regaling his subjects with talk of immortality and strength, he prepares for death, and where he should be thrifty, he spends – which is a source of great concern, since payment must surely depend on victory, and yet the nature of the work points more to the finality of defeat than to the glory of success.'

'You make too much of it,' he says. 'A man has the right to anticipate death, even the duty, since none shall escape it.' His mind has been in Florence these past weeks. There has been news of French cannons bombarding the city. His father should be in Anchiano. He thinks of Sandro, Domenico – inevitably, Lisa. He wonders where she is, what she is doing. In his mind she is still young, childlike, wearing a green dress and a misleading smile. He tells himself, this is not a true picture. She is older. He is older. Time comes back – but never the same way.

'Ever the optimist,' says the architect. 'But let's put your optimism to test for a moment. Florence is as much threatened by the French as Milan, but there is worse to fear in Florence these days than French cannons.'

'Fra Savonarola,' he says. 'The friar.'

'Yes: preacher of Hell and damnation. Now he uses the French armies in the place of Hell, saying God has sent them to punish the Florentines for their worldliness and wantonness. While I acknowledge that the association of the French cannons with the fires of Hell may not be too tenuous, nevertheless, you and I know where the source of the fire lies, do we not?'

Leonardo turns to look at the Duke. Sforza is in deep discussion with the prior, talking scripture, altarpieces: the greater glory. Only with him the Duke talks men, armoury: war. He wonders how the two can live side by side in the same head. Then he remembers the abstinence of Lent and Fra Alessandro's gluttony. Most people, he reminds himself, have two souls: one for other people and one for themselves. But it is too late for philosophy. Sforza has his sketches.

'And the inhabitants of Florence,' he says to Bramante, 'what of them?'

'The women are chastised for their beauty, the men for their taste,' the architect replies. 'If ever indeed there was a Hell on earth, then Savonarola has surely created it. Most women are either marrying in haste or leaving the city for good. For court holds no pleasure for either sex, and opportunities for trade as well as society are diminishing every day. Nobody dares buy either silk or leather, gold or silver. Feasts are few and far between and marriage celebrations such as the last one I heard recounted survive but one poor day, since any generous display of wealth brings patrols to your doors. All that remains is to wonder which outcome will be the worst: the arrival of the French king, or the rule of the kingdom of Savonarola's heaven.'

The candle flickers on the table. Having found a way in, a moth flutters at the flame. He grasps it between his fingers. 'A hawk moth,' he says, holding the wings gently.

'An omen of death,' says Bramante. 'Let it go.'

He laughs and opens his fingers. 'Superstition is weak wisdom,' he says. 'Call it an omen of change, if you like. This wedding you heard of – was any name given?'

'I believe it was one of the Giocondi,' says the architect, 'but I don't know the name of the bride, other than the fact that she was the oldest virgin in the city. That alone must have been a reason for a hasty marriage.'

The *bottega* has become a warehouse. Alongside the materials he had ordered for the bird – which still lie waiting to be used – is the latest delivery: iron, steel. Francesco as usual is the first to offload everything and check it through. This time there are no questions. He does not offer explanations.

He removes his attention from the bird and places it elsewhere. Before he was chasing time, now time has turned around and is devouring him. He hears hammering from the adjacent workshop and puts his hands over his ears. Work on the chariots has begun. Double time. Every spare hand. The noise of nails driven into wood, and beaten metal. Bang, bang, bang. He goes out and roams through the *bottega*. This is unthinkable, he tells Francesco. A man can't judge an angle without a quadrant. His voice is raised. He takes his cloak and leaves for Santa Maria delle Grazie, and the giant web.

Bramante is high up on a wooden beam, in the apse. The chapel is full of workmen. He dodges men and lengths of wood and enters the refectory, thankfully empty except for the monk clearing the tables. He sits on one of the benches and looks through the web of strings at the faint outline taking shape beneath it: twelve shadowy figures wait to be born on his wall canvas of lead plaster. Beyond them, windows overlook a distant landscape.

He watches the monk collect used plates. All his working life he has painted scripture. He is no nearer to faith now than he was the first time he sketched an angel. He has cut skin, sawn bone, followed the nerve to the brain. But it is not enough. He must look beyond what he can see, and imagine what he cannot. He rolls up his notes and puts them in the pouch of his belt. The Last Supper brings to mind another: Caterina coming in from the wind and the weather. A meal where each one sits, looks at his plate and speaks without talking.

The monk stretches across the table to clear his cup. He holds his arm. 'Tell me,' he says, 'the feast of the Passover. What does it mean to you?' The monk considers.

'Sacrifice,' he replies. Then, 'Memory, perhaps. Betrayal, certainly.'

'Thank you,' he says.

He wanders the streets of the city, and waits on the steps of the cathedral, watching those who enter and leave. Faces parade past him. Some are worn and twisted by age and life. Others are young and fresh, full of hope. He observes men talking in the square, and he waits for a fleeting expression, a moment of anger. As he sees it, he draws it; transposes it to paper. He looks for gesture: in the hand, the turn of a neck. He sees people seated outside houses and shops and records how they sit, how their bodies betray their thoughts, and transposes it to paper. As he sketches, a child runs up to him and says, 'Messer, will you draw me too?' He obliges; takes a small sheet and casts a critical eye over the face of the small boy.

'Which part of me are you drawing now?' asks the boy.

'Your eyes,' he replies. The boy stares directly into his. 'No,' he says. 'Don't look at me.' He turns back to find a point of reference. 'Do you see the face of that gargoyle, there on the parapet of the cathedral?'

'Yes,' says the boy.

'Good. Now look at that.' The boy's expression changes to disgust and horror. He finishes his sketch rapidly then executes another for himself. He hands the small piece of paper to the boy. 'There you are,' he says. The boy stares at it in surprise.

'Was I really that scared?'

Satisfied, he makes his way back to the Corte Vecchio. As he arrives he sees Filippo, the stable hand, talking urgently to Francesco. There's a problem. 'Messer Leonardo,' says Filippo, 'I think you should come with me.'

The search for Caterina's herbs took the last remaining strength from his father's mare. After long weeks of stable rest, she is no better. Her breath is hoarse; her wind is broken. 'What do you want me to do with her?' says Filippo.

He runs his hand over her back and looks into her eye. The pupil is dilated; white flashes around the rim of the retina. 'Take her to the slaughterhouse,' he says. He turns and walks away. Closing the stable door, he notices the wind on the ground, swirling dust into eddies and carrying leaves and twigs on its invisible current. Filippo offers him a ride back. It's all right, he says. He will walk. He arrives back at the end of the day. Francesco is there as always, ready with a question, but the figure of the apprentice is blurred so he brushes him aside. He closes the door to his room and spends the rest of the daylight learning Greek. When his head is exhausted by words and he can no longer think, he closes his eyes and sleeps.

There are people around him; some he knows, some he doesn't. He pushes through the maze of faces, and emerges into a meadow, bordered on every side by dense woodland. At first there is silence. Solitude. He hears the wind in the branches of trees and smells the wild rosemary it carries. In the sky above, swallows dip and rise, their wings like stretched silk. From inside the woodland on one side of the meadow comes a thundering of hooves, then a breaking of branches. Galloping wildly into the middle of the field, a riderless horse appears. At the sight of him, the horse runs faster. Attached to its sides are leather straps and wooden shafts pulling a wheeled chariot. On either side monstrous blades spin like knives. As the horse weaves past him, its breathing is raw and broken; he holds out his hand to grab the harness, but to no avail. He looks down at his hands. They are covered with blood and lined with fine cuts, like the wrinkles in the face of an old man, or the lines of laughter around the eyes of a child.

His eyes snap open. Hemmed in by the walls of the room, he must get out. He pulls a tunic over his shirt and goes out into the quiet courtyard. Beside the church tower is the San Gottardo bell tower. Patron saint of gout sufferers, he thinks. He remembers Andrea; nobody could suffer like him – although he has to admit that he is doing his best. He climbs the steps to the upper hall of the Corte Vecchio. From the balcony he climbs onto the roof easily. Behind him is the tower. In front of him is a straight drop of some twenty braccia. There is a brisk wind blowing; he holds up a hand to test the strength and looks down. He leans his body into the wind, feeling the pressure of the air beneath his chest. If he threw himself forward, he would drop like a stone and hit the paving below with the full force of all his weight. In spite of the wings of his bird and the achievement of his target weight, severe injury or death seems the most likely outcome.

Cold wind streams against his face. He looks up. The night stars, deceptively reachable, fill the bowl of the heavens. Inside him is empty space. He closes his eyes, numbed by despair and loneliness. If he were to jump now, wings or no wings, wouldn't it be simpler?

He moves his foot. It dislodges a piece of broken masonry that clatters down the side of the tower. He puts his hand to his head, berating his own stupidity. *A stone must be thrown.* Strapped into his bird, he would need a running jump to have a chance. Speed is necessary. Pressure alone is not enough. Upwards needs forwards. A bird flaps its wings to stop it from dropping; he must find another way. He peers through the dark to the courtyard below, takes a step back. He must revise his calculations, then build.

VII

Francesco turns a white face to him. 'Clear? What's clear?'

He leans across and presses his hand into Francesco's chest. 'Pressure,' he says.

He wonders what is wrong with Francesco. The man looks unwell. He looks around at the number of projects on the table. The blades for the chariots have been cut but not turned or sharpened. The Duke is staging a play before Lent. First it was Plautus's *Braggart Warrior*, now there is to be a change. Sforza wants *The Pot of Gold*. Ten costumes and five shields wasted. 'What shall we do with the shields?' asks Salai, disappointed. 'You can keep them for your private collection,' he replies, and his mind is filled with the sudden image of a warrior holding a shield on a blazing mountaintop. Francesco is supervising the building of the stage. Then there is the curtain. It must be raised and lowered. They need stronger pulleys; the fabric is heavy. He makes a mental note to help Francesco with the pulleys. There is the scaffolding for the Sala de la Asse, and frescos to finish in the Saletta Negra. But first they are to build the chariots.

He pushes everything else back except for pressure – air pressure. He picks up the drawing of the bird and his pages of notes. 'For a moment,' he says to Francesco, 'I thought I had it. But then I remembered the air.' He points to the base of the bat wing in the sketch. Structure is not enough. 'We need lift. Lift from beneath needs a change in air pressure. If it's the same on both sides, then there's only one way to go: down. Gravity. Weight. Less weight means less pressure, means more lift. The pressure of the bird against the air is the same as the pressure of the air against the bird. We have to make it less, but we need speed. With more speed and less weight, I think we can do it.'

Francesco is reading his notes. *The bird obeys the laws of mathematics: laws which man can reproduce but not with the same force . . . An object offers as much resistance to air as air does to the object. The beating of its wings against the air supports a heavy eagle in the highest and rarest atmosphere, close to the sphere of elemental fire. The air in motion over the sea fills the swelling sails and drives heavily laden ships. Thus a man with wings large enough and duly connected might learn to overcome the resistance of the air and by conquering it, rise above it.*

His apprentice's face is full of doubt: 'I don't know,' Francesco says. 'If you want to know what I really think, I think you are going to kill yourself, and I don't want to be there to see it.'

'A fair response,' he says. 'But I have no intention of killing myself.'

'To be honest,' says Francesco, 'what really worries me is not what we haven't built, but what we have. If killing has become the new objective of this *bottega*, then we seem to be excelling at it.'

Precision is the talent of the Milanese; Francesco has executed his drawings to perfection. The finished product stands beneath a cover in the upper-storey room. He had walked past it that night without even seeing it. Now Francesco removes the cover and they stare at it. It looks like a weapon of torture: apocalyptic; deadly blades stretching out either side like sabres.

Francesco turns to him. 'What are you doing, Leonardo? What are *we* doing?' The apprentice clasps his hands. 'I know it's a commission like any other; but it is like no other. What happens next?'

Francesco is bothering him. He has no time for it. 'The bird,' he says simply. 'And after that I have other work.' Francesco's idea of tomorrow is not his. At the back of his mind is a confused thought about getting back to Florence. He does not know what has brought it on when there is so much to do. Long tasks lie before him at the hospital. However Sforza sees it, he knows what must be done. Dissections are the key to saving lives. *Men need saving from themselves.* He made the vow at the age of ten and has been paying for it ever since. He has never backed away from an objective in his life. He's not about to start now.

Francesco shakes his head. 'What I mean to say is, what do we do after this? An altarpiece?'

He feels impatience rising up like a black current. 'Francesco, what are you trying to say?'

'There's another thing.' Francesco looks at him with that way he has of meeting things head on. 'The Duke sets his sights too high. He has debts. They're saying he'll use the bronze for the statue to settle them.'

There is too much to do. Francesco is wasting time. 'I will not listen to rumours,' he says. 'If you want other commissions, then find them. My hands are already full.'

Sforza has approved the first chariot and ordered the construction of twenty more. The Duke has sent for his best court physician, Giovanni Marliani from the University of Pavia. With his flowing white beard, the physician reminds him of pictures of Poseidon from old books he read as a child. Marliani uses a walking stick in place of a trident.

'I have wanted to meet you for many months, but it seems that you are a busy man and rarely at court. Perhaps it is useless then to extend an invitation to Pavia, since the Duke tells me that, for the present at least, he cannot spare you.'

'The Duke keeps me busy; I keep myself busy,' he replies. 'But nothing would give me greater pleasure than to see what work is being done in Pavia. I have heard of Luca Pacioli's advances in algebra and am eager to meet him. But time is always short.' He thinks of the hours in a day and a night – too few.

Marliani nods. 'I've seen your paintings, both those of Florence, since I am a well-travelled man, and your more recent works – your model of the horse and rider. They are outstand-ing, beyond compare. But the Duke tells me that you're also interested in the study of medicine, and anatomy in particular. Of course I can see the interest an artist would have in an under-standing of the human body – how else can you capture through sculpture the arrangement of muscle and the movement of limbs?'

He could have replied, observation tells me all I need to know for art. It is what I don't know that bothers me. But the image of him sitting on the cathedral steps with his notebook or taking five hours to groom a horse seems the wrong one.

'I study anatomy principally for medical reasons, not artistic ones.'

Marliani calls a servant for water. 'Is that so? And in what way are your reasons medical?'

'I believe that we need to understand the workings of the body in order to understand disease.'

'An interesting idea, which has of course been thought about in the past. Galen carried out extensive studies on animals, to great effect.'

'Galen conducted studies on the anatomy of pigs, certain species of monkey, but never on people,' he says.

'Naturally. But you are not suggesting that we start butchering human beings in order to understand why they fall sick?'

Butchering. He sees himself before the body of the pregnant woman, his last dissection. *Nothing but understanding had passed between them, and all was well.* 'If you need to call it butchering, then I suppose you must . . .'

'What do you call it, young man?'

'Science,' he offers.

In the courtyard of the castle, Sanseverino is lining up his men. There are raised voices, orders. He imagines Sanseverino's unit on the battlefield, at the head of a chariot. Then he wonders what Francesco is doing. He hasn't seen him all day.

'The wise man does not expose himself needlessly to danger,' says Marliani.

He turns back. 'I also read Aristotle. But that is not the solution to every problem. Dissection of a corpse for the greater good of mankind is the only way forward.'

'Then forgive me, but it is a way neither I nor any other physician I know will take,' Marliani replies. 'It is not that I am against the acquisition of knowledge, but you are talking about something entirely different.'

An old friend is back. He sees the pitted face of his elderly tutor, hears his solid footsteps on the gravel path. 'I suppose you mean heresy?' he says.

'Let me put it this way; man has an immortal soul which lies within his body. His soul belongs to God. His body, Messer Leonardo, does not belong to you.'

Marliani is on one side of the wall; he is on the other. Unscalable, he thinks. Find another wall to look at, he concludes. He passes by Santa Maria delle Grazie at Vespers, leaves the altar for the refectory. The wall is huge; he can see why Sforza wants a mural. The final result will lie so high above the occupants of the room that perspective must be manipulated, the table narrowed, the figures of the disciples brought together around the table in an arrangement that makes the impossible possible. Then there is the background. The eye must see more than men. There must be a world beyond the wall. As for the men themselves, he will make them talk. From his belt pouch, he brings out the sketch of the small boy on the cathedral steps. Every man has his story to tell. Fear is one of them. But as he gazes upon the wall and visualises the scene, he knows that there is more to it than that. Shadows crowd in on either side, but he can put no faces to them. Names, then? There is one perhaps, the worst of twelve, but he pushes it back, leaves the hall and the church and returns to his room. There he lies until dawn, plagued by troubled images of sketches he has made and of others yet to come.

The refectory has become a sanctuary from the frantic pace of the *bottega*. Francesco is working as usual, but says little. Every hand is hammering steel. He rises early and leaves silently, taking his bread with him. The refectory commission now occupies his entire mind, leaving room for nothing else, and that is how he wants it. Bramante works near him and the architect's conversation brings moments of lightness to a task that drains his resources. The apostles look down at him from the wall, listening to news they do not want to hear.

'Before I was an architect, I was a painter. Perhaps I mentioned it already?'

Bramante stands with his hands on his waist, observing his work.

'It is of no consequence to any but myself and no doubt a few disappointed patrons. One of my paintings, if memory serves me well, was even more useful at one point as a structural support. But that is another story to the one you are now engaged in, and I can see already that you are giving it your full attention.'

'Tell me,' he says, stepping down from the scaffold, 'where are the French? How far north?'

The French are winning battles while Sforza rages. 'They have passed Rome, but this far, the damage has been contained. Some are still encamped at the borders of Florence; others are already in Modena. The Duke needs Venice, as does Florence. If there were ever a reason to unite, we have one now,' says Bramante. 'Where the French move forward and attack, our troops withdraw. When we finally mount an attack, the French fight like dogs.'

'And Florence?'

'Florence, so far, has not been taken. But the fate of Piero de' Medici is uncertain. I have heard that Republicans led by the friar Savonarola have declared Florence a republic, and told Piero to pack his things and leave.' Bramante shakes his head.

'After everything the Medici have done for the city, it seems wrong that it should end like this.'

'He who talks loudest wins the day,' he replies. 'The friar is known for his speeches.'

Bramante is looking at him now that he has climbed down to ground level. 'You look thin,' the architect says. 'What is it? Too many berries?'

He laughs and thinks of telling Bramante the story of his target weight. He will take me for a madman, he decides, like everyone else. Butcher, heretic, lunatic.

He paints at dawn. Sometimes he stays all day, sometimes no longer than a few moments. And other times he comes to observe rather than paint. Vibrant colour has emerged on this surface he calls his giant gypsum sketchpad. He had spent hours rubbing down to a smooth plaster surface. He had covered it with a fine layer of white lead powder, instead of painting directly onto wet plaster in the normal manner. Now he paints with egg tempera. The base is experimental, but he feels reckless.

'Tell me,' he says, looking from Bramante to the gypsum sketchpad, 'what do you see?'

'Well there's a simple question. The feast of the Passover; the breaking of bread for the last time.'

'More than that,' he says. 'Tell me what you see first, when you look at it.'

Bramante stands back and considers. 'Jesus sits in the middle, his disciples all around. It is the Messiah one first sees; the others after.'

He smiles. 'That's because you're thinking of the subject. Now allow your eye to rest on the first place it chooses, and forget about the Passover.'

'The vanishing point,' says the architect. He gazes at the mural. 'The first thing I see is nothing of any importance; I see the hills.'

'Right, quite right,' he says. 'You do indeed see the hills, because that is what I have had you see. The eye is drawn beyond the right temple of the Messiah to the view behind.'

'I have the feeling that you're making me see something that isn't real. You've made space where there is no space.'

'The calculations weren't easy,' he agrees.

'Then I'm looking at an illusion,' says Bramante.

'An illusion of reality,' he corrects. He remembers his fake stars in the space of a canopy, and the reality of illusion. Little to choose between them, he thinks. He makes a note in his mind: optical studies.

'But it's the expressions on the faces of the apostles that tell the story,' adds the architect.

'So now what do you see when you look at the scene?'

He disappears down the aisle of the refectory but Bramante calls after him. 'I have it. A moment of truth, a revelation.' His voice is bigger than the room. 'One of you will betray me. But tell me, when will you finish Judas?'

He returns to the *bottega* and sits in his favourite chair by the window. He thinks of scripture: the Gospel of Judas. The sacrifice of Judas is old heresy. *You will sacrifice the man that clothes me.* Betrayal is necessary. John of Wittenberg, he says to himself, would have appreciated the irony. Leonardo da Vinci provides the Duke of Milan with a reason to save his soul. If Francesco is right, then with his promises of bronze the Duke has been stringing him along like a marionette. He has had enough of conjecture. He has had enough of doubt. *There is no safety in ownership.* He remembers Beatrice and gets up, feeling strangely weak at the idea of his chariots in the hands of Sforza. He passes his pile of silk taffeta and cane without looking, and takes up his cloak.

Ludovico Sforza, Duke of Milan, is wearing a five-day beard. The *condottiere* is alone in his chambers. There is no sign of woman, wife or mistress.

'You came before I could send for you. But I knew you would not be long in coming.'

'I have been busy with the mural.'

'And the Saletta? When will it be finished?'

'A month, perhaps longer. We are at full capacity,' he says, hearing his own voice. 'The chariots.' He adds, 'For the bronze, do you have a date?'

'Transportation in these trying times is no easy feat. By river would have been easier than overland. But while we wait, other work can be done.' The Duke throws a log of wood into the fireplace. 'In any case, for the time being I need you. I want you to accompany me out of town. I need your advice: a matter of strategy.'

Sforza stirs the fire with a poker and wipes his hands on a cloth. 'We leave at first light.'

The plains of Lombardy are home to many creatures: the wolf, the bear and the whistling marmot. There in the fertile soil grow wheat and maize. Higher up, the song of the cicada silences the cuckoo. The swallow feeds nectar of celandine to her chicks to cure their blindness, and vultures circle the plains on Alpine thermals.

Below the birds, the great Lombard rivers feed the lakes. The

Po, the Olona and the Lambro flow above ground; below ground there are other waters. These are the rivers of the past, which in years gone by were fed by the alluvial plains of this abundant country. Long ago the rivers retreated below ground, leaving their minerals behind to fertilise the land. Looking around, he wonders whether nature will one day stop giving, or whether people will ever stop taking.

The road out of Milan leads through tall, verdant wheat. It takes a full day to travel through this natural larder. He rides beside the Duke. On the flag before them the Sforza coat of arms curls in the wind. It's a strange insignia: man swallowed by serpent competes with eagle for the crown of the city. Sforza gestures to it.

'You observe the arms of the House of Sforza with much interest, I think. Which of these creatures is most to be feared – the eagle or the serpent?'

'That would depend on whether you were a mouse or a leopard.'

Sforza laughs. 'I expect more than cat and mouse from you, Leonardo. Your words have always shown ten times the wisdom of others, and I know that you always speak them fearlessly.'

He sits uncomfortably in the saddle. His first time on a horse in months. He thinks of black elder and the sacrifice of his father's horse. Above them wind is bringing bad weather. Clouds he cannot draw without paper darken others in his head.

'French soldiers are beyond those hills.' Sforza points south, at the blue peaks of the Apennines. 'They think they can scare us with their cannons and their culverins.' Sforza digs his spurs into the horse's side. 'But we shall have them.'

They follow well-worn paths beneath a ridge. 'Our soldiers have been defending this position for the past two days,' says Sforza. 'I wanted you to see it, so that you understand for yourself the importance of our defence.' Beyond the ridge of mountains, the slope drops into a valley. There, far beneath them, he hears a new sound. Smoke rings float lazily into the air, followed by the echo of cannon fire. A constant droning noise carries on the air, like the suffering of many people locked together. He thinks, this is the sound of battle. Looking down, he starts to discern movement. There is a mass of men, metal and horses, a twisted, moving canvas that merges, separates and merges again, in one human mass. They watch it for a moment in taut silence.

Sforza speaks. 'French gendarmes. You see, Leonardo, why I need you? For the *condottieri* war has always been an agreement between two men – a contract, if you like. But these armies know nothing of politics; they kill and plunder. Prisoners are not taken, they are slaughtered.' Sforza's face has lost its bravado. 'There's no ransom or exchange, no deal. Only death. So you see,' the Duke says, turning to face him, 'I have no choice. I need cannons; I need the bronze to cast them and I need the man to do it.' Sforza turns to give an order, glances at him, then points his face into the wind. 'The statue must wait. We have other work now.'

Sforza straps his sword to his side and puts on his helmet. 'You must stay here; the fray of battle is no place for a painter, but remember this hour as your finest. When the battle moves to Fornovo, as it must, your chariots and my cannons will bring the enemy to his knees. What greater monument can there be than that?' Sforza turns his horse down the hill, as the ground beneath his feet trembles with gunfire. Leonardo stares in horror at the scene below him. The grating sound of tack and cart and the dry thrust of spears bring his stomach to his mouth. This is not death, he thinks, but murder.

Sensing danger, his horse backs away. From the field below comes the sound of hooves. A horse without a rider is galloping towards them, its trapper torn. The horse weaves and bends, its stride unbalanced. Then he sees the reason: with one foot in a dangling stirrup, the headless body of a cavalier trails alongside, arms outstretched and leg twisted. The horse speeds up, eyes wide and white, mouth foaming.

He looks at the corpse in horror; with a flick of the rein, he turns his horse around. He rides without stopping until he has reached the other side of the hill. He finds a quiet meadow, dismounts and throws the reins over the branch of a tree. He leans against the trunk and slides to the ground. Above him soft ash leaves are brushed by the breeze. He puts his face in his hands and wonders why he is here, wishes himself in Florence. He pushes back the picture of thrusting spears and plunging swords. The right soldier, Sforza had said. On the battlefield there is none. He thinks, if I could cry a river of tears for all the miseries of men, it would not be enough.

Night falls, and with it, familiar sounds come to comfort him in the calm light of dusk. His horse grazes peacefully beside the tree, on a patch of russet grass. Crickets stir the foliage at his feet and a dormouse climbs the tree beside him. He falls asleep, waking later to a darkness brightened by moonlight. The moon is full, pale silver. He rises and drinks what little wine he has in his saddlebag and eats two small figs, as yet unripe, from a nearby tree. Then he closes his eyes until dawn, conscious of the east breeze on his face and thankful of the blessed distance he has put between himself and others.

At dawn he wakes refreshed. He stands up and stretches as though a burden has been lifted. The world seems new and as it should be. At his feet a lizard basks in early-morning sunshine; here and there a bird flutters to a nest.

He hears the hooves of horses drawing closer. It is a group of Sforza's men, clearly sent to find him.

'Messer Leonardo! The Duke asks for you,' says one. They look white and wasted, their mounts tired.

'Tell the Duke I shall make my own way back.' He shakes the leaves from his doublet and puts it on.

'But our orders are to bring you back. The Duke will be displeased.'

'Then he must be displeased,' he says. He mounts his horse and turns back to Milan.

When he arrives, he finds the *bottega* empty. No Francesco. He throws down his bag and walks round in circles. What now? In his mind he turns over his conversations with Sforza. Strong name, strong will. It is *he* who is weak. He finds a jug of water and washes his face, then takes a cloth to dry his hands, wiping away the dirt of the past few days. When he was a child, his father would hold out his hands and tell him they were strong. He looks at them now, wishing he could read in his palms some knowledge of the future, some sign, some grain of hope. He closes his fingers over thin air and illusion and his eyes rest on something else.

Salai's stash of objects. Pieces of fabric, masks, offcuts of silver, shields discarded from the *Braggart Warrior*. He picks one up. It takes him back again to the study in Anchiano. *I thought you could draw something on it for me: something to frighten away our enemies. Can you do that?* His father turns over the shield and sees a chimera: part lizard, part dog, part nine-year-old boy. He watches for the terror on his father's face. Time comes back, he thinks. He turns the shield over; there in the shine of the metal is the terror that is his: eyes livid, mouth open. *Takers of the souls of men, destroyers of their own.* A monster.

'You've not slept?'

Francesco shrugs his shoulders. 'Who sleeps?'

He has returned to the refectory and worked through most of the night, putting the final touches to the mural. Francesco speaks from below the scaffold. 'He makes a lonely figure, your Christ.' Francesco is right; Jesus sits surrounded but alone, the weight of treachery heavy on his shoulders. On his right hand is Judas, now complete, body tense, hand poised.

He turns to his apprentice. 'Forgive me Francesco. You were right; I was wrong.'

'The bronze,' Francesco says, bitterly.

'Worse than the bronze: me. I should have known.'

'Leonardo, you are a man like no other, but still a man. Men make mistakes.'

'Not any more,' he says, climbing down from the scaffold. 'I've been blind. I know it. But now my sight is restored.' He puts his hand on Francesco's shoulders. 'I have been looking in the wrong place, but it's not too late.'

When they return to the *bottega*, he takes up his notebooks to pack them away in the bottom of his trunk. An old habit. He picks up the last few pages from the locked drawer of his *scrittoio* – his drawing of the human heart, and the annotations beside it. With his pen he hurriedly adds a line. *The vessel of the soul lies not in the heart but in the brain.* He contemplates the words for a moment, then in his head writes another: *optics*. What is real, he asks himself, what we see, or what we think we see? The key to understanding is there. He binds the pages in leather and ties them with a strap. Then he turns to Francesco. 'I need you to help me pack, but first there's something we must do.'

Sforza's terracotta urns hold supplies of oil. He hands Francesco one of them and fills a bag with rags from a pile of old fabric. Then he turns to the rows of paper neatly lined up and ordered. He picks out the detailed drawings of the bird and the scale drawings of the chariots. 'What are you doing?' says Francesco in alarm.

He says nothing, but stokes up the stove that is still smouldering in the corner of the *bottega*. Then he folds up the sheets of paper and calmly places them in it. Gold flames flare up, devouring the paper in moments. Francesco is sitting down, shattered.

'This is only the beginning,' he says, and takes up the urn.

They leave the Corte Vecchio, passing the back of the guard and entering the inner courtyard of the castle, where the Duke's stables run along the perimeter of the building. They enter a section of yard where barns and shelters serve a store. There is barely any moon, but the shape of the chariots stands out clearly beneath the brown sacking that covers them.

He tears off strips of the fabric and passes them to Francesco, who douses them with the oil from the urn. These they scatter among the wood and metal of the chariots, pouring the rest of the oil onto the sacking.

'Fetch a torch,' he says. The courtyard is quiet. The guard is taking a rest during Sforza's absence. It's the last day of the Feralia: they will be setting out food for the dead for the feast of St Peter. Francesco returns with a flaming torch. He sets it to the oiled fabric here and there, passing from chariot to chariot until a line of blazing wood and metal has formed beneath the open stone shelter. The shelter is isolated; he has calculated the risk of fire spread. It seems minimal. The stables at least are safely away on the other side. He takes the plans and notes for the chariots and throws them onto the pyre. All that is left now are the preliminary sketches.

From the opposite end of the courtyard the sound of the guard rises up, voices call out. But by then the damage has been done. As they go around the other side of the building to leave, he glances back and notes with satisfaction that the fire is burning well. All that will be left at the end of it in testimony to his madness will be ashes and twisted metal.

'I hear you are leaving,' says Bramante. 'I would do the same. For I speak no French, nor have the desire to learn any.' His eyes drawn to the mural, the architect adds, 'Let them loot that. Only madmen would plunder a wall.'

He wraps his brushes carefully in a leather strap. Tomorrow he is leaving for Florence. 'For my part they can have it,' he says, 'I am done with Judas.'

'You will return, won't you?'

'That depends on Florence,' he says. He clasps the architect by the shoulder and embraces him.

'Give my best to the Republic,' says Bramante. 'But be careful; Savonarola's influence has lit up the city like nothing before. You are leaving one hot cauldron for another.'

'Then I shall feel at home.'

He and Francesco have packed his things. This is the hardest goodbye. He promises to send word, and asks Francesco to watch over Salai.

'When you see the Duke, give him this.' He has written to Sforza. A letter of resignation in which he takes his leave as delicately as possible, holding back anger and bitterness – replacing them with as much elegance as he can muster. An old commission calls him back to Florence, requiring his urgent attention. He is grateful for the patronage of the House of Sforza, but cannot satisfy its needs without compromising his own. 'The chariots,' he writes, 'were my mistake, and I have corrected it. I have asked Francesco to return enough money to cover most of what has been used and wasted. In this I would ask your understanding, and hope that the loss of the chariots will cause you less pain than the loss of the monument, the greatness of which must now be consigned to the past, and not the future.'

'And tidy up the work in progress,' he says to his apprentice, knowing that he will do it anyway. Francesco looks at the materials for the bird, which still lie ready and waiting to be used in a corner of the *bottega*: sheets of silk and piles of cane that look so light a breath of wind could sweep them away. 'Would it really have flown?' Francesco says, reading his thoughts.

He turns his back on the pile, makes ready to leave. 'Flight is a mathematical certainty. As are many things. But you have to want to know before you can understand.' He sees himself at the top of the San Gottardo tower, or soaring above a lake, and wonders whether – even airborne – he would have made sense to anyone. But there is no point in regret. The sketches of his flying machine are in the stove, by now burnt to nothing, and there they will remain. He manages a smile at the downcast face of his loyal apprentice. 'Besides, you did say it was dangerous, didn't you?'

Francesco nods, takes his arm and hands him food for the journey. As he rides out of the courtyard, he has the strangest sensation of eyes burning his back, as though from every window of every room someone is watching him leave.

San Casciano

I

The wheat store of Milan becomes home to oak and beech wood. The underground rivers that watered the wheat have found a way up to the surface to become gushing streams that lead him south. He sent his bags on ahead in a traveller's carriage for the price of a sketch and is now travelling light with no need of cart or servant, which in any case he no longer has the means to pay for. He had pressed money on Francesco, who took only half, suggesting he return the rest to the Duke. He left what he could for Salai. He sleeps in barns or in the open, stopping at inns along the way when he's hungry. He keeps to byways, crossing fields when he can, and cutting through forest when he is sure of the way. He keeps his eyes open for French gendarmes, but sees none.

South of the river Po, Lombardy becomes Emilia Romagna. The vast alluvial plains of the Po valley had made easy travelling, but now the land pushes up. The Apennines of Liguria sculpt the plains into rolling hills dense with forest. He does not need to see the wolves to know they are there; he hears the first of the howling as he descends the ridge into woods two days south of Pavia. The wolf is prowling the borders of its land, marking out territory. He is impatient to return to his own, but with every new sight the temptation to stop is too strong. He veers west to the coast, as much to avoid the presence of the French as to see the water. He feels the ocean on the horizon; smells it before he sees it. The horizon becomes light and open, the air salty. The sky drops below the next hill, as the Apennines descend steeply to the sea. He sits at the edge of the clifftop, watching the draw and wash of the current against the rocky coastline, and observing in both cliff and wave the effect of one on the other. He remembers the shallow banks of the streams of Anchiano. All his life water has fascinated him. Control water and you control everything, he thinks. But as he looks at this mass of water, this swell, this current, he feels small, insignificant. He dislikes the feeling, and stirs himself, suddenly aware of time passing.

He stops overnight, then moves back inland, heading towards Bologna. As he travels he takes out the compass he has constructed from iron, magnets and wood, and studies it. Packing away his notes, he rides on again. He passes a type of cart he has never seen before, drawn by a tired horse. Who conceived of that? he wonders. Shaking his head, he takes his notebook from his pouch and stops to write: *In Romagna, vehicles with four wheels are used, of which the two in front are small and two high ones are behind; an arrangement which is very unfavourable to the motion, because on the fore wheels more weight is laid than on those behind, as I showed before . . .*

He feels the sting of the darnadello, the Tuscan wind, upon his face. The western gate to Florence, Porta al Prato, is within sight along the northern bank of the river which feeds the meadow. He presses on.

At the gate to the city they ask him questions: his name –

which he gives without thinking; and his business – which he thinks about but doesn't give. Looking for work, he says, and leaves it at that. 'Not much work to be had,' the guard says, staring at his clean hands. He parts with a few soldi and gains entry. He puts back his pouch of money: even lighter than he thought. He passes under the great arch of the familiar stonewall. It was on a day like today that he first went through it, a residue of rain in a cloudy sky, the sun in and out. His father rode in front, him behind, struggling to get a better view of the shape of the Duomo.

Now he sees it clearly. Flashes of burnt amber in between the crushed masonry of houses and shops. He notices that most of these are shut up. It's a city of closure. Streets that were bristling with people give off an air of practised restraint. He passes a group of young women and children singing a lament. The youngest child is crying. He looks over his shoulder as he passes the group. 'Why are you crying?' he calls to the boy when he is level. 'For his sins,' answers the girl following behind. Which ones? he wonders.

He stops at the Via de' Macci. The door to the old *bottega* is locked. No hammering, no shouting, no sign of life. He tries to peer through the small glass panel in the wall on the side, imagining how his face must look from the inside of the building. A memory comes back of Andrea suggesting to him that a measurement needs to be double-checked, and twice is not four times. As he stares through the grimy opening he thinks he can make out a workbench, the shape of an old bust, a leather apron abandoned in a corner. He turns away.

In his hurry to be gone he has barely considered logistics. The money he had made from his last commission in the Sala delle Asse bore the stamp of Sforza. He had given it back. Whether he would be paid for the refectory mural, he did not even begin to wonder. Perhaps it will depend on how many culverins Sforza can manufacture out of seventy tons of bronze, he thinks bitterly. Thus his own purse, as so often in times past, is mostly empty. He will need work, a bleak prospect. In his letter to Sforza there was more of desire than reality. His old commission was a memory he drew out from a pile of others, jumbled together and pushed aside. His own lack of foresight irritates him. He can imagine a painting in an instant; geometry is clearer to him than night follows day. But ask him where he'll be this time next month, and he is lost. Who will pay for beauty when there are sins to worry about? Even scripture is problematic.

His feet have taken him without thinking to the vast stone construction of the Medici palazzo. The benches of credit are empty of people; the loggias shut up. The familiar entrance to the courtyard and the garden beyond is closed and barred, Lorenzo gone. His prospects are bleak. His possessions comprise a bag of belongings and a trunk containing a manuscript nobody wants to read. He wastes time thinking about an alternative history. Giuliano is alive and well; Lorenzo is in crimson and gold; the cave dweller comes up to the surface and he sees the trees and the beauty and the light, and he says, 'Here shall I stay.'

The Medici made me as they have destroyed me.

As though invisible ears have heard him, he feels the pressure of a hand on his shoulder and turns round.

The guard looks closely at him and points to the palazzo. 'What business do you have there?'

'None, now,' he answers.

'Then, in that case, I recommend you move on.' The guard looks down at his bag. 'If you have anything to burn, you should go to the Signoria at the end of the day.'

Unable to make much sense of this, he returns to the *borgo*, where his belongings await collection. When he has them, he wonders what to do with them. He thinks of the Via del Montecommune, his father's last place of residence. He gets his things loaded onto a cart, and goes on ahead. But once there, he finds that the lease has been passed on. Ser Piero has returned to Anchiano permanently, for reasons of health. He finds an inn down the next street and sits beside a spitting hearth, wondering if he should make the journey to Anchiano. But what will he find? The house on the hill will be smaller; the light in the little window opening that had guided him back at the end of so many days of childhood exploration will no longer be lit; his father will ask him why he did not stay and open his own *bottega* as they had planned. They might have a conversation.

From the window, shafts of light illuminate his despair. Somewhere in the square the familiar sound of the bell tower calls people to Mass. He leaves the hearth and the memories it brings and goes back out into the streets.

The churches are full for Mass. Santo Spirito, Santa Maria, Santa Croce: at the entrance to each, crowds gather and pour inside. The group of children he saw earlier in the day have reappeared in the Piazza della Signoria. Now they have an air of celebration, as though it is a festival day in Holy Week. Once he arrives in the centre of the piazza, he understands the reason.

The sight astonishes him to such a point that he has to draw nearer to confirm what his own eyes tell him, before he can take it in.

The sun has sunk beneath the level of tiled roofs and stone turrets. Florentines are filling the square. Some are holding sacks; others are holding swathes of fabric over their arms and some are even carrying objects in their hands: statuettes, candlesticks, books. In front of the loggia a larger crowd has assembled. He struggles through it, fighting back a distant memory of Florentine crowds, the hunters of Pazzi, Riario and Bandini, and the head on the spike. He is slowed by a trumpet sounding from the loggia. When it stops, he hears dry wood crackling and smoke rising.

Three fires are burning in the square. Guards stoke them with pitchforks, while others stand at the head of a long queue of people throwing fuel onto one or another of the fires. He walks level with the head of the queue. Someone tells him to get in line. The flames spew sparks and the crowd swarms sideways. He plunges forward.

'What are you doing?' Instinctively his arm stretches out and he grabs the leather-bound book that the guard is preparing to jettison. He stares at it in disbelief. 'Petrarca! You're burning Petrarca!' He looks into the flames licking wood, fabric and fur. He makes out the shape of a large gilt frame.

'Move over! It's not yours to burn.' The guard takes the book from his hand and flings it on the fire. The poems on the scorching pages melt into yellow and black, gone in an instant. He takes a step back; what form of Hell is this? He looks down the line of people. The guard pulls his arm. 'Name and street?'

'Wait!' Someone takes his other arm and places a large framed painting beneath it. A voice in his ear says, 'Give it to him.' He looks down at the painting; it is the portrait of a young woman. He notices the lines, the curve of the breast, the melancholic face, the beauty. He knows this style. This steady hand. But he's too slow. 'Make up your mind, painter,' the guard says, and takes it from his hands. The wood smoulders and crackles. Flames draw into the pigment, streaming up a rainbow of colour. Another hand draws him away. He turns and looks into the strained face of Sandro Botticelli. The guard calls after him, 'Messer, haven't you forgotten something?' Sandro takes soldi from his belt and tosses him a few coins. 'Penitent painters,' calls the guard, 'are welcome in the Kingdom of Heaven.'

He cannot say what shocks him more: the painting on the fire, or its creator turned destroyer. Sandro explains. 'We needed to make a show. Besides, I never liked that one.'

Sparks fill the edges of the piazza like dancing fireflies. 'I thought I might find you at the Tre Rane,' he says, 'like before.'

'Little chance of that,' Sandro tells him, 'it closed down.' He adds, 'Things have changed.'

He can see that. The painting has been devoured. Now a woman throws a leather cloak trimmed with fur onto the flames. Thick brown smoke swirls up from the cloak and makes the waiting crowd cough. 'Couldn't you find something easier to burn, Signora?' one calls out.

'You have been gone too long,' says Sandro, looking closely at his ageing face, his wiry hands veined by the sculpting of Sforza's monument. 'You left us behind.'

'You were too busy,' he replies, 'with Medici commissions.'

Sandro leads him to the river, along old familiar ways. A

woman beats a rug at an open doorway. The bells of the Duomo announce Mass. Sandro shrugs. 'Florence has a new master. There are no Medici here. There are other things to paint. More important things. Domenico of course is always busy,' he adds. 'Personally, I have contented myself with poverty, relatively speaking – which seems to be well suited to the times.' They stop at the riverbank and look at the darkening sky. 'Do you know, I have listened to him every Friday at San Marco since Epiphany, the friar Savonarola. It must be his voice I think. Something about it; something that keeps you there, listening, until you finally understand.' Leonardo searches his friend's face for signs of the rebellious son of the tanner, the stubborn young apprentice, but can find neither. Suddenly he feels his age. 'Tell me,' he says, 'how they do it? Burn books, paintings?'

'I think it's easier than you imagine,' says Sandro. 'They burned a man for heresy just before the feast of the Passover. If they can burn a man, they can burn a book.'

'Yes,' he replies, 'until someone else writes another.'

'How was Milan? How is the Duke?'

'In the hands of French gendarmes, how *can* a man be?'

'They blasted cannons all night from the hills at the eastern wall. By morning, Fra Savonarola had the Council eating out of his hand. As far as everyone else was concerned, Savonarola had saved the city. By sundown the hills were empty and Savonarola's fires were lit.'

He thinks of burning chariots, sketches of wings and the stove of ashes. *Savonarola burns his books; I burn mine.* 'If I ever chance to meet our friar,' he says, 'I shall make a point of thanking him.'

They spend the night in the rooms above Sandro's *bottega*. He notices the empty benches, the dusty floor, and sees Sandro standing there long ago, ready to cast another line of gold onto a tapestry of colour. He looks at the new studies on the scrittoio in the corner. Faces look back, etched with pain. The bodies of men in chains await judgement. Purgatory spreads before them: a wasteland of sulphur and rock. He tells himself that the world has swung off balance. In Milan there was too little virtue. Here there is too much. A flood is as bad as a drought. When he leaves Florence again, which he must, he will take Sandro with him.

II

He asks Sandro for a horse. But he is far from the stables of Sforza. Eventually Sandro returns with a thin Maremmano. He thanks him, then spends an hour worrying about the state of the horse, before finally riding out to Anchiano at a speed that matches his own hesitant state, and the horse's weak one. He rests overnight, under cover of a beech tree in case it should rain again. He finds that he enjoys sleeping out of doors less than he used to. The ground is becoming harder, or he is becoming softer. His body does not move as fast as before, but his mind moves faster. How many years does a man have? How many good years? If he is feeling his age, his father must be lamenting his.

He spots the house on the hill. Square and lonely, it dominates the valley. Years come back; time comes back. He takes a breath, gathers the rein and pushes on, up the winding path to the yard, past waving grasses and the squat olive groves he remembers, where cicadas hide in trees and lizards flit through tall fronds of meadow barley in search of sun.

He dismounts in the middle of the yard and leads the horse into the stable. There is no other horse there, only a pair of goats in the corner. He fills the trough with water and throws a handful of dried barley into the wooden basket beside it. He notices a broken model of a half-finished water mill forgotten on the shelf at the end of the barn, like a miniature shipwreck washed up on a shore. His, he thinks.

The coolness of the house is warmed by the smell of burning wax. On the right, his father's study overlooks the front yard and the barn to the left. His father has taken to his bed. The servant says it was a hard winter: crops frozen in the ground. No point in setting foot out of doors at least until Epiphany.

'You've been long in coming,' his father says.

He places a pillow behind his father's back and helps him sit up. This is his father's bedchamber, a room he has rarely entered. There is a fireplace smaller than the one downstairs. On a scrittoio in a corner is a carved documents case, a candlestick, a number of pens and a pot of ink.

'The last transaction I did was for Ghirlandaio. A contract,' his father says, staring at him. 'That isn't much of a beard.'

'I don't like wearing a beard,' he replies. 'If I ever grow one, it will be out of lassitude.' His father's face is buried beneath a straggling beard. Only his eyes haven't changed.

'Where are you staying?'

'Sandro, above the studio. Florence.'

'Ah, Sandro's workshop. Yes.'

How many words, he thinks, does a man say in a lifetime? And how many does he keep back? He asks after Albiera.

'In the city. She'll be back by nightfall. You're staying of course.'

He takes his bag to his old bedchamber on the other side of the house. On the table by the window opening is a piece of charcoal. He picks it up and turns it over in his fingers. The chamber seems smaller than it used to be, but that's only to be expected, since now he's viewing it from a different perspective.

His father gets up. Albiera returns and drops her basket at the sight of him. 'We've all grown old,' she says, 'but you have grown thin.' They eat a meal of meat and bread and vegetables from Albiera's garden. He reminds them that he doesn't eat meat. As they sit round together, thoughts of food bother him. He would like to say his mother couldn't eat so she came to stay with him. But even then she couldn't eat. Then he remembers that these are old wounds, and a glance at Albiera's face puts them aside. His mother is dead, he tells himself. Only the living count.

He sits beside the fire with his father in the study. Old friends line the shelves, books he looked at but didn't read. Now his Greek is perfect.

His father says, 'So what have you done?' It's a good question and he thinks about it. The right answer is 'Too much but not enough', but instead he says, 'Commissions for the Duke, a mural, a number of portraits.' His father nods. Then, 'But what have you really done?'

Albiera lights a lamp and places it between them on the table. 'What I've always done,' he says. He looks at his father. 'Looked for answers in the dark.' A moth settles on the lamp. He watches it spread its wings.

He lies down on the bed, then gets up before he blows out the lamp. He runs his hand along the wall. He pulls out the loose stone and feels in the dark space until his hand touches wood. He pulls it out. A spidery board that looks more like a cemetery. The bodies of butterflies partially consumed by time and insects. Only a few are intact. '*Papilio Macaone*,' he reads aloud. He puts his hand back in the space of the wall and pulls out the rest of the stash, a roll of old paper tied up with string. He opens the sheets and smiles. He reads his old script. Mirror or no mirror is all the same to him. There is a sketch: the faded arc of a rainbow, in every tone of grey. Beside it he had written a line of annotation, in fine charcoal. *The raindrops are round. So is the colour.* He rolls up the paper, puts it in his bag, snuffs out the light and closes his eyes. As he thinks of things that are round, his mind traces the line of a continuous spiral in the dark, until daylight filters in through the cracks of stone in the wall of the room and settles on the floor in broken circles around him.

When he leaves, his father asks him, 'Why don't you live a little? Take a wife, father a child?' The view from the hill will never change. It stretches over valley and woodland, taking in mountains and sky. There is Monte Albano to the east, distant hills the colour of water and ash. I am living, he thinks. 'I'll think about it,' he says. Then his father stuffs a bundle in his hand. 'Something I've been meaning to give you. When I first gave it to you, I was worried. Now I think you were right. We're always afraid when we don't understand. God is on your side, my son. Don't worry about me. There's nothing you can do about it, whatever you might think. I'm just old, that's all.'

He rides level with the hills of San Pantaleo. Old habit turns his head towards his mother's house. At a distance, it looks more like a ruin. He drops down into the valley. He stops to wash his face and hands in the stream and opens his bag. There is his father's bundle, and the roll of old paper with his drawing of the rainbow. He pulls out the bundle. Wrapped inside it is a small round shield, in the centre of which is a simply drawn but well-proportioned picture of a creature: part lizard, part dog, part cockerel. He sits back on the bank of the stream and looks into the current. His father didn't burn it. He shakes his head. Time comes back, and shows the way ahead. Not the fire, he thinks. Of course. The colour, the light. *The rainbow.*

A sound makes him jump. He turns round, expecting to see the figure of a small girl in a green dress, but it's the sound of gurgling water, the rustle of a bird in a branch. He gets back on the horse with a feeling of urgent purpose. If Sandro's horse can manage the pace, he could be back in Florence by nightfall.

'Your best hope of work is outside the city walls,' says Sandro. 'There are still families ready to pay for what they want. Machiavelli, Acciaioli, these are old names. The Medici may be gone, but their flags have not been entirely destroyed, only stashed aside. The Acciaioli will almost certainly put a commission your way. These days they are one of the few who still have the stomach for feasting, and the purse to pay for it – if you can manage a little conversation.'

'You forget I've been in Milan—' he says, '—the city that sharpens the wits. If you don't say the right thing there, you may as well leave.'

They are travelling south to Montespertoli in a cart. Having spent two weeks with Sandro, he is glad to put a little distance between his old friend and the friar's sermons, which the artist attends with a devotion he once reserved for his work. Florence has fallen into darkness. The light has gone out. Lorenzo lies in a marble vault, cold and still.

'Since you mention old names,' he says, staring ahead at the track, 'here's one for you. Lisa Gherardini.'

'Gherardini, Lisa. Yes, I know her. There was a wedding some time ago. Let me think. Married Giocondo, Francesco di Zanobi. Nobody invited me, naturally. But I have a feeling Domenico went.'

'Did he?' He says nothing. He has heard the name before. Silk merchants – what else? He thinks briefly about the right cut of cloth, shakes his head; he looks at the slow-flowing stream, the soft grey line of alder to his right, and thinks of all the years in between.

They branch off onto the Via Volterrana. People are pruning olive trees. The hillsides are scattered with grey trees and delicate leaves; branches make piles in clearings, ready to be set ablaze by nightfall. It is almost the feast of the Annunciation. Sandro jumps down and returns with a handful of last season's olives. Leonardo laughs. 'You'll have a hard time swallowing those until they're broken and cured.' Sandro stares at his hands, that are holding a strange-looking object. 'What is that?'

'A camera obscura,' he explains. He holds it against the eye of the artist. 'The image that passes through the pinhole is inverted, then reflected by a mirror inside the box onto this screen, here.'

'Plato?'

'No,' he says, 'Aristotle.' Sandro smiles.

'I thought the pinhole had to be round?'

'I made it square deliberately, to check the result.'

'And?'

'It makes no difference; the light comes through round.' He draws a shape in his mind: first a circle, then a spiral. The spiral becomes a shell, a delicate coil of pearl. He puts down the camera and looks at the country as it passes by. A thought takes shape. There is nothing square in nature. Everything is curved. He gazes into space.

Sandro says, 'If you want to tell me what you're thinking, I would like to know. There is something else too that I would like to know. Why do you want to find *la Gioconda*?'

III

Lisa Gherardini is now Lisa di Zanobi del Giocondo. A suitor has been found. Since he has no intention of taking a wife, fathering a child, things are as they should be. He thinks of a reply for Sandro. He finds it strange, but it seems right. 'She has a painting of mine.'

Sandro replies, 'Is it one I've seen?'

'No,' he says, 'but that's because it hasn't been painted.' Some paintings are complete before they're finished. Some are never over. This one has taken a lifetime to begin. He wonders how many years a man has. How many good years.

Sandro is leading the way through a broad door into a courtyard, where buildings form a series of allotments, each with a small garden alongside a stone dwelling; a stone wall. The main body of the castle is arranged at the end of the courtyard, where a bell tower is raised above a small chapel. They enter the chapel first. His eyes adjust. An altar forms at the end of a short nave. A basilica, stone benches, stone walls.

'I wanted to show you,' Sandro says. They are standing in front of a large canvas. Even in the semi-obscurity of the chapel, the colour is luminous, fresh. The red hair of Venus is tossed by absent breezes. Roses ride the currents of invisible winds. '*The Birth of Venus*,' Sandro says, 'goddess of love. I brought her here to save her from Savonarola's fires. Or perhaps, what I really mean is, I brought her here so that I wouldn't feel obliged to throw her on.'

He places his hand on Sandro's shoulder and imagines the death of Venus. He says, 'I'm glad to hear it.' As he looks at the painting he feels a rush of hope. Right now he would do anything to turn back time. He steps for a moment into Sandro's world and finds it hard to leave. But his mind becomes crowded with images. The face at the window, a girl in a green dress beside the river, Lorenzo's cave dweller beneath the light of a million stars in a real night sky. He pushes these back and steps out. There is no such thing as Paradise.

In spite of his fears, the fires of vanity had not been burning long enough to strip Florence of her beauty. 'You'd do better to call them the bonfires of renewal,' says a merchant. 'My wife has been throwing out everything she doesn't like, and is expecting a new wardrobe as soon as I've sold my next shipment.'

Life goes on for the wealthy and the privileged. They are gathered in the main body of the castle, where the grand salon gives onto a loggia filled with plants and cultivated flowers: jasmine and deadly nightshade, broad fig and cool fern. Outside in the courtyard a spit roast is turning on a stick.

'Everyone from miles around must be here this evening,' Sandro says. 'And I suppose that includes Giocondo. Let's hope that each one has an invitation.'

'Or that the walls of the castle are high enough to ward off prying eyes,' Leonardo adds, looking around the room. 'Too little penitence and too much pleasure.'

Acciaioli, their host, is a man of elegance. He takes the trouble to point it out. 'My family has been at the service of the Medici since the time of my grandfather. Lorenzo of course was a great man – the only man I knew who could entertain two rivals simultaneously without upsetting either. But there is another I would like you to meet, if I can just remove him from *that* conversation.'

He catches the end of it: '... strung up before the year is out ... Now he's printing it on paper. Can you believe it? Rome will have to move fast ...'

Niccolò Machiavelli is delicate, impenetrable. His eyes, which look through things until he finds them interesting, come to rest on Leonardo's face, and stay there. 'You need no introduction,' this delicate man says, 'Leonardo the Florentine. Or do you prefer to be known by your earlier name, da Vinci? No, no, I doubt that. Times change and people must change with them. Leonardo the Milanese, then?'

'Call me what suits you,' he says. 'It's one and the same to me. Although change is not something I am good at.'

'That, in the present state of affairs, is not good news. But you look as though you need a distraction. Perhaps there is something I can do?'

'Possibly; I'm looking for someone.'

'It's possible that you're looking, or it's possible that I can help? Here's a solution: why don't you start by telling me what it is, or who it is you're looking for? Then we may, between the both of us, arrive at a decision.'

He smiles. What kind of answer would he like? he asks – a truthful answer, or one that is possibly true?

'Then let me tell you. You are looking for something you have lost, and wish to find.'

'Partly right,' he acknowledges. 'But more complicated than that.'

'Life is simple only to the simple-minded,' says Niccolò. 'But I believe that you, Leonardo da Vinci, have made it even more complicated than it is, or must be.'

'How do you mean?' he asks.

'By leaving the Duke of Milan to face the French with nothing but a band of renegade soldiers, a badly equipped army and a mausoleum.' He did not build the mausoleum. 'No, but there were other things that you did not build, and others you destroyed. My question is this: Which do we value highest? Your conscience or our state?'

He has no time to give an answer. Acciaioli has his shoulder. 'There he is,' he says. 'May I introduce — although I think you must already know — Monna Lisa di Zanobi del Giocondo?' Lisa Gherardini. Girl turned woman. Married woman. He feels he no longer knows her. Then he looks in her eyes and realises he does.

'Leonardo. It has been too long. What has kept you away?' She knows the answer. Her eyes search his face; her smile is unchanged: elusive, wistful. She is glad to see him.

Is love possible? Is it he who cannot love a woman, or is it the other way round? His next thought is, the days are too short. There is too much to do. If he has used up all the hours in one day, he will move on to the next. If he has used up the night, there will be other nights. Those at the Ospedale Maggiore. The grimy window. The table of the dead. Besides, this is not his passion. His passion is a pile of ashes in the stove of the Corte

Vecchio. He is standing on a Milanese rooftop. The wind bears his body and he leans into empty space. Give him wings and he will fly. His wings, not hers.

'I've been busy,' he says. 'But then, so have you.'

'And of course, Francesco di Zanobi del Giocondo, whom you have yet to meet.'

Acciaioli is waiting. Niccolò is watching. Francesco del Giocondo is observing him with interest. He is tall, imposing. Makes a point of elegance. 'I have heard you are a great portrait painter. Then we could not have come upon you at a better moment. I mentioned only yesterday that I want a portrait of my wife. Now it seems we've found the perfect man to do it. Will you oblige us?'

He has a brief recollection of standing before Lisa's father – of calculating the likelihood that he will end up on the cobbles of the road. Things have turned full circle, as nature, or fate, would have it.

'Don't press him too strongly,' says Niccolò, 'He's weighing up the case. Well, Messer Leonardo, will it be yes, no, or possibly?'

'Machiavelli is a dangerous man,' Sandro says. 'You want him as a friend: exercise caution. You don't want him as an enemy. He's quietly wealthy, intelligent and too much of either to involve himself in the normal occupations of life.'

'He's an interesting character,' he says. 'Different doesn't mean dangerous.' He could fill fifty pages of his journal with that.

'At least you found what you were looking for,' says Sandro. 'Your portrait. Although I don't see why the interest; there are a hundred such women on every street of Florence.'

But already his mind is gone. Racing backwards. They are back in the cart, passing through countryside. He is holding the camera obscura. His mind is full of circles. They spin and turn and take on the colours of the countryside he passes: the cobalt of a stream; grass touched by sunlight, grass under cloud; violet mountains; violent sunsets. The answer is in the rainbow. Move a little, and you see the rainbow; move again, and you don't. Two eyes, one canvas. The secret of sight. What is real, the thing that you see, or the act of seeing? *There are a hundred such women on every street of Florence.*

'Yes,' he says, 'a hundred, perhaps, but only one canvas.'

Acciaioli gives them bed and board. The other guests leave. Niccolò catches him in the courtyard. 'There is something I was meaning to tell you. But perhaps you know already? The friar Savonarola has called for all heretical documents and books to be burned. Knowing as I do the scope of your studies, I felt it wise to warn you personally, since you are here. Milan is immune to law, but Florence is still shackled to the Church, and now in spirit as in pocket. You may find my words not to your liking, but you will like the methods of Savonarola even less. I wish you good night. We shall talk again I hope.'

He goes to his bedchamber and takes a sheet of paper from the drawer of Acciaioli's immaculate scrittoio. He dips his pen in the ink and writes the following words, right to left: *Curvilinear Perspective. The fifth day of the Calends of March: First entry.*

Niccolò calls in on him the following morning. 'I've been up all night worrying about you. Can I offer you a ride back to

Florence? I have a carriage waiting. I think it will be more comfortable than Messer Sandro's cart.'

'Thanks, but I'll take the cart,' he says.

'If you wish. Then I'll meet you on your arrival. I know a good table where they still serve good food.'

They take their leave of Acciaioli. 'Did you get what you wanted?' the Count asks him.

'What do you mean?' he replies.

'The woman?' says Acciaioli. 'She does have something about her, doesn't she? A certain attractive – how can I put it? – appeal.'

He thinks of Beatrice and pities Francesco del Giocondo. *There is no safety in ownership.* They set off, Niccolò following in his carriage. Their horse develops a limp. They stop and he straps up the leg with a piece of cloth. Niccolò waits with them, offering advice. Their journey is slowed down. It takes the best part of the day to get back to Florence, by which time Niccolò's table has stopped serving. 'Never mind; we're just in time for Vespers. Come with me. There's something I want you to see.'

Deftly, Niccolò turns the subject around to what he wants to talk about. The scholar has the will and drive of Lorenzo, but his mastery of metaphor is not so delicate. 'Tell me, were you looking for commissions or did the wife of del Giocondo simply fall into your lap?' He asks what kind of a question that is. 'You were never known for your approachability,' replies Niccolò. 'But I think that del Giocondo does not know you at all. Or let us say, his wife has not enlightened him. After all,' Niccolò adds, 'not every man's wife is worth painting. I would have thought you, of all people, would understand that.'

Beatrice, he thinks. The Crivelli portrait. The scholar knows everything. He asks, 'Did you bring me here to ask questions about my commissions?'

'I did not,' says Niccolò. 'I brought you here because I wanted you to see it for yourself.' To see what? Niccolò bends down and picks up a pamphlet of printed paper. The sermons of the friar fill the sheet: the citizens of Florence live in the shadow of Satan, in the grip of sin, the only outcome of which is Hell and damnation.

'I have heard that you have more work on paper than the rest of the scholars of this city put together. And that your notes, which run to heresy, contain some of the most unusual and valuable findings ever to come to light,' Niccolò says, staring intently. 'Is this true?'

Because if it is, then he should consider that, with these pamphlets, Fra Savonarola has already shaken the foundations of the Holy Roman Empire. Nations are built on knowledge just as surely as institutions are destroyed by it. If unified, the states of Italy would be stronger than either France or Spain. 'Paint your portrait,' Niccolò continues, 'and it will be forgotten in a year. But share your ideas, and you will be remembered as the one who saved Italy from the French, the one who frightened away the enemies of a people, the one who built a nation.'

Illuminated in gold on the pages of a manuscript he has never written, he stands upon a blazing mountaintop, his shield – like the tablet of all the wisdom of Moses – stashed in safety beneath his cloak, ready to be drawn in battle in the face of some new enemy. Who is it now? he wonders. He looks at Niccolò and his paper pamphlet. 'You spoke earlier of reputation, and you were not wrong. I know I have one. I have had one all my life.'

He spots the small boy he had seen on his arrival in Florence. He is carrying an olive twig in one hand, while the other hand is in his mouth. He thinks of his father. *Live a little.* Take a wife; father a child. Too late, he thinks. There has been too much to do. He says, 'As a child I made a vow that I would do everything in my power to save people. I have carried out dissections in search of a cure; I have scoured every hilltop and river to understand God's earth. I have asked every question, and struggled to find its answer. Now give me one good reason why I, Leonardo from either Vinci, Florence or Milan, should share the work of a lifetime with people who have so completely misunderstood it?'

Niccolò has no answer to offer; although Leonardo is in no doubt that this is a man who will think of one in time. The church of the convent of San Marco is austere. There is barely any sculpture, no painted glass. 'There is the library,' says Niccolò, 'and the frescos of Fra Angelico, for those that are cloistered. But I think you shall find enough to look at on the outside.' There is truth in that. When they reach the piazza a huge crowd is waiting. Girolamo Savonarola makes his appearance at the doors of the convent. The crowd cheers him like a hero. 'The posture of a monk, the nose of an eagle, the voice of a crow,' says Niccolò.

'Cast out your sins now, before time passes and forgiveness comes too late for you to save yourselves. For when the day comes, you will be held to account for those crimes which you have committed, and the same it is for those who commit them in God's name, and for those who rule their kingdom by any law but the law of God.'

A woman from the back of the crowd shouts, 'Praise to God

and Fra Savonarola!' Those at the front cheer. Those at the back applaud.

'You must cast aside all those ornamentations of your lives that are called worldly. You must make your deportment one of chastity, simplicity, obedience to God. Or there will be no mercy, no pardon – no escape from the fires of damnation. Yours will be the journey down to Hell; your resting place will be fire, but you will have no rest; your body will be sulphurous ash; your soul will wander for ever in the wasteland of Hell, destined to endure the torment of demons. You must repent of your sins. Florence is safe, but you are yet in danger. The shadow of sin and vanity is long and deep; the path to heaven requires sacrifice and dedication. But the reward is great. So I say to you now, God is with you. You stand in the shadow of the Devil, but if you let me, I will guide you on to safety. Therefore I ask only this of you: understand that there is no wealth greater than God's love, no power stronger than his, and no knowledge truer. This is my promise. Go now and tend to your children, make your work good and honest, and you will have nothing to fear.'

'Nothing to fear? I'm already terrified,' says Niccolò, turning to him discreetly. The crowd is starting to disperse. Some of the younger women are singing, while others, both men and women, as Niccolò has observed, wear looks of abject terror.

The small boy in the square sees him, runs up and hands him the olive twig.

He takes it and smiles. 'I'm glad to see you're not crying.'

'But I was in the night,' answers the boy. 'I thought the devils would come and take me away. So I hid under my blanket and said Ave Marias. But she says' – the boy points to his sister – 'that

Ave Marias make no difference and if they don't come one night, they'll come the next.' The boy begins to howl. The girl comes up and grabs her brother by the arm.

'Why do you frighten your brother?' he says to her. 'He's innocent. He's only a child.'

'That makes no difference,' replies the girl. 'He stole spice cakes from the counter of a shop.'

'Well, I'm sure that's a pardonable offence.'

'Who are you to judge what's pardonable?' A guard is listening at his shoulder. Niccolò steps up beside him.

'He's only trying to calm the child.'

'Well,' says the guard, looking at Leonardo, 'are you?'

Years of scripture bear down on him. Fra Alessandro and his stick. He has a reckless desire to put Niccolò's sermon to the test. 'I'm trying to efface the visions of terror needlessly instilled in the mind of this innocent child by the friar,' he replies. Niccolò takes a quiet breath. The guard calls another.

'You can say that to his face.'

IV

Flanked by guards, they cross the piazza and enter the convent through the sacristy. 'I hope the boy feels better,' mutters Niccolò. 'That will be some consolation.'

Girolamo Savonarola is standing by the empty grate of the sacristy fireplace. The central table of the room is covered with books of prayer, paper and pens. The compelling voice has given way to silent, brooding authority. He glances at the habit of the friar; the fastening around the middle is broad and the monk stands stiffly. Flagellation, he thinks; he's wearing a cingulum. Savonarola waves the guard back and stares at him. 'You had something to say?'

'Most men of learning have something to say,' he replies. 'But whether it's worth listening to depends on the man.'

'I know you. Leonardo the Florentine. Verrocchio's student. There is an admirable beauty in your paintings, although they are overworked for my taste.'

'I paint what I see; in nature as in scripture. I prefer to look for the truth in both, rather than satisfy myself with the falsities and misconceptions of others.'

Savonarola walks up to the table. 'So, you think you are qualified to interpret scripture as it suits you? Like a heretic?'

'Neither more nor less than yourself. Scripture was written by men; it can be interpreted by men. It is then subject to the judgement of men. Since that is so, we must all be guilty of heresy.' Have I gone too far, he wonders, or not far enough?

'How dare you fill these rooms with such filth?' the friar says. 'I speak the word of God. There is only one guilty man here, and that is yourself.'

'Faith is one thing; bigotry is another. I am both a man of science and a believer,' he says quietly. 'When I paint, I see the hand of God; when I examine the body of a human being, I see the hand of God. But what I will not see is what I'm told to see. The same should follow for everyone, even children.' He stops and considers. 'Especially children. That is all.'

'Fine. Then you leave me no choice.' Savonarola summons the guard. 'Bring the child from the square,' the friar says, icily. 'Punishment is part of education.'

Niccolò takes Savonarola's arm. 'Just one moment. If I may, I too would like to speak.'

'Please do,' says the friar. 'There's enough room on the pyre for two.'

Niccolò lays his cloak over the back of a chair. 'May I sit down? Thank you.'

'I know you. You work at the Signoria,' Savonarola says. 'A clerk?'

'Yes. My family have been *gonfalonieri* for generations,' Niccolò adds, as though it were a thing of little importance. 'And having listened carefully to what has been said, I cannot help but feel that a most important area of interest has been ignored. That is to say, an area of common interest. The true nature of the problem facing all of us in this room, including yourself, Fra Girolamo, is one of change. Florence is changing, our state is changing; our country is changing. One day our Church will be forced to change. Such things are inevitable, I think. Still, our first concern must be to keep out those foreign invaders who would destroy and pillage all that we have struggled to build. Florence has become a republic,' says Niccolò, leaning back comfortably in his chair. 'To survive, the fabric of her society must remain intact. Anything else will mean war. If we do not manage our own affairs intelligently, then we will fall at the feet of foreign invaders, a fact that has already been borne out.' Niccolò Machiavelli glances from the friar to him. 'The French have been repelled, but that does not mean that they won't return. And when they do, we need to be ready. Divisions will serve no other purpose than to make us weak. Leonardo does not recant the teachings of Christ. He has declared himself a man of faith. Why create hostility between ourselves to no purpose?'

'There is faith and there is Hermetic faith,' says Savonarola. 'He will be cast down, I will not. The difference between us is there. But I will give him time to reflect once he is alone in the Alberghettino. There is no substitute for incarceration. It gives a man time to find God.'

'Then let us come to some other arrangement.' Niccolò takes out his pouch of coins. 'Let me make a donation to the convent, a payment to the poor?'

Savonarola looks at him without flinching. 'You can make all the donations you want,' the friar says, 'I am beyond temptation.'

'Very well,' says Niccolò, drawing back. 'But I think you're forgetting something. Messer Leonardo was a favourite of the court of Lorenzo. He will be a champion of the Paleschi. Arrest him and you will have to arrest others: Messer Ghirlandaio, Messer Botticelli. The list of artists could be long. The fires would dwarf your bonfires of vanity. What will people say then? Perhaps they will take to your sermons with less . . . enthusiasm?'

Savonarola stiffens in his habit. It is a good argument. As he watches him, Leonardo imagines the biting cuts of the belt, the twisting of the rope against ulcerated flesh.

'If you think that popularity will save you,' says the friar, 'then you must take your chances. But the chapter is not closed on this conversation. This page stays open. Remember that.'

They leave the piazza for the river. The Arno is fast flowing. Where it leaves the city walls it will widen and slow. There, barges will ferry back and forth. People, animals, bags of grain, sacks of wheat flour. Children will be playing on the edge of the water, out of range of Savonarola's voice. Florence has become a city of torment. Niccolò Machiavelli is talking about close calls. The wrong strategy. All that matters is the end result. If the end result is to roast as a heretic, then the strategy needs to be revised. There is no virtue. Even the friar, with his puritanical zeal, will find out the hard way. Fra Savonarola cannot win, because his strategy does not take into account this one simple fact: men are born bad; they will die bad. Anyone who thinks he is a saint is fooling either others or himself. All that exists is power and who has it.

He asks, 'Is there no space in your calculation for principle?'

What is principle? argues Niccolò. There is no principle, only self-interest. If the friar wants to survive, he should play the right game with the right person.

'So,' he says, 'are you suggesting that I should have sold my skills to Sforza, done his bidding, played his game?'

Niccolò places both hands on his shoulders. 'I have already said that men like you can change the future. What's stopping you? What are you afraid of? God?'

They decide he must relocate. He gathers up his belongings from Sandro's studio. There is a monastery near Florence, the convent of Santa Maria della Pace. Near San Casciano. Franciscans, not Dominicans. If you seek refuge from one order, you will find it in the home of another. 'But he has a commission,' says Sandro. 'The Gioconda portrait.'

'Within easy reach of the monastery,' says Niccolò. 'I will make the arrangements. I can provide a horse, transportation. Leonardo is better out of Florence than in.'

Sandro hands him a letter. It is from Francesco. News from Milan. As he takes it, he realises how much he misses him. The news makes him sit on the edge of Sandro's bed, and takes away the last of his energy, the remnants of a shattered will. The French have invaded Milan. Beatrice is dying. Her child is still-born. The Duke, Francesco recounts, '... is unable to take in events. He can neither command his men, nor eat, nor sleep. Servants say he takes what meals he has standing up, refusing to allow himself the pleasure of repose.' They are leaving town. A *podere*: a small vineyard, which the Duke has made out in his name. He is taking Salai. But that is not all. As for his model of the Sforza horse, it has been shot to pieces by French gen-darmes. 'All I can say,' Francesco writes, 'is that if I could have prevented it by whatever means, I would have done so. But there was nothing to be done. They would have shot me just as easily. I could only watch as a desperate onlooker. All our work, Leonardo. The beauty, the majesty of our vision reduced to a target for culverins. As I write this letter, I weep. What else can I do? Without you here there is no comfort to be had even from art . . .'

He stands up, his legs unsteady. He imagines the clay horse, ravaged and dismembered. He closes his eyes and pushes it back. 'I should get back to Milan,' he says. 'Francesco has need of me.' He starts moving around, gathering things. Niccolò takes his letter.

'You're not going anywhere. It's too late. The Duke is past helping. Francesco is safe.'

By the time they reach the monastery, he's running a fever. He wonders whether the effort of speaking his mind has proven too much after so many years of silence. He has a vague memory of black elder beneath a bush, the dark odour of incense from the back of a quiet room. They lie him down in a cool dark place at the end of a long stone corridor. On the wall before him, a crucifix slips in and out of view. Swaying on the wall, it fights for his attention with the image of the fallen statue. But in the end the fever gets it all. He slips in and out of consciousness, until at length, he lets it go.

Bright circles cross his face. The soft warmth of gentle light is streaming in through the vertical opening beside the bed. He opens his eyes and wonders where he is. His first confused thought is Anchiano. Downstairs his father is telling Albiera to bring him water to bathe. Sandro takes his hand. 'Thanks be to

God you're out of that,' Sandro says, placing a damp cloth on his face. 'I'll get you some food. You haven't eaten in days.'

Through the slit of the opening, he sees something flutter into the room. A butterfly, grey wing tips. Startlingly blue. *Polyommatus icarus*, he murmurs. What are you bringing me: change – or luck? Polyommatus lands on his bed and settles there for a few moments. One heavy rainstorm and you're dead. He lies back on his pillow. Sandro comes back. A bowl comes into focus. The monks have made him soup.

He swallows the soup a spoonful at a time. The butterfly moves its wings. He gets up from his bed in Anchiano and goes over to the wall, where he feels around for a piece of board hidden in a crevice. Now he is running through a field, a child of seven, net in hand. He has made the net from pieces of wood, gauze and resin. 'Do you know,' he tells Sandro, 'when I was a child, I chased butterflies.' Beyond the window, butterflies are emerging from their chrysalis. They hatch as one creature; they become another. They receive no affection; they offer none. They must survive alone. Sandro reaches out to pick it up. He stops his hand. Pick it up, he says, and it will never fly again.

A few days later, he is on his feet. He takes his notebook and a piece of charcoal. He walks to get his strength back, but cannot manage more than two hours before he returns to the monastery, exhausted and sweating. The rhythm of work settles back into him, but different from before. His mind feels slower, his hands weaker. 'I need to do sculpture,' he tells Sandro, 'or I won't even be able to hold a brush.' It occurs to him that Sandro hasn't picked one up in weeks. 'I'm busy with a study,' Sandro says.

Sandro hasn't spoken of Savonarola since Florence, but there are other means of self-flagellation than the cingulum.

The monks cultivate honey and grow vegetables. He wanders into the grounds. He sits beside one of the hives and writes.

Insects: Bees live together in communities. They are destroyed that we might take the honey from them. The more that is taken from them, the more they produce. This is the paradox of nature.

Prophecies: A great portion of bodies that have been alive will pass into the bodies of other animals; which is as much as to say, that the deserted tenements will pass piecemeal into the inhabited ones, furnishing them with good things, and carrying with them their evils. That is to say the life of man is formed from things eaten, and these carry with them that part of man, which dies.

The bright circles of light come back with greater insistence. He understands that he has work to do. He spends the next five nights working. The new notes on curvilinear perspective are growing. But the dissections on optics in Milan have not taken him where he wants to be. He needs to do more. He rediscovers the hills of Florence. It is not Monte Albano. There are fewer rivers, more sources. Hot springs surge up into turgid pools. The water comes from far below ground. Nature has warmed it. There are fewer mountains, more hills. He sits on the side of one of them. At his feet are poppies, orchids.

He makes notes in the notebook he carries round with him for short descriptions. He takes the camera obscura with its square pinhole, and looks at the reflected image. Square hole, round light. Light is curved. The rainbow is curved. The shape of nature is curved. A blade of grass, the horizon. He puts down the camera and looks at the water at his feet. It too bends to a curve.

The curve bends to a circle. The circle goes on for ever. From sky to land; from land to river. From river to ocean; from ocean to sky. That is nature. He draws plane curves. He could be drawing the earth, round, not flat. He stops, stares at the page. Is this God he's drawing, or science? He draws a circle and fills it with a grid. Then he redraws the circle and bends the lines. Linear perspective is not enough. He looks through the pinhole of the camera. Two eyes, one canvas. The secret of sight. Vision and perspective are one.

His hand shakes. He puts down the camera. When we see with our eyes, we see two images through two curved lenses. The image becomes one. Like the camera, it is inverted, sent to the brain and corrected. Two become one; reality becomes inversion, inversion becomes reality. With one important change: it is not the same reality. Nothing we see is real. It is only a version of what is real. As he thinks about this, his head spins. Do we see the truth? He walks back to the monastery and works through until daybreak on the manuscript seeded by a rainbow and now growing in depth and scope with every week that passes. The night is full of cicadas. They call to him from the leaves and branches of trees, from grassy crevices and the warm stone walls of the monastery, in harmonic accord.

The monks provide him with soldering irons, and in a corner of one of the outbuildings he creates a small workshop. Sandro has returned to Florence. But he will be back at dusk with Niccolò. When they arrive he feels like a child. 'I've something to show you. Sit here on the bench, while I set it up.'

Sandro says, 'What is that? A camera obscura?'

'No,' he says, 'a magic lantern.'

'Since when have you been a magician?' asks Niccolò.

'Science, not magic,' he corrects. He takes the painted pieces of glass he has prepared. One is a landscape, the view from the top of the hill. Another is a flower, the lily of the Annunciation. The third piece is *Polyommatus icarus*, the butterfly on the bed. He lights a small oil lamp behind the lens and slots the first piece of glass into place. On the white wall of the chamber an image appears. 'The projection of sight,' he says. 'This is what we see.'

Niccolò is captivated. 'It's flat.'

'Yes,' he replies, pleased. 'It is, isn't it?'

Sandro says, 'What about movement, shape?'

'The missing calculation,' he replies, 'is up to us.'

'We imagine the rest?' asks Niccolò.

'More or less.'

'If you made it move,' says Niccolò, 'how would you know it wasn't real?'

'That's the thing,' he replies. 'It isn't.'

The monks notice his workbench, an improvised slab of wood in a corner of a barn. Time comes back, he thinks. 'Messer Leonardo, your reputation as a painter is known to us all, and we have a request to ask of you. Lend your hand to the work of God. We may not pay you what you want, but hope that you will over-look such a small detail in the knowledge that there is no greater praise to offer than one man's work.'

He thinks of his work. Rolled up in the crevice of a wall, packed in a trunk, carried from place to place, his manuscript has never left him. Stashed away like a guilty secret, kept from public knowledge like a crime. But now, things might change. He senses it in the air around him. Nature has opened herself to him. The rainbow is within sight. He will give the monks their praise, he thinks. He will sharpen up his hand, his mind: his eye. Then he will be ready.

He nods thanks to the monks as they furnish him with charcoal and cotton paper. 'What would you like me to draw?'

'The chapel of Giacomini Tebalducci is in need of an altarpiece. The church has suggested the Madonna and Saint Anne.'

V

He works on sketches in the barn at the back of the monastery. Streaming through open doors and framed by wood, the light takes him back to the barn of his mother's house, and his first slab of panel. Memory gives way to the moment. The pace is frantic. He draws lines, shapes, more lines. They come together in an image. Two days later, he moves outside, working in a corner of the cloister, where he can hear birds, smell grass. He takes the charcoal in between his left finger and thumb, steps up to the cotton canvas and starts to draw, keeping the same pace as before. The preparatory sketch is large, nearly as tall as he is. After hours of work, his hand is limp and shaking. Figures emerge, the Virgin and Saint Anne, the newborn Christ and John the Baptist. The drawing of one is the response to the other. Saint Anne turns to face the Virgin Mary; her hand is raised and her forefinger points upwards.

Sandro has returned to watch him as he works. He feels the chasm between them re-formed and re-shaped. Once it was blood, colour. Now it's an entire body. Veins; arteries; bone; flesh; a pumping heart. 'Is it possible,' Sandro asks, 'four figures so close, so real?' Then, looking curiously at his part-drawn gesture, his finger pointing skywards, 'What does it signify?'

He speaks over his shoulder. 'What would you like it to signify?'

'The presence of God?' Sandro suggests.

'It's something I've been meaning to discuss with you.' He puts down his charcoal and opens his bag. From it he pulls out the circular shield his father returned to him and hands it to Sandro. 'I've been wondering what to do with this. Now I think you should have it.' Sandro looks at the faded picture.

'I thought I was drawing a monster,' he explains. 'But in reality, it's a chimera. A creature of deception. A fraud.'

Sandro's studies are taking form. Dante's *Inferno* fills his nights. In the cool room of the peaceful monastery, Sandro's Hell finds expression, and it worries him. 'I was going to ask you to keep it by your side while you work,' he says. Sandro humours him, but he knows that he will need more than a magic lantern to chase away those shadows.

'So what about your gesture?' Sandro says. 'Your pointing finger.'

'Think of it as a warning,' he replies.

When he has finished the preparatory drawing, the monks pass judgement. 'Will it transfer to canvas or panel?' they enquire. He looks at the multitude of lines, the complexity of the strokes and the depth of expression.

'I don't think so,' he remarks.

'It doesn't matter,' says one. 'Altarpieces can be re-commissioned. This sketch is one of a kind. If you have no objection, I think we would like to keep it the way it is.'

The next morning he takes Niccolò's horse and rides to the Machiavelli villa in the hills, south, two hours away. He needs poplar wood, directions to the home of Francesco de Zanobi del Giocondo. He acquires both. He coats the poplar panel with mastic and turpentine. This he lets dry. He fills a flask with aqua vitae into which he dissolves a small quantity of arsenic. Then he coats the panel with the solution. He lights a flame, and over it heats linseed oil. When this has boiled, he applies it over the top. Once it is a little dry, he rubs it down with a cloth. To this he applies a coat of varnish, which he washes over with urine and leaves to dry a final time. He selects pigments: green; yellow ochre; turmeric; vermilion; cinnabar. He collects oil of mustard seed from a storage jar, picks up his brushes and his bundle, and leaves the monastery.

The villa of Francesco del Giocondo is on a hill. There is a loggia, which looks out over the valley below. 'We pass the worst of the winter in the city,' Lisa's husband assures him. 'The summer months we usually spend here, since the air is cooler.' The merchant slips into his favourite line of conversation: commerce disguised as nature. 'Are you interested in nature, Messer Leonardo?'

'A little,' he says. He is looking round this salon, which is decorated with more silk than he can remember seeing all together in one place. Del Giocondo is also wearing it: silk hose and silk taffeta doublet.

'The silkworm is an astonishing creature,' the merchant continues. 'The children of the moth, I call them. A mere two to three days is all it takes for the silkworm to produce its silk. Imagine that. Such beauty in such a short space of time.'

'Yes,' he replies. He thinks: and such riches from such beauty in such a short space of time. 'But you might have to wait a little longer than that for your portrait.'

Del Giocondo laughs. 'I'm not a difficult man to deal with, although I do have certain expectations, certain requirements. Before we draw up our agreement, perhaps we should go through them?'

They sit at one end of a long table, and Del Giocondo brings out his contract. 'I have a notary at hand,' the merchant says. 'All you really need to do is take a look and sign.'

It contains the usual details: subject, colours, background. He reads down the lines quickly. 'Fine,' he says.

'Excellent. I have not exactly stipulated the clothing, but I have assigned a particular dress for the occasion. Silk taffeta, as you would expect.' Del Giocondo smiles. 'A merchant must display his goods. I think you'll find the colour agreeable. A light red. Lifts the complexion of a woman I think. I have allowed a little freedom for you to choose the exact background, having only gone so far as to specify that you use one or another of the draperies in this room. Which one you choose is up to you.'

'Thank you,' he says.

'Now, as to the matter of payment: I am a generous man. Money is not an issue of debate on my side. Name your price and you shall have it.'

'That is more than fair. Shall we say ten florins?'

'Ten florins? Messer Leonardo – you sell yourself too cheaply. That is a low figure for a portrait. At least allow me to pay you an advance?'

'I would prefer to wait until the moment of delivery,' he says.

Del Giocondo gets up. 'Very well, as you wish. This has been a simple transaction. And you are a modest man. But if that is how you want it, then I shall request the presence of the notary and you will be free to start.'

'There is one more thing. Each artist has his own way of working. I prefer to leave the discovery of a portrait until completion. For me, a portrait belongs to the painter until it has been finished. Do you agree?'

Del Giocondo raises his hands. 'Of course,' he says. 'Silk of the silkworm until it is harvested.'

All of his time is going into optics. He is either in the hills or at his desk. The tenets of linear perspective, once so central to his work, now seem rigid, limited. Organic life needs a different viewpoint. When he is in the hills, it is clear, obvious. But once he gets back to his desk, complexity weighs him down. He fills sheet after sheet, but knows that there is too little certainty, too much assumption. This drives him out again.

He thinks about the future. Where do I go from here? he wonders. He is no longer as young as he was. With all the years that have passed, he is still waiting for the right commissions. So what does he really want? A houseful of silk? Build an army? He has already answered those questions. The others have been answered for him: butcher, heretic, lunatic. Now, with Savonarola in control of the city, there is nothing here to detain him but Lisa's portrait. 'How long,' he says to Niccolò, 'can a man hide himself away?' A month, a year, ten years? Between Florence and Milan, this hidden corner of countryside is the only safe place. 'I might go overseas,' he says. 'Travel east.' He imagines the other side of the Mediterranean, land he does not know.

'Why would you do that,' asks Niccolò, offended, 'when the French are at our door with their cannons?' He considers explaining the lessons of Milan, but decides that Niccolò will not want to hear them. The scholar asks to see his notes on vision and perspective, then stares at the script, right to left. 'Do you do this for yourself or for others?'

He replies, 'Once I did it for secrecy.' But secrecy has become a habit hard to break.

He hands Niccolò a mirror. The scholar flits through the pages of paper, stopping here and there at a calculation, a drawing or a section of manuscript. Then, 'I know a good publisher, if only you wrote legibly.'

When he sleeps that night, he worries about the future. If he has to say what he is afraid of, he knows it will be neither God, as Niccolò suspects, nor Savonarola's hellfire, as Sandro fears, but the thing that frightens him most: people.

In his dream, he is holding a vast book of knowledge, pages of paper. As he reads, he notices that the script is darkening. From right to left, the words begin to burn. Line after line is scorched away until he is left with nothing but the carcass of an empty leather book, and the memory of what he thought he knew.

'Sit here in the shade,' he says. 'If you are in sunlight, I can't see you.' Madonna Lisa is wearing a pale red dress. He looks at her complexion. 'According to your husband, red is your colour.'

'According to my husband,' she replies, 'you are an easy man.' He smiles. She is watching him, waiting for an opportunity to pass judgement. Now she finds one. 'You don't smile as often as you used to. What has put you out of humour all these long years?' Solitude, he thinks. Loneliness. 'Work,' he says. 'The inability of people to open their minds.'

'You never did say what you really thought, did you?'

He corrects her. 'This is a preparatory sketch. If you change the expression on your face, I will have to find it again. And since there are as many different variations of expression as there are stars in the sky, I will not have an easy time.'

'Which expression would you like?' she says.

She is sitting in front of dark yellow silk drapery, the exact colour of honey. The fabric has an imprint of swirling leaves entwined over branches. Incidental, he thinks. His pen shows something else, flowing water and forest, rocks and mountains, a landscape free from ownership.

'Will you come back tomorrow?' she asks him.

When he gets back to the monastery he finds a man waiting for him in the refectory. 'We have offered him food,' says a monk, 'since he said he was a friend of yours.'

Francesco, he thinks. But it is not Francesco. He's wearing a long grey cloak over a black, broad-shouldered doublet. John of Wittenberg.

'I heard you have been ill. How are you now?'

'Is that why you came?' he says. 'To ask me how I am?'

'Yes, among other things. I also came to ask you about freedom, space. Did you have your fill of it in Milan? Did the Duke give you what you wanted?'

Too much freedom, he thinks. Too much space. 'At a price,' he says, 'which I refused to pay.'

'Then you are to be congratulated,' says Wittenberg.

'Not according to some.'

'Each fights his corner,' replies the foreigner lightly. His accent is as hard to listen to as it was before. But his judgement then, Leonardo admits to himself unwillingly, was hard to fault.

'Let me tell you what brings me here. As an emissary of our order, I have come to learn more of Fra Savonarola and his teaching.'

Teaching, he thinks? 'Preaching, you mean? If there is a child in Florence that can still sleep at night without fear of his demons, I will be surprised.'

Wittenberg crosses his hands. 'You disapprove of his methods?'

'I've never liked hellfire,' he says.

Wittenberg pulls a sheet of paper from his bag.

'That I have seen,' Leonardo says.

Wittenberg says, 'It is an inspired tactic. The power of the written word. But one man cannot bring down the Church of Rome. That would take an army of men.'

He thinks, that depends on the manuscript.

'Messer Machiavelli tells me that you have work ready for publishing.'

'According to the Church, my thoughts are heresy,' he says. 'Who will print heresy?'

'There are other men of faith who understand the value of new ideas, new ways,' says Wittenberg. 'Fra Savonarola is not change, but the seed of change. One day there will be others to challenge Rome's thinking. There will be other pamphlets. And besides, this is still Florence. There is more than one scribe in the city.'

Curvilinear perspective does not question God. It questions how we see him, not if we see him. Perhaps Wittenberg is right. Perhaps he has spent too many years watching the figure of his old tutor retreating down the stony track in the dark; too many years waiting for the sword of Damocles to drop on his head.

'Pacini is a publisher with a reputation for choosing his own friends,' Wittenberg says. 'Our first port of call. I'll come back when I have engaged him.' The tall man stands up to go. 'Niccolò Machiavelli told me where to find you. You can reach me through him whenever you need to.' Wittenberg throws his cloak over his arm. 'Your Tuscan sun is hot.' Then, looking towards the door, 'I wonder how you manage to work at all.'

The pages of his manuscript are spread out on his scrittoio. He binds them together and starts a new sheet. Two eyes, one canvas. He writes: *The canvas is the brain.* The first magic lantern came from the East. Texts translated from Arabic provide him with the best explanations for what he has observed in dissection, but he needs to understand what happens on the canvas. He takes up his pen. *Dissection of the human eye*, he writes, *has shown that the image is sent from the retina to the brain and there it forms a new image: a single canvas of vision and perspective as one. But this canvas can contain errors, slips of sight, thus leading to tricks of the mind, or illusions. What we see is not necessarily the truth.*

What do we see first, he considers. He leaves his chamber and goes out into the garden, where the monks have finished matins and are tending to their bees, with veils of gauze over their faces. He offers to help. The monks explain. 'Before we take the honey, we must drive the bees out with smoke. Then we can harvest the bees' miracle.' One of them places a gauze veil over his face. He stands in the early sunlight and lifts the gauze. 'Forgive me,' he says. 'There is something I have to do.'

He walks off, his mind speeding up. Vision can be blurred. He stops and fixes his eyes on the leaves of a tree ahead of him. He focuses on one leaf and sees every vein and mark; the sun catches it and turns it bright green. Then he stops focusing on the leaf and looks straight ahead, allowing himself to see the rest of the tree, rather than only the leaf. The leaf becomes blurred, as though a veil of gauze has dropped over it. Now he can see the tree. He notices that it takes him longer to focus on a single leaf than it does for him to see the tree. I see the tree first, then the leaf, he thinks. He tries to remember everything he has seen, views from mountaintops, the walls of caves, the stars of the night sky when he has slept beneath the canopy of nature. Images viewed at the edge of vision are seen faster but with less accuracy, he considers, while images that we focus on are seen through the centre of the retina, but take longer to appear.

He passes back through the garden and opens the small wooden door of his workshop. He needs to make a second lantern. It takes a full day. He needs new slides. The subject must be right. Shadow against light, he decides, and draws a moth in black and grey charcoal, one on each slide, one slide in each lantern. Two eyes, one canvas. He positions both of the lanterns towards the white wall of his chamber, lights the lamps and waits for the flame to settle. When it does, he slips a further blackened slide between the light and the moth. On the wall canvas he sees two images, one after the other, but one picture: a flying moth.

A full week has passed since he has visited the Del Giocondo villa. His reception this time is cool. It is the feast of the Passover; the house is decked with flowers, white lilies, blue irises and stalks of wheat. Now that he has the main elements of the preparatory sketch in place, he focuses on her face. He looks up at her leaden expression.

'You could try a smile,' he suggests. But today there is no smile. She widens her lips in a half-hearted effort. 'Since when does tomorrow become next week?' she asks him. He smiles on the other side of the paper. A far-off memory of Lisa leaving a cave because she didn't get the shells she wanted.

'Don't worry,' he says, from behind the paper, 'I can manage the smile.'

He stays for the Passover feast. They give him lamb and fish. He eats the fish but not the lamb. 'I don't eat meat,' he explains.

Del Giocondo asks, 'How is the portrait going?'

'Well,' he replies.

'When will you be finished?'

He watches Lisa over the table and thinks, what is it like to be loved by a woman? He imagines it's like seeing the leaf without the tree, or a flying moth. It's what you want to see, or what you think you see.

He completes his work on the new manuscript. He knows it will never be over, but feels that he has gone as far as he can without further dissections, and better instruments. He has tried using a glass lens to see detail more clearly, but most of the time it's like covering his eyes with gauze. Conjecture is fruitless without a way of testing. Observation has its merits, but observing the instrument of observation is like trying to see into the back of your head with your own eyes. Dissection here in Florence is not only dangerous, it is now materially impossible. The time is not right. Patience is necessary.

It is Holy Saturday in the Piazza della Signoria. The murder of Guiliano de' Medici has become old history in a city that now has other problems. The Pazzi family, disgraced since the time of the massacre, have bought back their reputation by a mixture of seduction and money. 'They are lighting the oxcart this year. The Pazzi have promised gunpowder,' says Sandro. The city is heaving; the population eager for whatever pleasure the choking abstentions of Savonarola will permit. With the Medici gone, the gold dolphins of the Pazzi coat of arms are carried into the square.

'People forget fast,' he says. It doesn't seem so very long ago to him that crowds streamed through the streets baying for the blood of Pazzi. They stay and watch by the Baptistery, where the oxcart stands ready to receive the dove of fire from the holy flame. The explosion makes him jump, transports him to a hillside south of Milan with Sforza on his horse, a battalion of gendarmes and cannons below. There the ground trembled with death, here the crowd screams with pleasure. He touches the bag slung over his shoulder and wonders whether its contents, his manuscript, will unleash a wave of excitement to rival that caused by gunpowder. He feels a strong urge to return to the safety of the monastery and lock the manuscript up with the rest of his notebooks, which have sat for so long in the bottom of his trunk. Now Niccolò is coming over to join them.

'Another edition,' says Niccolò, producing a handful of pamphlets. 'Another master coup by our friar: "Citizens of Florence, freed from the clutches of evil, join us in prayer for the souls of those for whom wealth and glory still spread the poison of sin and corruption . . ."' He looks at his bag. 'You've brought the manuscript?'

Wittenberg is standing outside the entrance door to one of the better-built houses on the Via Ghibellina. They convene to an upper room. 'Messer Leonardo,' says Pacini, 'the pleasure is mine.' They talk philosophy for a time. The pros and cons of a republic. Then he takes out his manuscript.

'The subject is optics, perspective,' he says.

'Optics or perspective?' asks Pacini.

'Both,' he says.

Pacini looks at the writing, then again blankly at him. 'What is this?' he says. 'Italian?'

'This is how I write,' he explains. 'How I have always written.' The scribe takes the paper and looks at it in horror. 'With the assistance of a mirror,' he says, 'transcription is relatively simple.' The scribe nods, unconvinced. Pacini takes it back.

'We will see how easily it can be done. Drop in when you are next in town.'

They walk out of the door. The air is filled with the smell of gunpowder. A hazy smoke tinged with sulphur and grey hangs over the city. He visits Sandro and finds him embroiled in discussion with a customer over a statuette. The oxcart celebration has been cut short. The pageant is over and people are going home to tend holy fire in their own hearths. It seems only yesterday that Lorenzo paraded the city streets in crimson and gold like a god. He, Leonardo, was young then. He was the Maestro's apprentice, the son of the notary. He remembers that Lorenzo was wearing a silk scarf embroidered with a motto: *Tempus revenio*. Only the observant picked it out. Only speakers of Latin remembered it. He had learnt his first words of Latin from his tutor, Fra Alessandro. But that was long ago now. The days when Andrea gave him a sword and modelled him as David. With one fair stroke he would vanquish Goliath. He is still holding the sword. He is still waiting.

Two weeks later. He has transferred the preparatory sketch to the panel. Lisa has been more patient with him, and no longer asks him difficult questions, such as: Why haven't you married? Don't you want to be a father? What kind of a life is that? My life, he tells her. The only one I know, he thinks. He explains his ideas on perspective. Tells her that nature is curved, reality is illusion. She looks back at him on paper as though she knows everything, and yet she knows nothing at all.

'When can I look at it?' she asks.

'When I've finished,' he replies, but is not certain she would like the result. She would probably accuse him of painting a version of her that isn't real. The dress is too old, she might say. Or, the background is wrong. He would have to disagree. The world behind the subject is a world of circles, light, colour;

curved nature. The woman in red sitting before him has become the girl in the green dress by the rivers of Anchiano, unchanged and unchangeable. This is what he sees. This is as real as it gets.

As time passes, a feeling of urgency grows within him. He takes Niccolò's horse into the city, shortening his journey by cutting across country. Straight ahead, on the horizon line, a veil of rain has cut the sky in two. The sun is lost in a haze of fine cloud, flaked across the sky in light brush strokes. Through the veil of rain, the iridescent arc of a rainbow appears, clear but incomplete. He stops and watches. Spherical drops of water refract light. The colours that he sees are a function of where he stands, how he sees. One more step, he thinks, and I will miss the beauty.

He rides through Porta Pisana and finds his way back to Pacini. He pulls the bell and waits. The scribe sees him in. Ser Pacini, he is told, is not there at the moment. He asks for news of his manuscript. What has been done? The scribe appears surprised. It was collected the previous week, for fear that the style of the script might become public knowledge and cause too much scandal. People, never mind manuscripts, have been burned for less.

His manuscript has disappeared. His pages of notes, his discoveries, his calculations. Every grain of thought gone from his hands, slipped through his fingers. He shakes his head in disbelief.

'Is there a message?'

'No more than what I've told you already.'

He turns away from the door and leans against the wall. Despair follows disbelief. He runs his hands over his face. To rewrite the manuscript would be a monumental task. He is not even sure whether he could do it a second time. He pays a visit to Niccolò.

'The manuscript is surely in safe hands. Wittenberg must have it. In any event, you would do better to concentrate your work on subjects of greater value, such as weaponry, armoury. If the French continue to sack our cities, there will be no art left to look at.'

He returns to the monastery and packs his trunk. He takes out the rest of his notebooks and puts them on the table in front of him. He rationalises, casts aside emotion, deception, in favour of logic: the lessons of Milan. These pages could build a nation. He takes himself back to the time of the monster, the time of the vow. He is no longer sure he is up to the task. All his life he has had to fight against the current. One day he will drown.

The words of Niccolò Machiavelli, he considers, are more dangerous than heresy. What kind of future do such men seek? He does not want to think about it, but he knows that it is not his future. He shakes his head. No art left to look at? Not quite. Not yet.

Francesco di Zanobi del Giocondo puts down his pen. It is late and he has had a trying day. Things are never as simple as they appear. A man can never be certain of anything. He reads the last entry of his journal: *After many weeks of patience on the part of my wife, the artist came to the end of his commission in a way that left the entire household uncertain of his return, since he did not announce the work as over but simply left with no word of a return and took the painting with him. This incident has been a source of great irritation to myself, not least because I felt unable to place a complaint, since no payment had been given and none asked for. In the end, I can only conclude that the painting must have been of little merit and even a source of embarrassment to the artist, who was clearly too unhappy with the result of his work to share it.*

Acknowledgements

I would like to thank my agent, Anna Webber, and Martin Kemp.

3⁰⁰ Gen 3/16-TD